the words
between us

Center Point
Large Print

Also by Erin Bartels and available from
Center Point Large Print:

We Hope for Better Things

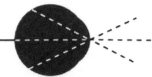

**This Large Print Book carries the
Seal of Approval of N.A.V.H.**

the words between us

a novel

erin bartels

CENTER POINT LARGE PRINT
THORNDIKE, MAINE

This Center Point Large Print edition
is published in the year 2019 by arrangement with
Revell, a division of Baker Publishing Group.

Scripture quotations, whether quoted or paraphrased by
the characters, are from The Holy Bible, English Standard
Version® (ESV®), copyright © 2001 by Crossway, a
publishing ministry of Good News Publishers. Used by
permission. All rights reserved. ESV Text Edition: 2016.

The text of this Large Print edition is unabridged.
In other aspects, this book may vary
from the original edition.
Printed in the United States of America
on permanent paper.
Set in 16-point Times New Roman type.

ISBN: 978-1-64358-395-2

The Library of Congress has cataloged this record under
Library of Congress Control Number: 2019946832

For Zach
who has even more books than I do

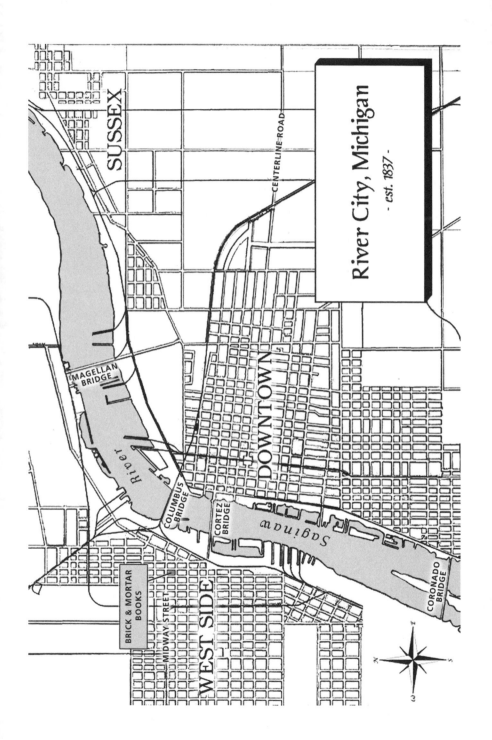

Second hand books are wild books,
homeless books.
—Virginia Woolf

1

now

Most people only die once. But my father is not most people. He is a monster.

He first died on a Wednesday in November 2001, when his sentence was handed down—*We the members of the jury find Norman Windsor, on three counts of murder in the first degree, guilty; on the charge of extortion, guilty; on the charge of obstruction of justice, guilty; on the charge of conspiring with enemies of the United States of America, guilty.* And on and on it went. Or so I imagine. I wasn't there. The teenage daughters of the condemned generally are not present at such events.

Now, nearly eighteen years later, he will be executed. It's the first thought I can separate from my dreams this morning, though I've tried for weeks as the date approached to ignore it.

I dress quickly in yesterday's clothes without turning on the news. I don't want to see the mob hoisting signs, the guards standing stone-faced at the prison entrance, interviews with grim relatives of the dead. All I want is for this day to be over, for that part of my life to be over. So I shut the past in behind the door, descend the creaking stairs, and emerge as always in the back room of Brick & Mortar Books, where my real family resides in black text upon yellowed pages, always ready to pick up our conversation where we last left off.

"Good morning, Professor." The African Grey parrot offers his familiar crackly greeting.

"Good morning, Professor." I open the cage door, wondering not for the first time who is imitating whom.

The Professor climbs onto the perch above the cage and produces the sound of a crowd cheering. I change his paper, refresh his water, and give him a terrible used pulp paperback to shred into ribbons. Every morning is the same, and there's comfort in that. Even today.

I know the store will be dead—even more so than usual—but I can't afford to stay closed, even if it is the day after Saint Patrick's Day in River City, Michigan. I have never understood why the feast day of an Irish saint is so popular here, as nearly all the Catholics who settled in the area have unpronounceable surnames that end in *ski*. Maybe they all just need a big party to forget the misery of March for a day. Even the Lutheran church three blocks south canceled services so its members could walk in the parade. And many of those same people who painted their faces green and donned blinking four-leaf clover antennae as they marched down Centerline Road instead of going to church were on this side of the river later that night, guzzling green beer and kissing plenty of people who aren't actually Irish, despite T-shirts asserting ancestry to the contrary.

Of all the storefronts on this section of Midway Street, there are only five that do not serve alcohol: a pet salon, a custom lighting store, a bank, an aromatherapy shop, and my bookstore. Every other business along this quarter-mile spur of Midway is a bar, making it the destination of choice for about half the sleepy city on any given weekend and about eighty percent on Saint Patrick's Day. Not that the high traffic translates into high sales for me. They stay in the bars. I stay with my books.

Armed with more than a few years of experience with the aftermath of Saint Paddy's, I pull on a pair of bright yellow rubber gloves— *Ladies and gentlemen of the jury, Exhibit A: the gloves Mr. Windsor wore when carrying out the strangulation of Mr. Lambert*—and head toward the front door with a triple-thick garbage bag and a broom. But there's another matter to attend to before I can clean up all the trash.

I knock on the glass near the ear of a woman who is slumped against the door. "Hey!"

She doesn't move.

Back through the store, through the maze of boxes in the back room, through the metal receiving door out to the alley. A stiff breeze whips up a torn paper shamrock chain, along with the stench of beer and vomit. I hug the east wall of the store, passing beneath the pockmarked remains of a mural of a billowing American flag. I stop. There, on the very lowest white stripe, a profane word is scrawled in black spray paint. I add the removal of the word to my mental checklist and keep walking.

The wind hits me hard as I turn onto Midway. Long shadows cast by light posts in the rising sun point toward the spire of St. Germain Catholic Church, just visible over the tops of the still bare trees, and graze the edge of the woman's coat. She is curled up tight, as if she were developing inside an egg. Glittery green shoes poke out beneath her black parka. Her bottle-blonde hair, streaked with green dye, was probably stunning last night. Now it is matted down around her face. I poke her with my broom. She shrinks a little further into her egg.

"Hey, wake up!"

Slender fingers push back the bird's nest of hair. One brown eye squints up at me. "Hey, Robin. There you are."

Sarah Kukla is as slim as she was in high school, but as I hoist her to her sparkly feet she weighs three hundred pounds.

"I was knocking. You never answered."

Her breath almost makes me drop her back onto the pavement.

"I can't hear knocking at this door when I'm upstairs. You should have called."

Leaning her body against mine, I manage to open the front door and dump her into a thread-bare armchair. Her parka falls open, revealing black fishnets under an impossibly short green dress that looks like it was sprayed onto her body. Her cheeks and nose glow red. Her emerald eye shadow smudged with black eyeliner makes her look more like she had dressed for Halloween than Saint Paddy's.

"Where were you last night?" I ask.

"Everywhere," she moans.

"Come on. I'll take you upstairs. You can wash up and get some coffee."

Even a massive hangover cannot hide Sarah's surprise at this offer. In my seven years at 1433 Midway I've never invited her or anyone else up. But I can't send her back home to her son like this. Anyway, I do have a human decency clause in my unwritten personal privacy policy. I'm not a monster.

"Let me get The Professor back in his cage. If I'm not around for too long he chews up good books."

The parrot is not impressed by this break in his routine and lets me know with a sharp bite on my thumb. I don't grudge him his irritation. I kind of wish I could simply bite Sarah's thumb and send her on her way. But I tell myself once more that it's probably not her fault she is the way she is and I should have some compassion.

Somehow we make it up the steep staircase and into my apartment, where she looks around with an expression that grows ever more disappointed. "It's so plain."

"What were you expecting?"

"I dunno. It used to be more—" She looks away. "Never mind."

She slouches onto the couch, kicks off her shoes, and pulls a fleece blanket over her head. I don't know what this place looked like when she spent all her time here, before it was a bookstore, before I came back to town. But I know from the snores drifting back to the kitchen that I can't ask her now. I don't have the heart to wake her when the coffee is done, so I creep back downstairs to gather in the remains of last night.

Each new gust of wind brings me more confetti and cigarette butts skidding along the concrete like staggering drunken partiers. I tuck it all into the trash bag along with broken glass, wadded-up tissues, and a single black shoe. I'll have to do it again in a few hours when the wind brings more. It doesn't bother me like it used to. It's just part of the rhythm of this place.

A sharp beeping ceases, one of those sounds

you don't notice until it's gone. In the silence left behind I realize that the ice on the river has finally melted. I know it without looking. Rivers have voices, and this morning the Saginaw is grumbling.

At the end of the street, a tow truck ascends the boat launch at Marina Five, dragging the rusty blue pickup I saw still parked on the thinning ice yesterday. The last of the ice fishermen leans toward the truck, hand at his heart, as one might hover over a dead body to search for one more breath, one more twitch of the eyelids, something that might indicate that there was still time to tell him you loved him. Only there wasn't.

No, he's just getting a pack of cigarettes from his breast pocket.

I watch until all that's left of the story is wet gravel. Next year it might be a Jeep or an ice shanty. It will probably be in February rather than March—winter had lingered so long this year. But it wouldn't be nothing. This too is part of the routine—when the ice gives way, when what was solid ground suddenly cracks and shifts and turns deadly.

There had been a tow truck in my father's case, pulling a black sedan from a different river—*May I direct your attention to Exhibit B?* It was anything but routine. I saw it splashed across the front page of the *Boston Globe*, read the gruesome details in neat columns of text that left leaden dust beneath my fingernails. I didn't go to school the next day.

When I can't fit even one more stray sequin into the bag, I tie the plastic handles and stretch my back. That's when I see it, in a skeletal crab apple tree on the other side of the street—the first robin. Spring. All signs point to it. A winter, no matter how long, cannot last forever. The longed-for bird tips his head at me and lifts off against the wind. I deposit the trash in the alley dumpster, fish out my scrub brush and graffiti remover—it's not the first time—and get to work on the wall.

Half an hour later I turn on the lights and let The Professor back out of his cage. Ignoring his muttered cursing, I flip the Open sign and settle down behind the cash register with a hundred-year-old copy of *Aurora Leigh* as company.

The spine crackles and the sweet perfume of time drifts up to my nose. The lines slip under my eyes like a mother duck and her brood slipping down the river. Word by word, Aurora lives and loves as she first did under Elizabeth Barrett Browning's graceful pen.

Three quiet hours later—not even a visit from Mr. Sutton, the only person I could call a regular customer with any integrity—the bells on the front door jingle. The Professor squawks, "Hello!"

"I got the mail," comes Dawt Pi's heavily

accented voice as she rounds a shelf. "I thought you were going to put that sign out."

She tucks her tiny purse under the counter before reaching up for The Professor. The bird edges over and makes his way down her arm to her shoulder. He'll spend the next half hour carefully preening her straight, oil-black hair. He never does this to me. If he sat for more than a couple minutes on my shoulder, I would probably end up missing half my ear.

"What sign?"

"That sign. You said you were going to put it out. On the sidewalk."

I put down my book. "Sorry. I was a little distracted this morning."

"I will get it." She retrieves a chalkboard easel nearly as tall as she is and a box of colored chalk from the back room. "You want me to do it?"

I know she is still not confident about the peculiar spellings of her adopted country's language, so I love her for offering. "I can do it. What did we decide?"

"Hardcover one dollar, paperback fifty cents."

I sigh. We will lose money. Still, I kneel at the easel to write out the words I hope will draw people into my beloved store. The past few years have been tough, but I'm determined to weather the storm.

"You want to look at this mail? There's a package for you."

17

I stand and tear open the large, padded manila envelope Dawt Pi slid across the counter to me. It's obviously a book. I carefully unwrap the brown paper from around it to reveal a vivid red and white dust jacket adorned with a stylized carousel horse beneath a bold yellow title.

"Oh my."

"What is it?"

I can hardly breathe when I see the copyright page. "Oh my."

"What?"

"It's a first printing, first edition *Catcher in the Rye*."

"Is that good?"

I shouldn't expect a recent refugee from Myanmar to know better, but I give her an incredulous look all the same. "This could be worth a lot." I flip over the envelope. No name, just a return address in California. "Why would someone just send this to me?" Starting at the back of the book, I flip through the pages. "Oh no."

"What?"

"There's underlining. That'll affect the value. Though it's in pencil, so we could . . ."

The moment I see the coffee-ring stain on page twenty-three, I drop the book on the counter.

"What?" Dawt Pi's now exasperated voice cuts through the fog that is swiftly gathering in my mind.

The bird on her shoulder voices his own question. "What does our survey say?"

But I can only manage one word in response. "Peter."

2

then

Death has always captivated me. My dead goldfish, one fin breaking through the surface, as though he had discovered he couldn't breathe underwater and was reaching out for someone to save him. The dead bird beneath my bedroom window, her last moment imprinted on the glass for months. The rubbery frog splayed on the board in my eighth-grade science classroom, his little hands and feet and skin pinned down so he couldn't stop my prodding. Always a body, but with something missing, something twisted out of order. It was that off bit that made me wonder. What was really missing other than breath? Because it wasn't just that. I could hook that frog up to a machine that would pump little poofs of air into his tiny lungs, but he wouldn't really be living. It was something else.

I wondered about this as I scuffed through the cemetery in my new backyard. Below my feet lay dozens of bodies, just missing one vital thing. Beyond the cemetery, perhaps a hundred yards off the road, stood a dead house. It wasn't just empty; it was dead. It was missing that same thing the fish and the bird and the frog and all these people were missing. But what it was exactly, I couldn't say.

My new home was closer to the road: a trailer occupied by a lumpy old woman I just had to trust was really my grandmother, and a parrot that glared at me whenever I dared come out of my cramped room.

"Does it talk?" I had asked when I arrived a week earlier.

"Sure does. If he has something to say."

But the bird, whom "Grandma" rather grandly called The Professor—you could hear the capital *T* in *The*—didn't talk to me. Instead he growled if I got within two feet of the cage, which I had to do in order to go anywhere because the cage was enormous and the trailer was not. So I retreated outside, bound by Grandma's three unbending rules: "Don't sit on the tombstones, don't fall in the ditch, and don't go playing in that old house. It's condemned."

The land that the trailer, the cemetery, and the dead house occupied was practically the only acre of untilled land in sight, a small ship in a sea of corn and sugar beets. I'd only been in Sussex, Michigan, for six days, but for a precocious fourteen-year-old girl from Amherst, Massachusetts, it had already been too long. Despite its tony name, which I figured would promise a certain level of sophistication or at least charm, Sussex appeared to be little more than a provincial suburb of the equally unremarkable River City to the immediate west. The streets back in Amherst were lined with ancient oaks, grand old homes, and venerable university buildings. The streets of Sussex were lined with ditches, a primitive drainage strategy in a place that wanted to be what it really was—a swamp. The grandest house I'd seen so far was the one decomposing just twenty or thirty yards beyond the headstones. Not one part of this town felt alive. How could my mother have grown up here?

With nothing else to do, I wove through the gravestones and attempted to pronounce the names I read. Andrzejewski. Wieczorkowski. Mikolajczak. I picked at the long grass around the stones that needed trimming and wished I had a book. But Grandma apparently didn't believe in them. The only things to be found in the trailer resembling books were the worn and curled *TV Guides* piled in a prickly, half-unraveled basket on the coffee table. Eventually, bored nearly to my own death, I leaned back against a tree, fell asleep in the heavy summer air, and dreamt that I lived in a ditch, which wasn't far from reality.

The sound of a car door awakened me. I watched a teenage boy walk twenty paces and kneel in front of a slab of shiny black granite. His mouth began to move like he was praying, but he kept his eyes open. He talked to the stone for a minute, then pulled a thick hardcover book from a backpack and placed it on the ground. He stood up and our eyes met across the rows of the dead.

He waved. "Hey."

"Hey," I returned.

He examined me with confident blue eyes set in a summer-tanned face. I could tell immediately that he was popular. And I was sure he could tell that I would not be.

He glanced around a moment. "What are you doing way out here?"

"Just taking a walk." I tried to approximate his accent, contracting my round New England vowels and stringing the words together like the pearls on my mother's favorite necklace. *Jus taykin awok*.

He raised his eyebrows and indicated the trailer by the road. "Do you live there?"

"I rode my bike." I indicated a vague area behind me where I'd parked my nonexistent bike. "Who died? Your grandma?" I made "your" into "yer" and dropped the "nd" in "grandma." I thought it sounded pretty authentic.

"My mom."

"Oh." I stopped thinking about accents. "Sorry."

He furrowed his brow. "Where are you from?"

"Out east. Just moved here."

"You going to Kennedy?"

"What's that?"

He laughed. "The high school."

"Oh, yeah. I guess so."

"I'll see you around then." He started off.

"What did she die of?"

He turned back to face me. "Aneurysm."

"Do you come talk to her often?"

He smiled slightly. "Today's her first birthday since she died. I had to get out of the house. My dad's not handling it real well."

I nodded. "What's it like? To lose a parent?"

The little smile melted away. "What do you think? It's the worst. Listen, I gotta go. I have football practice. It's hell week. Catch you around."

When he was gone, I knelt in front of the gravestone he'd been talking to. *Emily Rose Flynt. Born August 20, 1954. Died December 10, 1999. Beloved wife and mother.* On the browning grass lay the book *The Complete Poems of Emily Dickinson.* Strange. What were the chances that this particular book should find its way to me?

I opened the cover, releasing the sweet scent of old paper, then flipped through the pages, stopping here and there to read the strange and beautiful words. Of course a football player would leave something like this on the ground, little considering that the words hidden within might actually matter to some people, that perhaps it should not be left exposed to the elements.

So of course I had to take it.

• • •

The next day Grandma got my mom's old bike out of the shed behind her trailer. Now it would be mine—likely the only thing of hers I would ever own. The tires were bald but held enough air for me to attempt the terrifying ditch-lined roads into the village of Sussex. I coasted down each bland street in town until I found Kennedy High School. Shouts, grunts, and whistles drifting on the humid air led me to the football field, where twenty or thirty guys were smashing into tackling dummies on the only green grass in sight.

I climbed to the top of the metal bleachers— the highest point in the county, I was sure—and surveyed the landscape. Boring little houses lined up neatly on parallel streets to the west, nothing but farms to the east. The football field was the dividing point, the last outpost of civilization before a vast wilderness of corn and sky.

In the midst of all the identical practice jerseys below, I thought I spotted the guy with the dead mom. The height and build were right, and the tufts of sandy brown hair poking out beneath the helmet. He moved like he knew where he was going. When the helmets came off twenty minutes later, I saw I was right. I descended the stands as the coach barked that there was only one more practice until school started and they had better get ready for the real work come next week. The huddle broke up. Most of the players

25

dragged their feet back toward the locker rooms, dog-tired in the thick late summer heat. Then one red jersey broke from the pack and veered in my direction at a trot.

"Hey." He ran his fingers through his sweat-slicked hair and then hooked them on the chain-link fence between us. "What are you doing here?"

"I came to check out the school."

"Yeah? What do you think?"

"It's all right, I guess." I glanced back at the low-slung, featureless brick building. "It's pretty . . . sixties."

"It was built in the sixties. What did your old school look like?"

"Like an *old school*. Like a school should look."

He laughed.

"Is the football team any good?" I asked.

"Sometimes."

"Are you any good?"

"Always."

A cocky grin, so much like my father's. He started toward the school. I followed, walking my mother's old bike along the other side of the fence.

"I'm Peter Flynt."

"Robin. Dickinson."

That was a lie. The first lie I would have to tell, but certainly not the last. Back when things

26

started getting really bad, I had been advised by a social worker to take a new last name in order to avoid any association with my disgraced parents. It would make things easier on me. As if they could be easy. The social worker suggested my mom's maiden name. But Gray? Robin Gray? How boring. How utterly without backstory potential. Dickinson was far more suitable. I was from Amherst, after all.

A few weeks later I was given a packet containing my new identity. I practiced saying my new name in front of the mirror. It wasn't easy, and even if I said Dickinson, I still thought Windsor.

"Dickinson? Like the poet. My mom loved Dickinson." He motioned to the school building hunching beyond the grass. "She was an English teacher here."

I understood the book now. We reached the end of the fence and continued walking side by side, the bike and my lie now the only things between us.

Grandma lied too. To her friends at church, to her priest—well, maybe not to her priest, but he wasn't allowed to tell other people her business anyway, so I was okay there. To her friends I was some shirttail relative—fourth cousin thrice removed, et cetera—who had fallen on hard times and moved in to help her around the house because she was getting old and decrepit. Maybe she wasn't really decrepit, but she was awful crotchety. All these lies were okay because they were for my protection.

"You must have lots of books at your house," I said.

"Tons. My dad put them all away in boxes, though. He can't look at them. Reminds him of her. But I thought maybe I should read them all, to honor her. So I'm pulling them out of the basement and reading each one, even if I've read it before for English class."

We reached a rusty metal door.

"You like to read?" he asked.

"Yeah. I had to leave all my books."

"Why?"

I hesitated. I couldn't tell him that practically everything in my house had either been commandeered as possible evidence or was to be sold off to help defray mounting court costs. Or that I had to be spirited out of Amherst under cover of darkness to this hick town only God knew about to prevent the media jackals from tracking me.

"I mean I had to leave my favorite library."

"Hey, stay here. I'll only be like ten minutes."

He disappeared through the door without waiting to see if I would obey his command. But I did. I had nothing else to do. And I liked this guy. I leaned the bike up against the wall and examined the salmon-colored bricks. Like bricks of Spam. Tiny red mites hurried over the hot surface. Even they had a bit of that undefined something that would escape their little bodies if I smooshed them with my thumb, so I didn't.

Eventually Peter appeared in the doorway in his own clothes and street shoes, duffel bag slung over one shoulder. He held a book with a bright red, white, and yellow cover. "You ever read this?"

I shook my head.

"It's good." He pushed it into my hands.

"What's it about?"

"It's about this kid who leaves his prep school and has a bunch of adventures in New York City all on his own even though he's only like fifteen. And he eviscerates people along the way when he figures out they're all pretending to be something they're not. It's great."

Peter didn't look like a guy who could pronounce the word *eviscerate,* let alone use it correctly in a sentence. But then, his mom had been an English teacher. The book sounded like something I should read. It sounded like the situation in which I found myself, adrift and alone with a pretty powerful desire to eviscerate certain duplicitous people. If only I was in New York City instead of Nowheresville, Michigan.

"Is there a library in Sussex?"

"There are a couple in River City. One on either side of the river. But you can read this copy."

"But it's your mom's."

29

"I trust you."

"You don't even know me."

He shrugged.

"How will I give it back to you?"

"We're going to the same school. I'll see you around."

He headed off to the parking lot with a wave, leaving me and my inherited bike and my untested trustworthiness leaning against the Spam wall. He had spoken to me all of ten minutes total in two days and seemed confident that I was dependable. I had spent fourteen years with my parents and had never suspected a thing. How could I have been so stupid?

Crushing dozens of mites in the process, I slid down the wall into the dry grass right then and there, and started to read.

3

now

"What is peter?"

The question sounds like it's coming from beyond a closed door.

"Who," I say. "Who is Peter."

"Please state your answer in the form of a question," The Professor admonishes.

"Oh, Peter, like the disciple," says Dawt Pi. "Who is Peter?"

"He's . . . just someone I knew who liked this book." I am starting to regroup. "I think we can still sell this with the markings. They're pretty light. There's nothing we can do about the coffee stain. We may not get as much, but it's a valuable book all the same. We should list it online. I don't know if anyone in this town would pay what it's worth."

"What is it about?"

"It's about a boy who leaves his boarding school and, well . . . he complains about a lot of people . . . He's trying to protect a younger girl—his sister."

"From what?"

31

I think of the curse word spray painted on the wall outside. "Life, I guess. Like he wants her to be able to stay innocent for as long as possible, keep her safe from the bad things of the world and the bad people."

Dawt Pi frowns. In the refugee camp, she began working at the age of twelve to help keep her six younger brothers and sisters fed. After years of trying to save as much as possible, her family could only afford to send one person to the United States. As the oldest child, Dawt Pi came alone at age nineteen to a country that worshiped youth rather than sending them to work. The reverence for childhood here is as incomprehensible to her as child labor is to Americans.

"Does he protect her?" Dawt Pi asks.

"No," I realize now, though I don't think I really understood it when I read it in the death throes of that long-ago summer when my life had changed forever. "He can't protect her. Nothing can."

I slide *The Catcher in the Rye* onto the shelf behind the counter where I keep the few truly valuable books. I will research its worth later. For now I realize that my best hope for understanding why Peter Flynt has reestablished contact with me is upstairs under a blanket and probably drooling on my throw pillows.

"Can you hold down the fort a few minutes? I have to run upstairs."

"What is hold down the fort?"

"Oh, um, watch the store and serve the customers while I'm gone."

Dawt Pi nods and I trot up the stairs to my apartment. The TV switches off when I open the door, but not before I see that it's on a news channel.

"Sorry, Robin. I didn't know you were coming."

I ignore Sarah's apology. It's not what I want to talk about right now anyway. "How are you feeling?"

"Awful." Sarah's squinty gaze follows me to the kitchen. "What about you?"

I avoid her bloodshot eyes. There's nothing worse than getting pitied by a complete train wreck of a person. "I'm fine. Didn't you drink any of this coffee?"

"I can't get off the couch."

"It's cold. I'll make some more. Sorry I left you here alone so long."

"It's okay. I was watching . . . Do you want to talk about it?"

"No." I fill the coffeemaker with fresh grounds and water and turn it on. "So, how was last night? See anyone back in town for the festivities?"

"A few. Did you know Ashley got divorced?"

"Which Ashley?"

"Galicki. She's staying with her mom. Mitch is in town too. They ended up at the same bar

33

last night—Pepper's, I think—and it was super awkward for everyone."

"That's rough. Anyone else?"

"I saw Mr. Pietka!"

"At the bar?"

"Yeah. He was talking to Julie Szczepanik. Like *talking* talking."

"I don't think I know her."

"That's right. You were gone by then."

"Wasn't he married?"

"Still is."

"Oh." Time to dive in. "You ever see Peter anymore?"

Sarah hesitates. "We've talked on the phone a time or two."

"Lately?"

She narrows her eyes at me. "Why?"

"Just curious." I pull two clean mugs from the cupboard. "It's been a long time."

"What did you expect? You really messed him up."

"Good."

It has been my standard answer to any creeping regret I've felt for the last eighteen years. I thought with practice that ambivalence would become a genuine feeling. But even on the day I'd cut all ties with Peter Flynt, I hadn't truly felt I was doing the right thing.

"Only he sent me a book. Totally out of the blue."

Sarah shrugs and busies herself with a loose thread at the hem of the blanket. "Can't help you there."

"You're not connected on social media or anything?"

"No. He's off the grid. Kind of like you."

The coffeemaker beeps and I pour two cups. Sarah sips. In the silence I sense the wisp of something she's not telling me. It's a common feeling any time I am with her, but it's always hard to tell if the reticence to talk about certain things is coming from me or from her. We both lug around our own share of baggage.

The bell rings on the door downstairs. Dawt Pi is fine by herself, but I hate to miss a customer.

"I have to get back. Stay as long as you need to. Take a shower if you want."

"Do I look that bad?"

"Yeah."

Sarah nods slightly. "Hey, where's that painting I gave you?"

It's down in the back room. In a box. Where no one will see it.

"It's down in the store. On the wall. Didn't you see it?"

"No."

"I'll point it out."

I shut the door behind me and make the dark descent to the store. The Professor is back on his perch and Dawt Pi is standing on her step stool

35

behind the tall counter. Her fingers rest on top of *The Catcher in the Rye*, now down from the shelf and under the examination of a rather portly bearded man in a trucker cap and a camouflage coat over a plaid flannel.

"How much is it?"

"Very valuable," Dawt Pi says, tripping a little over the pronunciation.

"We're not sure yet." I slip the book out from under her hands. "I need to do some research before we can make this available."

"I liked that book in school," the man says. "I didn't know it came so big, though. The one I read was littler."

"Generally students read a cheap mass market edition. There are far fewer of these hardcovers, and it's rare to get one with an intact dust jacket in this condition. I'm sure there are a few of the mass market edition on the shelves. They're only fifty cents today."

"How much is that one? Ballpark?"

I don't really want to say it out loud around Dawt Pi. She's told me how little the average subsistence farmer in Myanmar makes in a year, and I know how much money she needs to get plane tickets for her parents and siblings once they're finally cleared for immigration, how impossible it must seem to her to save that much after living expenses. So I say it as quietly as possible, slurring the words together in the hopes that she won't be able to separate them.

"Prollyroundfivethousindollars."

He laughs out loud. "Dang! Who would pay that much for a book?"

I feel heat blossoming in my face. "There are people who collect rare books."

"No one I know."

I don't doubt this, but I don't say it. "Dawt Pi, can you show this gentleman to the classics section?" To him I say, "I'm sure you'll find several things that might work for you."

"I ain't really looking," the man says. "I'm waiting on my mom's dog. It's getting groomed down the street. But I'll take a look."

He follows Dawt Pi, and I scoot off to the back room to find Sarah's painting. It's exactly where I left it last June. An odd combination of fairly random items spackled together and adhered to a piece of plywood, then slathered over with black and red paint and sprinkled with silver glitter. The creation is not something I would choose to look at more than once, let alone hang up in a place where I spend all of my time. It reminds me of a car accident. I find a spot of wall by the mysteries, remove a poster for a classic film I've never seen, and replace it with Sarah's piece.

Moments later the big guy is at the register digging in his pockets. He slaps two quarters beside a dog-eared mass market copy of *The Catcher in the Rye*.

"Fifty-three cents with tax," Dawt Pi says.

"It's fine." I slide the quarters off the counter and open the cash register.

The man shoves the book in his back pocket and walks out into the wind.

Dawt Pi puts her hands on her hips. "We have to pay for tax."

"It's just three cents."

"Just three cents to you." She steps down from the stool and walks away.

I slip the hardcover of *The Catcher in the Rye* onto the shelf again, this time with the spine to the back to hide it from prying eyes. Then I pull out my prehistoric laptop and begin to research its value. Several minutes later the bell rings.

"Can I help you?"

"Just browsing."

The woman hugs her long wool coat close to her body and begins a circuit of the shelves, not quite slow enough to be browsing, in my mind. I watch her for a moment. She glances at me twice.

"Are you looking for something in particular, ma'am?"

"Now that you mention it." She approaches the counter. "You're Robin Windsor, right?"

Every pore prickles. This can't be happening again.

"I work for WRST," she continues, pulling a little notepad and pen from her pocket, "and

I was wondering if you have a statement about what today means for you."

I know I'm glaring at her.

"Just a few words?" she says through her smile.

A few words?

"I'd like you to leave," I say.

Dawt Pi walks up beside me and grasps my hand.

"I'm sorry," the woman says. "I know today must be difficult, but if I could get a few words about how you feel about your father's—"

"I want you to leave."

The woman opens her mouth to speak again, but Dawt Pi plants herself between us and pushes the much taller woman toward the door. "Out. We call the police."

A moment later I feel a gust of cold air as the reporter stumbles onto the sidewalk. Dawt Pi locks the front door, flips the sign to Closed, and marches back to where I am frozen behind the desk.

"Who was that?" she asks.

But I can't answer. All I can think of is the last time I heard the name Robin Windsor spoken by a reporter. I see Dawt Pi's lips moving, but all I hear is the scrape, scrape, scrape of bricks being removed from my carefully built walls of anonymity. Peter Flynt is making contact. A reporter knows exactly who I am and where to find me. It can't be a coincidence.

Through the large picture window at the front of the store, I see a news van parked by the curb. With effort, I focus in on Dawt Pi.

"Turn off the lights."

4

then

I didn't see Peter at all on the first day of school. Freshman and senior lockers were in different hallways, we had none of the same classes, and while underclassmen filled the cafeteria at lunch time, upperclassmen could leave to go scarf down McDonald's or Taco Bell. I sat alone at the end of a long cafeteria table with a Styrofoam tray of clammy fries and cardboard pizza, until a girl with dirty blonde hair and glasses had mercy on me.

"I'm Ashley."

"Robin."

"You're new."

"Bingo."

"Come over to my table. I'll introduce you to some people."

She took my tray of food before I could answer. I followed her to a table occupied by four pleasant faces. They looked like people who might enjoy a good story, and if I was going to reinvent myself in the wake of the Norman and Lindy Windsor scandal, I needed an audience.

"This is Robin . . ."

"Dickinson," I supplied. "Like the poet."

A few nods and one blank stare from a girl whose hair was redder than my own.

"She's a relative, a great-great-great aunt," I continued. This seemed to impress them. "I just moved here from the East Coast. My parents died at sea."

A couple gasps.

"That's horrible!" Ashley said.

I nodded gravely. "They were on a romantic evening cruise for their anniversary when a sudden storm blew in from the North Atlantic. Their yacht was dashed upon the rocks far north of the port. A rescue party couldn't be sent out for two days as the storm raged on." The chewing of food ceased around the table. "When they finally found them, they were half eaten by sharks." I let my voice break a little on the last word, and the red-haired girl put her arm around me.

"How awful!"

I let out a shuddering breath. "So I've come to live with another relative of mine, though she's nothing like old Great-Great-Great-Aunt Emily was. She's an old woman who has lived alone for so long she can hardly have a conversation with another human being. Most of the time she just talks to her parrot. It's terribly depressing."

Someone pushed a cupcake in my direction.

They were hooked. I was now a romantically tragic figure, a victim of cruel circumstance, and the relative of someone famous to boot.

"But wasn't Emily Dickinson a recluse too?" one of them said.

I ignored her. "Tell me about you."

For the next twenty minutes, I was filled in on the particulars of my new friends. I also got an earful about people at other tables.

"What about Peter Flynt?" I said when I felt them winding up. "Know anything about him?"

"He's a senior," Jenni-with-an-*i* said. "His mom died. She was my sister's favorite teacher."

"He's the quarterback on the football team," said Ashley.

"He's pretty nice," said Brianna.

"He's a tool," said Eric.

"You're just jealous," said Jenny-with-a-*y*. "How do you know him?"

"I met him last week. In the cemetery."

"That's *so* sad," Brianna said.

Eric expelled a puff of air.

The bell rang. Ashley took me by the arm and showed me to my next class. I went home that day feeling that maybe it would all work out. I didn't have to live the rest of my days as a sideshow to my parents' three-ring crime circus. I could write myself a new story. I would be Robin Dickinson, orphan with a heart of gold. And I would give myself a happy ending.

• • •

The next morning, I walked out of my way to the senior lockers before the first bell rang. Peter lounged with a group of guys on one of the large carpeted platforms I'd heard a girl in my algebra class wistfully call The Islands. Freshmen and sophomores couldn't sit on The Islands. I stood quietly to the side, book in hand, and waited for him to notice me. He didn't, but one of his friends did.

"Who are you?" It was less of a question about my name than a challenge to my existence.

Peter looked up. "Oh, hey, Robin." He stood and placed himself between me and the five sets of eyes that were now assessing me. "What are you doing over here?"

"I came to give this back." I held up *The Catcher in the Rye.*

"Hey, Red," said one of the guys on the island, "you new here?"

"Peter, you *know* this girl?" said another.

Peter half turned toward his friends. "I met her over the summer."

"Oh yeah?" a new voice said. "Did you get some of that?"

"You know he did," said the guy who had spoken first.

The island erupted in laughter, and a few people at nearby lockers swiveled their heads toward the commotion. Peter turned back to me, and as he did I saw the last vestiges of a smirk and suggestively raised eyebrows before he schooled his features to meet my gaze. He rolled his eyes apologetically but said nothing.

Everything was ruined. In the space of thirty seconds. Ruined. Despite my little cadre of friends from the day before who ate up the tragic story of my fake past, my reputation had just been sealed at Kennedy High School. I wouldn't be the mysterious orphaned relation of Emily Dickinson. I would be the slut. And Peter Flynt would be the stud.

"Here." I shoved the book into his chest, catching him off guard and sending him backward into the unyielding island where he fell, hard. I stalked off amid whistles and jeers, shaking from the adrenaline a little more with every step. At my locker I kept going, past all the happy, chatty students and into the bathroom where I shut myself into a stall, kicked a dent into the metal door, and refused to cry the fat, burning, angry tears that clamored to get out.

I endured the rest of the day, aware that between every class the rumor that I had done stuff with Peter Flynt spread like the flu. Maybe something about being related to Emily Dickinson would slip in there as well, but that wouldn't be my defining characteristic.

The moment the last bell rang, I sped home on my mother's bike and headed straight for the grave of Emily Rose Flynt to confront her for failing to teach her son chivalry or even common decency. But the day had already drained my reservoir of anger. All I had left was loneliness and misery and confusion.

I sat down on top of the grave and pushed the heels of my palms into my eyes. My own mother was seven hundred miles away in the Federal Corrections Institute in Danbury, Connecticut. She had taught me good manners and the importance of loyalty. Loyalty to my father had landed her behind bars. She wasn't dead, but she might as well have been. When I needed her, she couldn't be there for me. And by the time she got out, I wouldn't need her anymore.

A shadow oozed onto the grass by my feet.

"I thought I might find you out here."

Peter Flynt held out his hand. I ignored it and got up on my own. "Don't you have football practice? What do you want?"

"Well, for starters, I'd like you to get off of my mom's grave."

I took a step to the side.

"And then I want to apologize for the way my friends acted. They—"

"I don't care about your friends. Apologize for yourself. You should have said something. You should have set them straight. You should have—"

"Yeah, I know. I'm sorry. Look, I want to make

it up to you." He rummaged in his backpack and pulled out *The Catcher in the Rye*. "Here, you can keep it."

"What makes you think I want to keep it?"

"You don't?"

"I didn't say that."

He smiled and waved it around like he was offering a treat to a dog. I took it.

"And I have another one for you I finished."

He pulled out a small pulp paperback and handed it to me. On the cover was a boy, hands in his pockets, standing in front of a gnarled tree at the edge of a lake. The stately building in the background was flanked by rust-orange trees. Big, blocky capital letters spelled out *A Separate Peace*.

"It's set at a boarding school in New Hampshire. An old school. You said you were from the East Coast, so I thought maybe you'd like it."

"This doesn't fix things, you know."

He scratched the back of his neck. "Well, I can't go back in time and undo it, and I've already said I was sorry. What else do you want me to do?"

"Set the record straight with your idiot friends—and everyone else who already thinks I'm a complete slut, which is everyone."

"I'll do my best. Promise." Peter looked at the grave. "Where's the book?"

I waved the two books in my hand.

"No, I left a book here last week and it's gone." He started looking around at the neighboring graves, as if his mother had perhaps loaned it to another corpse.

"You mean the Emily Dickinson poems?"

He snapped back to me. "Yeah, have you seen it?"

"I have it."

"You took it?"

I planted my free hand on my hip. "It could have gotten rained on. I can give it back."

Peter seemed to be considering this. "Keep it. I can barely understand a word of it. Half-crazed ravings of a lovelorn recluse."

"You know, for a dumb jock you talk like you're kind of smart."

He gave me a half smile. "I am smart."

"So why don't you understand Emily Dickinson?"

"To be honest, I haven't tried real hard. I'm just not super into poetry. I like novels."

I smiled. "Well, maybe you're not so smart, then."

"Excuse me?"

"Poetry is to novels as champagne is to grape juice."

He laughed. "Like you've ever had champagne. Did you like *The Catcher in the Rye*?"

I screwed up my face. "I like the writing okay. But I hate Holden Caulfield."

"What?" Peter looked stricken. "How can you say that?"

"He's a jerk. He thinks he's special, but he's just as phony as all the rest of them."

"Okay, but you'll like *A Separate Peace*."

"If you say so."

Peter glanced at his watch. "Coach is gonna kill me. I'll see you later." He took off running.

I waved *The Catcher in the Rye* over my head. "What do you want for this?"

"Nothing!"

I'm not sure why, but the thought of Peter Flynt just giving me something didn't sit well. Maybe it was because it wasn't really his to give. What would his dad think of him giving away his mom's books? What would she think if she could think anymore? Or maybe it was because when my perfect life in Amherst was crumbling down around me, I finally realized that all the gifts my family had enjoyed—the trips to five-star hotels in New York City, the tickets to sold-out Broadway shows, the electronics, the jewelry— had been less about friendship and generosity and more about currying favor and covering tracks.

For the first time in my life, I had no money. But I did have something I could offer in return. I tucked the two books into my backpack, pulled out a notebook and pen, and began to write.

5

now

What is going on down here?" Sarah's
voice.

"How did you get in here?" Dawt Pi's.

"Robin let me in this morning. I've been
upstairs. Are those news vans?"

The street is indeed lined with vans emblazoned
with the logos of local news affiliates. Women in
tight skirts and wool coats totter around on too-
high heels like newborn deer. Beefy men point
bulky video cameras at them. The phone has not
stopped ringing in twenty minutes. The Professor
alternates between a high-pitched squeal like
a trumpet fall and looking at me for a reaction.
Parrots love drama, and this is more than he's
had in years.

Behind the counter, I sit on the floor with my
knees to my chest.

"There was a reporter in here," Dawt Pi says.
"She would not leave, so I pushed her out."

"Good," says Sarah. "It's no one's business."

"What is going on?" Dawt Pi asks.

I feel Sarah's long fingers on my shoulder and

50

look up to her winter-pale face. Now devoid of makeup, the scar beneath her left eye is clearly visible. Her wet hair is pulled back. The green is still there, faded from the shade of an actual shamrock to a shamrock shake. She is wearing my clothes—a pair of sweatpants that look like capris on her long legs and a T-shirt that is much too small, with no bra underneath. I can only assume her spray-on dress from last night would not accommodate one.

"You go upstairs," she says. "We'll stay here. We won't answer the door or the phone."

"You don't have to stay. Go out the back. It'll lock behind you."

"You don't want to be trapped in here alone. Who knows how long they'll be out there?"

"We will stay with you," Dawt Pi declares.

I force myself to my feet. I don't want to hang around in my apartment with anyone. I don't want to talk about it, and I don't want to have to avoid talking about it. I want to be alone. I'm best alone. But sometimes you do things you don't want to do in order to please your friends. People think that once you're an adult, stuff like that stops. It doesn't. It just changes.

"You can come up with me."

"What about The Professor?" Dawt Pi asks.

"Bring him with you. This is too much."

I lock the register to protect the fifty cents I earned today. As we pass through the labyrinth of shelves, I point out Sarah's painting. She stops to admire it before following me upstairs.

Once inside my apartment, Sarah scoops up her outfit from last night, which she had left in a tiny puddle on the floor in front of the bathroom, and stuffs it into the pocket of the coat she hung on the back of a chair. It actually fits in a pocket.

"Is anyone hungry?" she asks.

"No," Dawt Pi and I say in unison. In the two years I've known her, I've never seen Dawt Pi eat.

Dawt Pi puts The Professor on the perch on top of the smaller cage I keep in the apartment and pulls me to the couch. "Let me do your hair." She releases my waist-length hair from its standard loose side braid and sends Sarah to find a brush. Dawt Pi slowly draws the brush from crown to tip until every strand has been through the bristles. Finally she asks, "Why are all those people here?"

I take a deep breath and let it out in a whoosh. I can say it. "My father is being executed today."

Dawt Pi stops brushing. "Oh, Robin. I am so sorry. I have lost someone that way."

"It's not the same. My dad's a criminal. Not a martyr."

Across the room Sarah mouths *murder* to her, but of course I see it too since Dawt Pi sits directly behind me.

"Three murders," I say. "But those almost aren't as bad as what he was trying to cover up with them."

I pause to access the memories. I've avoided reading about it for so long, trying to forget. But it's all still there, just under the surface, a cold-flowing river beneath the ice.

"He was a senator, chair of the Armed Services Committee in the 1990s. He ran covert arms sales to what turned out to be al-Qaeda—though nobody really made that connection when he was first arrested—and he was skimming liberally off the top."

"What does that mean?" Dawt Pi asks.

"It means he kept a bunch of the money from selling weapons to terrorists for himself. After the embassy bombing in Kenya, some people who knew apparently threatened to talk. So he killed them. He killed three people to silence them." I feel a tightening in my throat. "But I've always wondered how many other deaths he must be responsible for."

"Robin, they didn't use those weapons on 9/11," Sarah says.

She's right. They didn't. But I of all people know that everything we do has consequences we couldn't have predicted at the time.

"Maybe not," I say. "But for all I know those weapons were used to kill someone who could have stopped it."

"Your father was not responsible for 9/11," Sarah says.

"If that were true, I doubt he'd have ended up with a death sentence. No one executes a senator."

"Unless they're just looking for someone to blame," she says, "to show people someone's being punished. I mean, the first trial was a mistrial. That jury apparently didn't agree he'd even done the things he was accused of. It wasn't until after 9/11 that—"

"Don't defend him," I snap. "The most expensive lawyers in the country couldn't defend him, so I doubt you'll do any better."

Sarah opens her mouth again, then shuts it.

"Sorry," I say.

She waves the apology away. "Don't worry about it."

Quiet settles in the room like dust. There's more to say, more guilt to go around. But nothing I'm ready to admit out loud. I hear the clock tick, the rhythmic slide of the brush, Sarah flipping the pages of the *New Yorker*, looking for the cartoons. But they are all the sounds of quiet.

I doubt it bothers Dawt Pi. She never talks to fill a silence. It's one of the reasons I took to her right away. She never pries, never makes idle conversation like Americans do. She never comments on the weather, never asks how I am doing, never inquires if a shirt or a pair of shoes is new. Never asks about my past. I can only assume it's because she doesn't want me to ask about hers. When I start a new book, she asks me what it's about, and my brief summaries always suffice to relieve her curiosity.

Predictably, Sarah is the one who breaks. "So how's the store going?"

"Not great," I say honestly.

Dawt Pi puts the brush down and begins separating my hair into chunks, tossing some of it over my shoulders, some over my face.

"I'm going to have to close by the end of the year unless River City residents suddenly lose all access to the internet."

"Really?" She sounds genuinely distressed. "I'd hate for you to not be in this place. I told you I used to take lessons here when it was an art studio."

I nod. There had been plenty of other people who had come in over the years and told me about it too, their comments accompanied either by a wink and a nudge—the men—or by a sour look of disapproval—the women. It was always a delicate dance trying to get them to stop talking without putting them off to coming back into the store for more books.

"Why can't you just sell books on the internet?" Sarah asks.

"I do. Just not enough."

"You own this place, right? So all you have to pay is water, heat, and electricity?"

"And for inventory. And taxes. And an employee."

"I told her I could find another job," Dawt Pi says.

"And *I* told *her* we could manage a bit longer," I say.

"Well, I guess if it's not working it's not working," Sarah says. "What's your plan?"

Plan? When have I ever had a plan?

"I've tried everything I can think of. Sales, advertisements, promos. I don't want to lose it. It's all I've got."

"You have The Professor," Dawt Pi says sweetly.

"Good morning, Professor," the parrot says. He's snuck down from the perch and is now pacing along the top of the TV, his claws scraping the smooth surface.

"If I didn't see the occasional person come through that door, I wouldn't interact with anybody *but* The Professor," I say.

"Your problem is that you never leave," Sarah says, oblivious to the fact that my comment was merely a poor attempt at levity. "You should get out more. You're surrounded by bars full of people, and you wall yourself off with a bunch of books."

I shrug. "Books are filled with people."

"It's not the same. They're not real."

"They've always been real to me. I realize that an extrovert such as yourself can never understand why I would choose books over the bar. But trust me when I say I'm happy this way. I like living in my little world."

Sarah looks doubtful. "What you need is some sort of big infusion of cash."

I almost laugh at this. My financial situation over the years seems to be one of the few secrets I have managed to keep from everyone—with the exception of The Professor. But that well is dry now, and part of me is relieved.

Sarah taps a green fingernail on her teeth as Dawt Pi finishes braiding my hair. "I'm going to figure this out. You can't lose this place. It's got too much history."

I don't point out to Sarah that she has never bought so much as a magazine in order to support my business. Back in high school she might have gotten an earful for hypocrisy like that. But not now. What's the point? Saying what you really think just leads to trouble.

"Listen, I appreciate you two wanting to keep me company, but it's getting late. Go home to your son, Sarah. I'm too tired for any more talk. I'm going back to bed."

Sarah stands. "I have to use the bathroom first."

"Will you put The Professor back on his perch? I think he's gotten himself stuck."

"Uck. No. I'm not touching that bird."

I hear the medicine cabinet squeak open and the sound of rummaging in drawers.

"What are you looking for?" I ask loud enough for her to hear beyond the bathroom door.

Dawt Pi twists the chunky braids she has created into a high bun that feels like a crown. I wish she had her family here to go home to. Come to think of it, I wish I had a family to go home to.

Sarah emerges from the bathroom, slips on her quilted parka, and shoves her hands into the pockets. She inserts her feet into those glittery green high heels, made even more ridiculous for the too-short gray sweats she's now wearing, and walks to the door. "Come on, Dawt Pi. I'll drive you home."

Dawt Pi finishes the bun, magically securing the ends without rubber bands or bobby pins, and grasps my hand. "God loves you, Robin. I pray for you—every day."

I can't answer her without releasing the tears that are swiftly building up behind my eyes like a river behind a dam. I wish I was so sure that God looked at me with anything but fathomless disappointment.

She puts The Professor back on his perch and kisses his stone-gray beak, an impertinence from anyone else, but Dawt Pi seems to be the bird's one true love. Then she and Sarah are gone.

I stand against the wall and peek through a crack in the curtain. Down below, the little media mob wheels like a flock of grackles as Dawt Pi and Sarah come into view. From up here I can see that Sarah needs to get her roots done. The reporters follow them all the way to the car, but once Sarah starts the engine and inches away from the curb they wander off.

By this time the bars on Midway are all open and the regular patrons are beginning to drift in. There are plenty of people for the news crews to peck at. It doesn't matter if they can speak with even a modicum of authority as long as they can provide sound bites.

I imagine what they might say about me.

"Oh yeah, that girl's a troubled soul, all right. Quiet. Keeps mostly to herself."

"I always knew there was something wrong with her."

"You know, I heard she was the one who actually pulled the trigger, but no one could prove it and she was a minor, so they let her go."

"There's a bookstore on this street?"

Why do I care what others think of me, as though the neurological activity in all those random brains has any actual bearing on my own reality? And yet, I do. I always have.

Though I know I'll regret it, I pick up the remote and push the power button. The Professor flaps with excitement. He loves TV, and he hardly gets to watch it anymore. The news station Sarah had been watching earlier flashes onto the screen. I almost turn it off again, but a carefully coiffed woman with too-bright lipstick is already speaking.

"Disgraced US senator and convicted multiple murderer Norman Windsor, scheduled for lethal injection today, has been granted a stay of execution. We go now to correspondent Marcia Barron outside the federal penitentiary in Terre Haute, Indiana, where Norman Windsor has been held since his sentencing in November 2001."

I tent my hands over my nose and mouth and squeeze my eyes shut.

It would not end today. It would never end.

The first robin of spring was a lie.

6

then

Smells of popcorn and cigarettes and rotting leaves mingled in the dark space beneath the bleachers. Above me the marching band shuffled off the stands, dislodging a shower of empty cups that had previously held chocolate so blisteringly hot that if you sipped it too soon you wouldn't be able to taste anything for the next thirty-six hours. With the band gone, I got my first clear view of the game I'd been half listening to for close to an hour. Crouched and ready for the snap of the football, Peter shouted out the play in a string of nearly unintelligible syllables.

I didn't care about football, but I did care about Peter. He'd made good on his promise to set the record straight with his friends regarding our relationship, if you could even call it that. I'd given him the combination to my locker, and every few days I opened it in the morning to find a new book waiting for me on the bottom shelf. Each time I finished a novel, I slipped a poem on a folded-up piece of spiral note-book paper dated like a check through one of the slits in his locker. My payment for each book.

With the terms of our literary commerce defined and the steady stream of books coming my way, I had no time to worry about the fact that I had so little in common with the kids I met on the first day of school that we hadn't managed to move past the occasional nod in the hallway into the territory of real friends. I still sat with them at lunch, but only as a spectator. When the last bell rang, they went to play practice and volleyball and the game consoles in their basements, while I quickly got my homework out of the way so I could pick up where I had left off the night before.

In the absence of real society, I made my own out of the imagined people Peter Flynt slid into my locker. They entered like corpses on a slab, but they came to life in my mind with each turn of the page. With their willing help, I began to forget my terrible life in favor of their spectacular lives. And because Peter continued to lay these offerings at my feet, I had come to each home game and watched him through the legs of the supportive crowd. I never added my voice to their cheers or groans, but I was there.

The half ended. Glossy jerseys yielded the field to stiff woolen uniforms embellished with gold fringe. The light filtering beneath the bleachers exposed my as-yet-unseen company. Junior highers roamed like stray dogs down here. They couldn't be bothered with the game, but it was the only thing to do on a Friday night in Sussex. A gaggle of girls here, a huddle of boys there, and the occasional couple edging off to dark corners.

Soon the band returned to their seats, shrouding me once more in darkness, and the game continued. The speakers spat out Peter's name and number regularly until the game was won. Cheers went up and the fight song played one last time as the crowd began its creaking descent from the bleachers out to the parking lot. Ten or fifteen minutes later, the field went black. I hated the thought of having to push through the crowd to leave, so I didn't move from my spot until the only remaining sources of illumination were the crescent moon, the stars, and a single floodlight above the closed concession window.

I was about to get my bike when I heard footsteps shuffling through the trash.

"So this is where you've been hiding out." Peter was silhouetted against the floodlight and closing in on me.

"Nice game," I said, because people say that.

"Did you even see any of it?"

"Enough."

"I saw your bike. Figured you had to be here somewhere."

Peter leaned back against one of the beams that supported his enormous fan base. With his face turned to the light, I could see that he still sported faint smudges of eye black. I wanted to wipe it off with my thumb. Instead I put my hands in my coat pockets.

"Wish I'd known you were watching."

He picked a piece of newspaper confetti out of my hair, letting his fingers brush my cheek. It was the first time we had touched without the buffer of a book between us. Our eyes met for a moment and he leaned in. I guess he was waiting for me to close the rest of the short distance. I thought of the rumors from the first day of school, of what a kiss might mean for our literary arrangement.

When I didn't move toward him, he leaned back again and crossed his arms over his chest. "So, are you going to go to homecoming with me or what?"

I snickered without meaning to. I wasn't shocked to be asked—three guys had asked already, I imagine because they still assumed I was easy despite Peter's efforts to convince them otherwise—but I was surprised to be asked by Peter Flynt. On game days his number twenty-two had been riding around on the boney back of Sarah Kukla.

"I doubt it."

"Well, that's blunt. Why not?"

"Dances are lame." I was glad it was dark because I wasn't sure I could sell that line in a well-lit place. All girls wanted to go to home-coming with the quarterback, didn't they?

"You know, people are saying you're not into guys because you turned down so many of them for homecoming. I thought maybe you'd want to prove them wrong."

"There are always rumors." Though I hadn't started that particular one.

He tilted his head. "There are a lot of rumors about you."

"Oh yeah?"

"Yeah. Like that your mom murdered your dad after catching him with his secretary, that you're the descendent of some illegitimate child Emily Dickinson had with a minister, that your parents died at sea, that your dad is a mob boss, that he's some corrupt senator who whacked people who had too much dirt on him, that you're actually twenty but you got held back more than anyone else ever has, that you're actually twelve but you're super smart so they put you in high school. And my personal favorite, that you're actually the oldest child of Charles and Diana and therefore the true rightful heir of the English crown, but your jealous brothers tried to suffocate you in your sleep, so you escaped to America."

"That is a good one."

He fixed me with a hard stare. "So who are you, really?"

"Why do you care?" I asked lightly.

Peter mirrored my stance and put his hands in his pockets. "I was the first one in this town to meet you. I feel like I should know. People ask me sometimes and I have no good answer. And I know all this other crap isn't true. I want to set people straight."

"I see. So you just want to make sure people know the truth."

"Exactly."

"And what makes you think I want people to know the truth?"

"Why wouldn't you?" Then he seemed to answer his own question. "It can't be that bad."

I shrugged, even though no amount of shrugging could dislodge the weight of what I knew to be true. That my family was disgraced, that my parents were doing time, that my life and friends and home had been stolen from me. That everything was horrible and there was nothing I could do about it.

"It's no one's business. You know what they say: 'Knowledge is power.' If I'm the only one who knows, then I have the power."

"No, if you're the only one who knows, people are going to think you're a snob and they won't talk to you. You can't be friends with someone who never talks about themselves, and when they do it's a bunch of lies."

"I talk about myself all the time."

He snorted. "Yeah, sure."

"Don't you read any of those poems I give you?"

66

"They're about the books, aren't they?"

"They're also about me. Each one is like a little slice of me, like those cross sections of seaweed you look at through the microscope in biology. I can't believe you haven't picked up on any of that." I gave him a playful poke in the chest. "You know, you're sitting on a gold mine there. Someday I'll be as famous as Emily Dickinson and you'll have a whole stack of original poems in my own hand."

"Is that so? Well, fat lot of good it'll do me. People will ask me, 'What was she like?' and I'll have to say things like, 'I dunno. She was pretty quiet, kept mostly to herself,' like they do about serial killers."

I scoffed. "I guess you'll just have to get better at reading. The books—you read them all first. They're about me too."

Peter let out an exasperated sigh. "How are the books about you? They were all written before you were born, even if you did get held back six times."

"You mean you've read all these books and you never found yourself in them?"

"What?"

"When you read a novel, you don't see yourself in it? You don't identify with any of the characters or the situations or the feelings?"

"The last book I read was *Lord of the Flies*. So no, Robin, I don't see myself as a murderous grade-schooler on a lawless deserted island. Before that it was—"

"*The Great Gatsby*." I was nearly finished with it myself.

"Yeah, and I don't see myself as some pathetic poseur who's obsessed with a girl he can't have."

I leaned into the light, close to his face, close enough to give him that kiss he had wanted, and smiled. "You sure about that?"

7

now

Ashamed as it makes me to admit it, I am secretly relieved the next morning to read about a deadly volcanic eruption in Indonesia, something to draw the great and terrible eye of the public away from me. But a night of little sleep and The Professor's outraged squawking at having been confined to the smaller cage in my apartment have given me one of those headaches where the ceiling swirls and the light pricks your nerves and any movement sends you into a pain vortex.

I scuffle into the bathroom, scan the medicine cabinet, and dig through drawers, but relief is nowhere to be found. That's what Sarah had been doing in here—snatching up pills. I don't know what would happen if one OD'd on migraine meds, but I guess it was nice of her to be concerned. She understands more than most people I know the temptations—and dangers—of self-medication.

I find a couple dusty pills at the bottom of my purse and chase them with a cup of tepid water from the bathroom sink. *Ladies and gentlemen of the jury, Exhibit C, the ricin capsule Norman Windsor slipped into Mr. Pritchard's drink.* One by one, I unravel the braids Dawt Pi wove into my hair. I lose my fingers in the ripples and remember the feel of my mother's hands in my hair on Sunday mornings. She must know about the stay of execution by now. There are TVs in prison. I should write to her.

Yet, what is there to say? Things are the same as ever, stretching on like a dream from which I just can't wake. Like coming to the end of a story, expecting the clean blankness of the inside back cover that would mark a pause between this imagined world and the real one, a sort of pressure chamber to help the reader reacclimate themselves to reality. But instead of the back cover you find yet more pages, more text, more tedious chapters to slog through. The story you can't seem to finish *is* reality. Norman Windsor, the great bogeyman, the conspiracy theorist's lynchpin, "Osama bin Laden's greatest ally," as one newspaper editorial had put it long ago, is still alive.

These aren't things you can write in a letter. Letters are for sharing news and chatting about your life. Neither my mother in prison nor I in my bookstore could have any news to share—each day is the same. That didn't stop her from writing to me at first, when I lived with my grandmother.

But I never read those letters. And when I left that tragic scene behind, I never gave her a new address. When you know someone's not to be trusted, it's hard to have a real conversation with them.

And yet, the impulse to write it all out throbs inside of me. If I could write it, I could be sure that it would end when it was supposed to. When I was a girl, I wrote reams of poetry. I hid myself in voices borrowed from the books I read. Peter's books. I placed all my jumbled thoughts and emotions into lines and cadences where they would remain fixed in place, obedient. All the love and anger and fear flowed out of me in black and blue ink pressed onto white paper, and then I could breathe again.

Then things changed, and I couldn't do it anymore. I wrote my last poem on a small slip of receipt paper torn from the first roll I'd inserted into my register at Brick & Mortar Books, the rough grain of the antique countertop transferred into my words by the pen. It held the whole weight of the hope I had that day. I taped it onto the first page of a clean notebook, thinking I would follow it up with more. But no more poetry came.

Will it come now, when I need it so badly? Can I pick up where I left off?

I wrench a dusty cardboard box down from the closet and pull out the first of many spiral notebooks I had filled in years past. There, waiting on the first page just where I left it, is my last poem. On the next, I had begun a journal in which I recorded the joyful tedium of my new business venture. Books bought or donated, shelves moved, organizational philosophies weighed, my first sale. Then it became something else entirely, something I never thought I'd write. A novel.

The year 2013 had been a big one for Brick & Mortar. The west branch of the River City library system had shut down, and my fledgling store was the recipient of boxes upon boxes of books. It had made the papers, so I saw an influx of customers who wanted to buy the old books they could have read for free a few months before. But one, a biography of Emily Dickinson, never made it to the shelves. I devoured it by night, amazed to find that the reclusive poet was actually quite famous in her own town. She didn't hoard all of her poems in the dark recesses of a desk but released them all over the country in letters to her friends—little gems, she called them. Tokens of herself offered up to select readers. Because while she desired solitude, she also coveted fame.

Her friendship with her sister-in-law, Susan, had struck a resonant chord somewhere deep inside me. I couldn't stop thinking of these two friends next door to each other, separated by walls but connected by words that traveled between them. I began to write their story, not as biography but as fiction.

Slowly I turn the pages, afraid to read, afraid that over the years the words that burned through me will have ashed over, lost their glow. My handwriting is so bad that it's a struggle to decipher every fifth word or so until about seven pages in, when, like reading Shakespeare or listening to someone speak in a heavy accent, I fit myself into the form of my slanted cursive words. Then I am flying.

I read for hours, notebook after notebook, and find my headache abating. The story is not as bad as I feared, but it's also not as good as I had once thought. I drone on for pages about houses and gardens. I wax poetic about the ache of unrequited love. I fail to convey a plot of any kind. I consider burning the whole lot, like Emily's sister burned the poet's letters at her behest after she died. But I am sitting upon 2,500 square feet filled top to bottom with paper and wood. A cathartic fire seems ill advised.

When I read the last sentence, I'm sure there must be some mistake. I thought I had finished it. I half recall a snappy final line that I swear I wrote down. But no. I leave Emily and Susan in their separate houses, gathering dust and cobwebs, fading a little from the sun that continuously streams through their unshaded windows.

Whatever happened to that last line I never penned, I can see why I left these two friends in suspended animation. I knew their friendship would end. I knew misunderstanding and illness and death would snatch it away from them. I could not put them through it. The end of a friendship—a true and soul-stirring friendship— is a terrible thing.

I file the notebooks away, their curling metal spines lined up like razor wire on a prison fence. There had been a picket fence between Emily and Susan over which a maid on one side might hand a letter to a stable boy on the other. Letters, despite them living just next door. I understand. So much easier to express truth on the page. No need to trouble with facial expressions and intonation and not having the right word at the right time. There is always time on paper.

I will not write a letter to my mother. Not now. I will not attempt a poem. But perhaps I can salvage this novelization of an expansive mind confined in a prosaic life. Perhaps I can write the end of it after all.

The next morning I wake to the promise of a return to business as usual—which is to say very little business at all. I reinstall The Professor in his roomy cage downstairs, put a sign in the front window—Absolutely No Reporters—and begin to draw up a new outline for my limping novel.

Dawt Pi arrives at eleven, carrying another thick, padded envelope in her hand. "Robin, I think your friend sent you another book."

8

then

Late one night a week before homecoming, I finished *For Whom the Bell Tolls*. I had plodded through most of it, feeling very much like I had been stuck in a mountain cave along with the tiresome characters for a month. But the last fifty pages or so made it all worth it, and when I read the last sentence I couldn't believe there was no more.

Still, I was starting to get testosterone fatigue. I broke from the pattern I had established of writing poems about the characters or the plot and instead penned something less subtle.

> Man said to Girl, The human race
> is known to me by voice and face
> so listen close to what I say
> by dark of night and light of day.
>
> Yes, said she, with reverent smile,
> that is indeed the truth, not guile,
> but if you look a little closer
> you may find I know some too, sir.

Haven't you a book or three
by someone who looks more like me
than Hemingway or Joyce or Faulkner,
say, the Brontës or Alice Walker?

For women make up half the globe—
I think you'll find if we disrobe
our brains, expose them to the light,
they are the same, by day or night.

Early Monday morning, I popped the paper through one of the slits in Peter's locker. The next day I opened my own locker to find the bottom shelf stacked with books. Austen, Hurston, Cather, Woolf, Walker, Lowry, Morrison, Brontë, Atwood, Rand, Gilman, du Maurier. I smiled at the tower of feminine names. But my smile quickly faded. I gathered them all up in my arms—no small feat for the sheer volume of pages—and headed for the senior wing.

Peter was sitting on a green island, elbows on his knees, talking to someone across from him. He was flanked by dull-looking guys, and directly behind him, with her skinny legs on either side of his and arms clutching his waist, was Sarah Kukla, the blonde cheerleader whose name had been paired with Peter's for weeks in rumors about homecoming.

I dumped the stack in front of him, and the books skidded out like shards of broken glass along the floor. "What's all this?" I asked.

He glanced around and subtly pried Sarah's fingers away from his stomach. "You said you wanted some books by women. I thought you'd be happy."

"So you've already read all of these?"

"No," he said slowly, "but you can have them."

"That's not how this works."

I ignored the sneer Sarah was directing toward me. The guy next to Peter snickered and got an elbow in the ribs in return. He scooted out of range and commenced smirking.

"But I'm never going to read all of that," Peter said.

"Why not?"

"It's stuff I wouldn't relate to. You know—childbirth and rape and dresses and dances."

"But I would?"

"Well, yeah. You're a girl."

"So I must want to read about rape and childbirth? Because that's part of my experience?"

"Well—"

"And when was the last time you saw me in a dress?"

"I—"

"And wasn't it *you* who asked *me* to go to a dance?" I briefly locked eyes with Sarah, who had swung around to fill in the empty spot left by Peter's retreating friend. "Take them back. Take them all back. And when you've read one, give it to me to read. If not, consider our deal done."

I spun around and stalked off down the hall to a chorus of *oooohs* as Peter's friends razzed him for getting dressed down by a freshman. I had never felt more powerful than at that moment, not even when I had knocked him off his feet in the first week of school.

The feeling didn't last long. The rest of the week my locker was empty.

At night when I would normally be reading, I instead sat glumly in the living room watching *Jeopardy* and *Wheel of Fortune* with my grandmother and The Professor. She was really good at *Wheel of Fortune*, really bad at *Jeopardy*. It didn't stop her—or the parrot—from shouting out answers in the form of a question to Alex Trebek, as though he might hear and pop out of the TV to award her the prize money. She never tried to make conversation with me, even during the commercials. Finally, though, on Thursday night when she turned off the TV, she spoke to me in her low, smoky voice.

"You going to the homecoming dance?"

"I hadn't planned on it."

"Why not?"

I shrugged.

"Because if you were going to the dance I was going to give you a little extra money to buy a dress."

A lump formed in my throat as I thought of how

I should have been shopping for homecoming at Nordstrom's with my mom. She would have gotten me any dress I wanted, plus shoes, a matching purse, and gorgeous jewelry—not fake either—then taken me out for tiramisu. What did they have here? JCPenney? Sears? I looked around at the tattered afghan, the worn couch, the scratched-up coffee table. If she had extra money, I could think of a lot better things to spend it on than a dress I would wear once.

"No need. But thank you."

"You're welcome!" squawked The Professor from the coffee table. Then he pooped on it.

The next day, most of the school was decked out in Kennedy High T-shirts, jerseys, or whatever was red in their closets. Others—gamers and stoners and some other kids who just didn't care—were wearing their normal clothes, but you only noticed them if you really looked, so subsumed were they by the boisterous intoxicating mixture of school spirit and hormones. I was in jeans and a black sweater.

During second hour the announcement came over the PA system that Peter Flynt had been elected homecoming king. Sarah Kukla was the queen. Of course. I got out of there the moment the last bell rang.

As the sun set that evening, I could hear the cheers of the crowd and the whistles of the referees down on the football field. Carried across the flat farmland on the autumn wind, the voices floated along, stopped above the trailer, and then crept in through the windows. For once I was glad to hear the TV switch on and the irritating sound of local commercials for law offices and car dealerships.

I was in bed that night by ten o'clock. I tried and failed to avoid wondering what Peter was doing at that moment, what I would be doing at that moment if I hadn't stupidly turned him down. It had been for nothing. I really had wanted to go with him. And the books had stopped anyway.

I must have drifted off at some point, because I was definitely awakened. For a moment I didn't know what had pulled me back from sleep, but then I heard a light knocking on my window. I peeked through the blinds and nearly screamed. Someone was out there, face inches from mine, features obscured by the darkness.

"Robin! It's Peter," came a muffled voice. "Come outside."

I hurried out of my room, turned on the porch light, and opened the door. "It's after midnight. What are you doing here?"

At Peter's silent perusal, I remembered that I was in nothing but an oversized Boston College T-shirt—the only thing I had of my dad's. I had cried for an hour the day I realized it no longer smelled like him. Peter was still in his tux and shiny black wingtips.

"I brought you something," he finally said. He pulled a paperback book from his waistband at the small of his back and held it out to me. "I read this. It's actually pretty good."

I saw the title, *Wuthering Heights*, but ignored it. "How did you know where I lived?"

"It wasn't all that hard to figure out. You do hang out in the graveyard more than a normal person. Figured you had to live close. Nothing's closer than this place. Plus I saw Jason Wisniewski mowing the cemetery grass once when I was visiting Mom. I thought maybe he had run into you. Cornered him in the bathroom at the dance and he said he'd seen you come out of the place with Snow White and the Seven Dwarves. Took me a minute to realize that he meant the Mary statue and the gnomes in the garden."

"Yeah, Martha really likes gnomes. And Mary."

"Who's Martha?"

"A cousin. She's who I live with."

"Oh." Peter looked like he was going to ask me why I lived with a cousin, but instead he held the book out to me again. "So do you want it or what?"

This time I took it. "Thanks." I hugged it against my chest. "Why didn't you just wait until Monday and put it in my locker?"

He put his hands in his pockets. "I dunno. I wanted to see you. The night didn't feel quite right. Whole week was off, really. I played terrible."

"Did you win?"

He gave me an incredulous look. "You didn't watch the game?"

"No."

He ran a hand through his hair. "Well, we won—barely—and only because the other team screwed up so much. Coach took me out during the third quarter and let Hayes finish out the game."

"Is the dance over?"

"Not quite."

"So where's Sarah?"

He waved his hand dismissively. "Probably dead drunk and sitting in Brad Ellis's lap."

"You left her there?"

"She left. With Brad. We only went together because we were pretty sure we would be the king and queen. I don't care about her or anything."

"She looked like she cared about you."

"She doesn't even really know me. She just latches on to people who she thinks will make her look good."

It was such an arrogant statement, but somehow I felt like Peter didn't realize it. And he did make people look good. He couldn't help it.

"Hey, want to go for a walk?" he asked.

"In this?" I tugged at the bottom of my night-shirt.

"It's not too cold out."

I slipped into a pair of flip-flops I had left outside a week ago, and we walked out across the small patch of lawn that separated the trailer from the cemetery. Through the treetops, the full moon cast shapes like scribbles on the ground. We were one good rainstorm away from the end of the fall color and the beginning of the frosted browns and grays of November.

Peter had been wrong when he said it wasn't cold. He was in a tailored jacket over a dress shirt and an undershirt, probably still trying to cool off after the game and the dance. I hugged my arms against my body but did not complain.

We strolled up and down the rows of graves. I didn't know what he was thinking—if he was looking for the right words to say to me, or if he was replaying the bad game or Sarah leaving the dance with another guy. Or was he wondering what I was thinking? When I really thought about how stuff was going on in other people's brains all the time, and that it wasn't the same as all the stuff going on in my brain, the world felt a bit unreal. All those bodies wandering about with thoughts of their own. Was that what all these dead people were missing? Electrical impulses in the brain? Breath and brain activity. Were those all that frog had needed?

We stopped in front of Emily Flynt's grave.

"My dad hasn't been out here at all that I know of."

I didn't say anything.

"He's always been an all-or-nothing guy. But I think that's wrong."

"What do you mean, 'all-or-nothing'?"

Peter took a deep breath and seemed to be deciding what it was he had meant. "He never does anything halfway. He never leaves something half done. You know?"

At my confused look, he went on.

"Like, when I said I wanted to play football, he wasn't like, 'That's cool, son. Be a good sport and have fun out there.' He started with an hour-long lecture about commitment—this is when I was going out for peewee football in like fourth grade—and drilled me and came to every game to take notes on what I did wrong and how I needed to improve. He was not happy about the game tonight."

"That's why you came out here instead of going home."

He shrugged and gave his head a little shake. "Not exactly. But yeah, it's hard to be around him. When Mom died, the next day he started cleaning out her closet and listed her car for sale and made an appointment with some appraiser to look through her jewelry. He had the whole house scrubbed of her within a month. He let me keep the books as long as he didn't see them. All-or-nothing. Look me in the eye and tell me that's not messed up."

For the barest breath of a moment I considered telling him about my dad to make him feel better about his. "Why is there a cemetery way out here anyway?" I asked instead. "There's no church."

"There used to be a little Methodist church where the gravel lot is now. It burned down a long time ago, and when they rebuilt they did it closer to town. But they still own the land out here, so I guess they'll keep burying people until it's filled up."

We walked on in silence, and I began to wonder where I would be buried. Not in Michigan. I belonged in some deep green place back east that was overgrown with moss and ivy, not in this field with its dry grass and too little shade. But would my mom be buried here someday? From Sussex you were made and to Sussex you shall return? And my dad—would any cemetery want to take him? Where did they bury murderers?

"You know," he said finally, "that last poem doesn't really cut it for Ernest Hemingway."

"I beg your pardon? I never signed a contract that said I had to write a certain kind of poem. You didn't even come up with the idea of paying with poems. I did. So I should be the one to set the rules."

"I'm just saying, it wasn't like the other ones.

All the rest have something to do with the plot of the book and, apparently, you, though for the life of me I can't really figure that all out. The last one doesn't fit with the rest of them."

"So? You want me to write another one?"

"Not necessarily."

"Then what?"

He tipped my face up to his. "I'd take something else."

I had to smile at his boldness. "I didn't give you one of those before. What makes you think I'll give you one now?"

"I dunno. Just a feeling. I've had a crappy week because of you. I played a crappy game because of you. I went to a crappy dance without you. Don't you want to make my night a little less crappy?"

I shivered involuntarily against the chill night air. Peter slipped off his jacket, slung it around my shoulders, and drew me closer in one deft move.

"Well?" he prompted.

I feigned indifference, but my heart was pounding. "Fine."

I closed my eyes. His lips touched mine. Then came the scream of screeching tires and the sickening sound of crumpling metal.

9

now

W hat is that one about?" Dawt Pi asks.
There is always a pause after this question as I quickly attempt to encapsulate an entire novel in one or two sentences and, if I'm being fairly conscientious, edit out the really complicated words. It's not easy. Each time, when I hear what comes out of my mouth—so inadequate, so small compared to what I had experienced while reading—I feel like I've snatched the story from the author's hands and trampled it underfoot.

Dawt Pi waits through the lengthening silence. When I read it at age fourteen, I thought that *A Separate Peace* was about fear. Maybe it was then—fear was my dominant emotion for much of that year. Now as I set it on the counter at arm's length I am broadsided by the realization that, at its simplest, it's about the deliberate betrayal of a friend—one who trusted you.

"It's about a boy who pushes his best friend out of a tree."

Dawt Pi screws up her face.

"That's just part of the plot," I clarify, feeling as

though I have punched John Knowles in the gut. "It's about more than that. It's about friendship and coming of age."

"Humph. Seems like a lot of your books are about that. They all start to sound the same. I don't understand why you need all these." She waves her hand to indicate that she is talking about the entire Brick & Mortar inventory.

"That's not fair. You may not have a lot of books in the Chin language, but you have stories."

"Stories that matter. The Bible. The history of our people. But we don't spend so much time making them up or so much money to buy them." She points to *The Catcher in the Rye* on the shelf behind me. "People don't spend more than a year's money on one book about a mean boy. We don't have stores and libraries full of books all about the same thing, that don't even sound nice to read about."

I have had plenty of opportunities in the last few years to be embarrassed at American excesses as Dawt Pi shifted my perspective on a lot of things—food, clothing, housing, transportation, entertainment. But when it comes to literature, I feel no shame. It may seem like an extravagance in a world riddled with poverty, injustice, and persecution, but those are the very realities that make it essential. I doubt I could convince Dawt Pi of this. In fact, my sadness over the gaping hole where her people's literary canon should be is only superseded by my frustration that this doesn't seem to bother her at all.

"Yes," I say, "these books are fiction, made up, imaginary. But they did happen—in the minds of the people who wrote them and the readers who turn the pages. They happen again and again, every time they are read. If I disappeared tomorrow, no one would miss me. But stories are alive, and some of them live forever."

Dawt Pi shakes her head and walks off. She has no desire to quibble about the existential qualities of literature. There are actually customers in the store for a change, drawn in by the commotion of the past few days. I suspect most have come to gawk. But soon I hear Dawt Pi stealthily guilting them into buying the books she thinks are all the same.

"You will feel much better about yourself when you go home if you at least buy something from the person you are spying on."

Her tactics prove effective in the short run— we sell more in one day than we have in the past two weeks—but I doubt many of the same people will return when faced with the prospect of interacting with the petite, pushy young woman with the exotic accent and almond eyes.

Every day for the next two weeks, Dawt Pi arrives precisely at eleven o'clock carrying the day's mail. And every day, another padded manila envelope containing a book is placed on the counter in front of me. They blow back into my life in the same order that Peter gave them to me long ago: first *The Catcher in the Rye* and *A Separate Peace*, followed by *Animal Farm*, *The Things They Carried*, *The Great Gatsby*, *Lord of the Flies*, *1984*, *Lolita*, *The Grapes of Wrath*, *Light in August*, *A Portrait of the Artist as a Young Man*, *For Whom the Bell Tolls*, *Wuthering Heights*. The postmarks inexplicably place their origins in California, Oregon, Washington, Idaho, Montana, Wyoming, Utah. They carry with them all my earliest memories of Peter, floating back into my life like paper boats.

Most of the books are not valuable like the first edition *Catcher* is. Some are pulp paperbacks that sold for less than a dollar when they were new. Others are hardcovers missing their jackets. The bottom edge of *Lolita* is warped and water damaged—I had been careless while reading it in the tub. I know without looking that all of them have light pencil underlines and occasional notes in Mrs. Flynt's precise penmanship, slightly darker brackets around phrases that Peter particularly liked, and the dog-ears, stars, exclamation points, and question marks I tended to add to the mix. Each one tells not only the story that the author had meant to convey—the one I find so difficult to encapsulate in a simple phrase for

91

Dawt Pi—but also the story of Emily Flynt's struggles, Peter Flynt's points of connection with his dead mother, and my own enraptured devotion to many of the very same lines of text that caught their eyes.

"What are you going to do with all of these?" Dawt Pi asks. "Are we going to sell them?"

It's a question that has been on my mind too.

"Only the one is really worth anything substantial."

"If you are going to keep them, you should bring them up to your apartment."

It would be the logical thing to do, but I can admit that logic has not always been my strength. Like so many of the characters in these books, I have often let my emotions drive. The truth is, I don't want to let Peter into my apartment. The few rooms I inhabit upstairs are all I seem to have left, my last bastion of privacy in a world bent on intrusion.

"I don't know. I think I'll probably end up selling them."

It makes the most sense. There was a reason I didn't keep those books in the first place, and nothing has changed since then. Nothing could change.

"Yeah," I say with more resolve. "Let's sell them."

I pull *Wuthering Heights* off the shelf and, starting at the back, flip through the pages to see how much writing is in it. It's not too bad. Four dollars wouldn't be asking too much. I flip to the front page to write the amount in the upper right-hand corner. But before I can position the pencil, I am assaulted by words written in black ink in Peter's bold hand, filling up the entirety of the inside cover. They are instantly familiar.

I am the consequence of love past
A love given freely
From one to another
Sent from this heart to that
Carried along Fortune's icy wind

I set my heart upon another
Chasing him down like prey
Caught up at break of day
Relaxed too long and he
Left me alone in the briar patch

I buried my love in Earth's belly
And sent out my anger
The putrid rolling waves
Of all my misplaced faith
Nevermore to trust his heart—or mine

At the bottom of the inside cover is a red-stamped notation: "Paid in Full."

I grab *For Whom the Bell Tolls* off the shelf and open the cover. My request for books by women is there in black ink. I look at *Light in August*, recalling how clever I thought it was to pen a haiku in payment for the long-winded Faulkner. There it is, floating in a pool of yellowed pulp paper.

> I carry myself
> in secret down dusty streets
> and everyone stares.

I open *The Great Gatsby*, and my mouth silently forms the words as I read.

> We build ourselves
> with pieces of truth
> laced with lies
> . . . or else the reverse.

> One tale here,
> one truth there,
> create something new
> . . . yet not quite true.

> When we're through
> No one will tell
> the *was* from *should*
> . . . because no one could.

They're all there. Every poem I wrote, each certified with that bold red stamp declaring the books paid for. I put my finger upon *The Catcher in the Rye*, close my eyes in a frantic, half-formed prayer, and pull it from the shelf. A slow breath. I open the front cover.

Nothing.

He must have known the value and chosen not to deface Salinger with the bad teenage poetry I had foolishly thought would one day be worth something. Or else he hadn't decided to add the poems until after he sent the first book. Either way, I could still sell it. I'm glad, of course. But not entirely. Had Peter lost the first poem I wrote for him? Had he thrown it away?

Dawt Pi reaches forward and slips a finger beneath the front flap of the dust jacket, releasing one more page that had been caught under it. Before the page has had time to land on the other side, I can already read the words that are inked, dark and permanent, on the inside cover. I'd chosen a modified Italian sonnet form, the most restrictive structure I could think of, in which to stuff Holden Caulfield's whiny self.

> In times like these it pays to know one's
>   mind;
> To trace one's inner thoughts upon clear
>   lines;
> To pause, reflect, and judge; to seek the
>   signs

That guide one toward the simple truths
    that bind

The heart to soul, the thought to word,
    remind
Us that each wretched one of us entwines
Disdain and pain and fear with love,
    combines
The self we are with one we have
    designed.

But focused as we are on others' faults,
We cannot help but launch our cruel
    assaults.
We pick apart each other piece by piece,
And through it feel a sensual release

Of pleasant chemicals within the brain.
Forget largesse. I'd rather just complain.

"What does this mean, Robin?" Dawt Pi asks
as she scans the words.

"It means we can't sell any of these," I say with
mingled devastation and relief. "And maybe it's
time to start looking for that other job."

10

then

I was eight years old when I realized that death had a sound. I'd find later that it had many voices, but the first one I recognized was when my neighbor's champion basset hound, Farley, was hit by a car. It wasn't the screeching of the tires—though sometimes that sound is the preamble to death. It was the sound the dog made. An unearthly, stomach-twisting mixture of pain and surprise and incomprehension. Beneath it all ran the ragged sound of something else— that thing that all dead things are missing— leaving that dog's body. At the moment of impact, Farley looked me in the eye where I sat on the front lawn, and I could swear it wasn't a dog at all looking at me. It was whatever left that dog. It was there. Then it wasn't. And the driver never stopped.

Death had a sound, and I heard it somewhere intertwined with that crunching metal the moment Peter and I kissed.

I slipped into the still-warm arms of Peter's jacket and took off after him toward the road. He ran so fast that in a moment I couldn't see him ahead of me as I stumbled through the cemetery in my flip-flops. When I came to the road, a wisp of smoke glowed red off to the left. I ran along the ditch toward the drive that led over it, then stopped. Just visible over the edge of the ditch on the other side of the asphalt, a tire was spinning slowly in the lurid red glow of a taillight. An engine rattled. A radio blared. In the moonlight, Peter scrambled back up the side of the ditch.

"Robin!" he screamed, not realizing how close I was. "Robin!"

I skittered across, terrified.

"Call 911!" His eyes were wild. "We need an ambulance."

I ran as fast as I could back to the trailer. The Professor squawked and flapped as I burst through the door. Hands shaking, I dialed 911 on the kitchen phone and sputtered out the awful words between labored breaths. The dispatcher was asking for details I didn't have, trying to be heard over The Professor's screeching, telling me to stay on the line. But I left the phone swaying at the end of its coiled cord and ran back out to Peter.

I crossed over to the scene of the accident and leaned over the ditch.

Then I wished I hadn't.

The passenger-side window had shattered across the motionless body of a girl. Blood stained her beautiful formal dress, covered her face, and dripped from one loose blonde curl. Her left hand lay limp at her side, a blood-streaked white bone in her forearm clearly protruding through her skin and catching the moonlight that had felt so romantic moments before. I could just make out the figure of a young man in the driver's seat next to her in the dark.

"The ambulance is on its way." I barely managed to push the words past the tightness in my throat.

Peter looked up at me, his eyes like sinkholes. "It's Sarah and Brad."

In a town as small as Sussex and a school as small as Kennedy, of course even I would know the people in this car. But that moment of knowing, really knowing, nearly knocked me backward. I couldn't ask if she was alive. I didn't want to know. All the same I was sure she must be dead. All the blood. You couldn't lose all that blood and survive.

Peter reached over Sarah's unmoving body and turned off the radio. In the sudden silence I could hear his feet splashing in the sludge at the bottom of the ditch. A vile fusion of stagnant water, gasoline, and beer mingling with the sweet scent of coolant and corn stubble drifted into my nose. I stood on the side of the road, useless, while Peter buried his face in his bloody hands and let out a deep, animal growl that quickly became a yell. It sounded far too much like that basset hound. He kicked the car hard with his soggy patent leather wingtips, cursed, then climbed out of the ditch and crumpled at my feet on the gravel shoulder.

What should I do? What did people do? These things were supposed to be handled by adults. When Farley had been run over, I ran inside to my mother. I thought she'd rush outside right away—to help the dog, to get the license plate, to question witnesses. But she didn't. She hugged me fiercely, put both soft hands on my tear-streaked cheeks, and said, "Are you okay?"

But no one said that to me now. I shoved the tears back inside. Stupid crybaby. Sarah and Brad were probably dead and all I could think about was myself?

Peter and I sat there in an eerie pocket of quiet despair for a long time. I avoided looking at his face, now striped with tears and Sarah's blood. Was I supposed to cup his cheeks? Ask him if he was okay? Of course he wasn't.

I saw lights in the distance, flashing like the glittering confetti shot from pressure canons at the start of each football game as the team broke through the paper and trotted onto the field. But instead of cheers, they were accompanied by the wail of sirens.

The next half hour I felt like I was watching something on TV. People in uniforms came and went on swift feet, barking orders and updates. I clung to the blanket an EMT had draped around my shoulders in lieu of my mother's absent arms. Sarah and Brad were extracted from the car and put on stretchers. Sarah was immediately put into the back of an ambulance and driven into the black night. Peter ran off without a word to follow them to the hospital in his car. The stretcher that held Brad did not move. There is no need to rush a corpse to a doctor.

When my father was arrested, it was quick and quiet. No lights, no sirens, no warning. Just men in navy jackets with yellow lettering and black handguns. Voices were raised, but not to shouting. No one cried out, no one swore. It was almost like everyone in the house had expected it— except me. I copied the sober expression I saw on my mother's face and stayed that way, silent and solemn through everything, even her arrest a few months later, until the day my grandmother met me in a tiny regional airport terminal and I was permitted to resume my childhood. Or what was left of it.

When I finally went back to the trailer, Grandma was seated at the kitchen table with an open book, a cigarette, and a cup of coffee. The phone had been hung up, The Professor calmed by a black sheet over his cage. Grandma put the mug down on the page to keep her spot. A few pages on the other side slowly fanned up.

"Crazy night," she said, raising the half-smoked

cigarette to her leathered lips. "You know those kids?"

I nodded.

She flicked the cigarette on the edge of an ashtray that, judging by the logo in the center, had been stolen from a hotel. "You okay?"

Finally. Someone asked the question. But it wasn't the same. This woman was not my mother.

"I'm fine."

She coughed violently, so violently and for so long I thought I might have to call 911 twice in one night. Then she recovered and pointed at the book. "I'm not sure you should be reading this. I hear it's banned in some places." She lifted the coffee cup and closed the cover, keeping her finger in her spot, so I could see the title.

"That's mine," I said. "What are you doing with it?"

She opened the book again and put her mug bookmark down. "What do you think I'm doing with it? I'm reading it. Is that a problem?"

"It's a problem that you took it from my room without even asking! And it's a problem that you're putting this on it!"

I made a grab for the coffee cup, seeing too late how full it was. In the jostling, a little sloshed over the side and slithered down the cup, forming a large brown C on the page. I snatched up the book and rushed for a paper towel, but it was too late. I let loose with one of my most exasperated sighs and stomped off to my bedroom, book in hand.

"Hey!" she shouted after me. "Whose tux is that? And why don't you have any pants on?"

I slammed my door and pushed all my books under the bed in short, tidy stacks. Then I lined up my shoes and tucked each pair under the bed skirt to shield my horde from further pilfering. If she thought I shouldn't be reading *The Catcher in the Rye*, she'd probably bring me to her priest for an exorcism if she read even a few pages of *Lolita*.

When I crawled back into bed, it was after 4:00 a.m. My body shook—from the cold night with no pants, the adrenaline, the exhaustion, from another disaster outside my control. Every time I closed my eyes I saw Sarah Kukla's bloody face, her white bone, her ruined dress. Was she still alive? Was Peter hunched over in the waiting room staring at his bloodstained cuffs? Was he pacing the hospital hallways, his wet shoes squeaking with every step? What were Brad Ellis's parents doing at that moment? Had they told his younger sister, a sophomore who had landed a large role in the fall play that was premiering in two weeks?

I wanted to call out for my dad, the soother of nighttime fears. But no amount of screaming could reach him where he was. So I just cried. All night. And most of the next morning while

Grandma was at church. She didn't make me go with her. "You can stay home just this once," she said. But there was nothing she was going to do to make me go the next Sunday or the next. I had nothing nice to say to God, so it was best if I didn't say anything at all.

On Monday morning we were all herded onto the gymnasium bleachers. For those who hadn't already heard, the red-eyed teachers would have been a clue. Principal Pietka read from an index card, probably too emotional to wing it as he did at other assemblies. Brad Ellis was dead. He had not been wearing his seat belt, we were told in a stern tone that seemed to accuse the entire student body of having conspired to convince him not to put it on. Sarah Kukla was still in the hospital with her shattered arm, broken ribs, internal bleeding, a fractured knee cap, and other injuries. Yes, alcohol had been involved.

As we shuffled back to our classes it seemed that everyone around me was in some stage of crying, whether holding back tears or openly weeping or wiping moisture from their eyes. I thought I should cry too. I tried. But I couldn't manage it. I was all out. I had never exchanged a word or a glance with Brad Ellis. The only interaction I'd had with Sarah Kukla was the one where she had to peel herself off of Peter in order to get a better angle from which to glare at me.

I didn't wish either of them harm. I just didn't know them enough to cry.

Not that that stopped anyone else. At some point during every class period for the rest of the day, and less so the rest of the week, some girl would burst into tears and be escorted down to the office beneath the comforting arm of a teacher or friend. We were all encouraged to talk to a school counselor and to be open with our parents about how we felt.

I considered writing to my mother, telling her about the whole thing. But I didn't want to talk to her. She should have been there. She should have already heard all about it and laid on my bed with me, stroking my hair, until I fell asleep. A letter would take days to get to Connecticut, and her response would take even more time to reach me. And a letter couldn't hug me, couldn't stroke my hair. So what good was it? All I wanted, all I needed, was another book from Peter.

Eventually we got the news that Sarah was conscious, then that she was improving daily, then that she was home. Peter started reading again, so I started reading again. Brad Ellis's little sister powered through her part in the play, which was apparently better attended than in years past. I'm sure they all told themselves they were supporting her in this difficult time. As I leaned against a wall in the cafeteria during inter-mission, sipping at a plastic cup of watered-down punch, I heard people whisper about her tragedy, about her irresponsible brother, about her poor parents. Had people whispered about me back in Amherst after I left? Was someone whispering about me even now?

The first dusting of snow came. Thanksgiving passed. Grandma and The Professor and I watched the parade on TV. We never talked about that late-night fight or the book or the coffee stain or my lack of pants. Then one day in mid-December she handed me a letter that looked like The Professor had gotten ahold of it.

"Your mother wants me to bring you to visit her."

I didn't answer her, just turned the next page of *The Handmaid's Tale.*

"We can go during your winter break, though I don't really want to drive in the snow."

"I'll save you the trouble."

"What do you mean?"

I looked up from my book. "I won't go."

Grandma sat down next to me on the couch and waited for me to look at her. I tried to ignore her, but once it was obvious I wouldn't get rid of her that way, I put down the book and looked her in the face.

"Robin," she said, "I know you're upset with your mother, but this is not the way to handle it."

"How would you know?" I snapped. "You got a

lot of experience with this sort of thing? Did your mom go to jail for trying to help your murderer dad avoid prison? You don't know anything about what I'm going through."

"Not exactly, no." She put a hand on mine. "But I have been the mother who was abandoned by her daughter."

I pulled my hand away and folded my arms across my chest.

"When your mother left Sussex it was for good," she said. "She didn't want to be associated with anything from back home, which included me. She never wrote me, never called, never invited me to visit her, never came back home for Christmas. The only time I saw her after she graduated from high school was at her wedding, and the only reason I was invited was because your father insisted."

"Why wouldn't she want to see you? Why didn't she ever talk about you?"

Grandma sighed. Then The Professor sighed.

"Our home was not always a happy one. Lindy's father was a manic-depressive. They call it something else now. Bipolar, I guess. And he was an alcoholic. It was hard living with him. He'd go from inviting everyone he knew over for a cookout and giving me just an hour to prepare for it to yelling and screaming and slamming doors. Lindy used to hide from him under her bed. And I guess I didn't know how to handle it

107

all. When Bob was raging and yelling about the house being a mess, I blamed Lindy and Kevin more often than not, so I got mad at them too. I probably should have been defending them. But I always sided with Bob, because if I didn't . . . it was just much worse for everyone. I don't blame her for wanting to pretend we didn't exist. But that doesn't mean it hasn't hurt. That's the one good thing to come of this whole mess with Norman. We're finally talking."

"Yeah, well, maybe I'll start talking to her when I do something really stupid with my life. As for right now, maybe she should start pretending that *I* don't exist."

I got up from the couch, went to my room, and slammed the door. Out my window the snow was falling, falling, falling. I opened up my book again and picked up where I'd left off. It was easy—I just opened to where my finger was, found the last line I'd read, and read the next sentence. If only someone had just put their finger in my life where it got interrupted so I could find the last line I'd said—*Good night, Mom! Good night, Dad!*—and keep going from there. Instead, someone had ripped the book in half and burned the end of it, and I was left hanging off the page, holding on for dear life, trying to figure out what came next.

11

now

The weather has warmed and activity around the marina has picked up. It's the time of year that wives wander up Midway Street looking for something to pass the time so they won't get roped into resealing the hull of a boat. I'll make more money this month than I have since Christmas, which admittedly isn't saying much. I push two old library carts filled with used paperbacks outside and position them on the sidewalk on either side of the door. Signs call out, "50¢ each, 3 for $1."

I linger, enjoying the warmth of the sun on my face, still so novel in April. Down on the river, a white sail catches a breeze as it approaches the Columbus Bridge, one of four drawbridges that connect the east and west sides of River City, inexplicably named for Spanish explorers who never set foot in Michigan. The sailboat will have one more bridge to clear before the river widens and spills into the Saginaw Bay and then into Lake Huron. And then who can say where it will go.

The drivers backed up on the bridge are surely cursing the man with the sailboat who made them all late with his leisure. The candy-striped arms with the blinking red lights lift, the cars roll like marbles over the bridge, and the day goes on. When they get to their destinations, everyone will understand. In the warm months in this town, "Sorry, I was stuck on the bridge" is a more common greeting than "Hello."

At ten o'clock I get my first customers of the day, and for the next couple hours things are fairly steady. A dozen or so books are plucked from the shelves and carried off to new homes. I send each one off with a silent charge: to live inside this reader in that long, drawn-out conversation across the miles and the ages. This is the impulse that led me to open a bookstore to begin with— to connect people with friends who will not fail them. Shy child, this is Madeleine L'Engle; she understands you. Overworked parent, this is J. R. R. Tolkien; he wants to take you on a trip. Budding conspiracy theorist, this is George Orwell; he believes you. Betrayed friend, this is Alexandre Dumas; you are right to be so angry.

A sick feeling lodges in my gut when I think how all of that could be gone soon. If I can't think of a way to get more customers into the store, my part in this mystical web of time travel and immortality will end. Another untimely interruption in life. But no matter how many sleepless nights I may have had in the past year, no matter how many sales I've had or ads I've taken out, I just can't seem to get enough traction.

The bell rings.

"You ever hear of this ArtPrize thing they've got going now in Grand Rapids?"

Sarah is already past me before I can turn around.

"It's this huge public art show—contest— where there's art all over the city, like in all different buildings and outside and everywhere." She heads for the mystery section and raises her voice to compensate for the insulating effect of the shelves. "And for two or three weeks it's open and people come from all over and they vote for their favorite."

"Yeah, I've heard of it."

"Do you think I could get something in it?"

"I don't see why not."

She emerges again carrying her painting. "Because I've been thinking that maybe that's what I need—something that makes a big splash. Then, if I win, I can quit my job and open my own studio and teach—the grand prize is $200,000. Can you imagine? And if I don't win, I still get my name out there. I just gotta get off my butt and go for it, you know?"

I nod supportively. Sarah's artwork is not necessarily something I'd vote for, but I can see that some people might.

She holds out the painting. "Picture this, only wall sized—a big wall, I'm talking huge."

"Okay, I can see that. What kind of . . . materials are you thinking of using?"

"This is the best part. What about an entire car—all in pieces, though. Like, exploded out, each piece separate. I bet I can get almost everything I need at a junkyard, and I bet I can get my uncle to help me pull it all apart."

"I bet you're right."

Sarah gazes at her painting, lost in the intoxicating effect of a new idea.

I feel a stab of jealousy and check the time. "Hey, would you mind watching the store while I run to the post office?"

"I can go there for you," she says without tearing her eyes from her artwork. "Give me the key to your box."

"No, I probably need to get a package from the front desk. I don't think they would give it to someone other than me or Dawt Pi."

"Why don't they put packages in your box?"

"Too small. I downsized about a year and a half ago. I wasn't getting anything but business-sized envelopes, so I didn't think it would be a problem. Dawt Pi checks at the desk for anything bigger."

"Where is she?" she says, finally looking up.

"I gave her the day off. She has an interview."

"What?"

"Better to do it now and not have any time where she's unemployed."

"But—are things really that bad?"

"I told you I'll be closed by the end of the year."

"No," she whined. "You love this place."

"Love isn't enough, Sarah. A store needs customers. It has to fill a need. Obviously there's not a big enough need to fill in this city. Everyone's reading ebooks. Or they order books online or go to the library or shop at the Barnes & Noble in Saginaw—and who knows how long that will even be around. Even big stores can't stay open, so it's no surprise I can't. Anyway, I've got to go to the post office, so could you sit at the register for me?"

She leans her painting against the counter. "You sure? Dawt Pi could pick it up tomorrow."

She could. I don't need to get it today. I could open two of them tomorrow. But I don't want to wait. When there's no mail on Sundays I feel anxious all day. I'm starting to depend on Peter's books, just as I had when I received them the first time, just as my grandmother had depended on cigarettes and The Professor depends on his morning paperback.

"I'd really appreciate it."

"Of course I'll do it," Sarah says, sitting on the stool behind the cash register. "I just didn't know if you really wanted to leave."

I laugh lightly. "It's not like I *never* leave. What do you think I eat up there? I'll be fine."

"Okay."

She doesn't sound sure, and I'm not as sure as I make myself out to be. I have spent so much of my life becoming invisible that it's a shock to the senses when I go out in public and people don't walk right through me. I do go grocery shopping out of necessity, but always late at night when there are few other customers and few clerks, and I always use the self-checkout.

"You can take my car," Sarah offers.

"I'll walk. I could use the exercise and the fresh air."

"Wait, what about this bird?"

"He won't bother you."

Sarah looks unconvinced.

"I'll only be twenty minutes."

It's a short walk to the post office. It's been so long since I've gotten the mail that I have to double-check I've got the right box before I turn the key in the lock. Two slim envelopes wait for me. Bills. I tuck them in my purse and head for the long counter behind which two workers stand ready to serve. I make my way to a short, plump woman with frizzy hair and large glasses about twenty years out of date, which is River City's fashion sweet spot.

"What can I do for ya, hon?"

"Any packages for Brick & Mortar Books?"

The woman narrows her eyes. "Where's Dorothy?"

"Excuse me?"

"Where's that little gal Dorothy?"

"You mean Dawt Pi?" I ask, carefully separating the syllables and pronouncing every letter.

"The little Oriental girl."

"That's Dawt Pi. She's in her twenties."

"Huh?"

"She's in her twenties. She's not a little girl. And people generally say Asian now."

The woman gives me a suspicious look. "She sick?"

"No, I gave her the day off. Do you have any packages for me?"

She eyeballs me. "I'll have to see some ID. I can't hand out packages willy-nilly to people. And I don't recognize you."

"I recognize her," says the tall bald man with fish eyes who has been watching our exchange from his perch at the next station. "Didn't you see her on the news?" At her blank look he adds, "*You* know," as if his insistence will retroactively change whether or not she had been watching the news a few weeks earlier. He turns to me. "Windsor, right?"

"Well, I'll go take a look in the back." The woman waddles off before I can correct her on the name or hand her the ID she insisted she needed, and I am left trying to avoid eye contact with the bald man in the preposterously short, government-issue tie.

I pretend to read a pamphlet on passports. Maybe when I sell the store I'll have enough money to get out of here, dye my hair blonde, start somewhere fresh. Again. My own personal witness protection program. The notion is as daunting as it is enticing.

The woman waddles back in. "Sorry, hon, but I got nothing for any Windsor."

I hold out my ID again. "It's actually Dickinson. Robin Dickinson."

"That your maiden name?" she says without looking at it.

"Yes," I lie. It's too much to explain.

She sighs and heads for the back again. The man is still staring at me.

Suddenly a tiny spark of the plucky person I once was pops in my chest. I whip my head up and stare him down. His bulgy eyes maintain their target for a moment until all at once it seems his brain catches up. He looks away and busies himself with some papers.

I turn, triumphant, to the round woman puffing her way back to the counter. She plops a padded manila envelope onto the desk in front of me. "There ya go, hon."

"Thank you."

The bald man does not look up as I pass, but

I'm sure as I push through the door that he is watching my exit.

Out on the sidewalk I check the postmark. Colorado. One state closer than the last. What is this game Peter's playing? I pull the red strip on the envelope and slide the book out. *Jane Eyre* by Charlotte Brontë. I remember exactly what Peter said to me back then. "Figured if that one by Emily Brontë was good, this one would be too."

I remember wondering as I read it whether he saw himself as the older Mr. Rochester, saw me as Jane. And I remember the chill that ran up my spine as I realized that the only underlined passages in the entire book were those involving Mr. Rochester's mad arsonist of a wife.

I open the cover, and sure enough, my payment poem is there.

A road drawn taut between horizons
moves me ever on
from one sun to the next,
suns that can't discern the rising
from the sinking down,
beginning from the end.

Flanked by fences delineating
my life's boundaries,
I walk along to then
when now is barely past being.

There's no wandering,
no asking why? or when?

Whether custom or misfortune's hand
propels me onward,
results are much the same:
I exist upon this hostile land,
walking dirt packed hard,
with nothing—save my name.

Perhaps someday I will come upon
a gap in the fence,
a burnt-out opening,
and light out, stumbling, on my own
to find evidence
I'm one of the living.

I close the book and quickly walk back to the store, memory at my heels.

Inside, I don't see Sarah at the desk or The Professor on his perch. What I do see is a large and elaborate manor constructed of chunky mass market romance and mystery novels. There are towers and parapets, gates and a grand hall lined with the spines of books that have a figure of some sort on them, like two stately rows of sexy statues. I find The Professor inside the structure, pacing back and forth before his throne of books.

Sarah appears with an armful of additional building materials. "You're back! How'd it go?"

"What is all this?" I wave my hand at the castle of books.

Sarah shrugs. "I got bored. And that bird kept moving around and running at me. I think he's disturbed. I didn't want to touch him, so I thought I'd at least contain him. Sorry. I'll put them all back."

"No, it's cool. Do you think that would fit in the front window? That could really draw attention."

Sarah looks doubtful. "I'd have to take it all apart and build it again."

"I'll help. You were going to have to take it all down anyway." I start to remove the two books closest to me.

"Not there!" Sarah shouts, but it's too late. Half the castle comes tumbling down. The Professor flaps and swears and poops on the countertop. "Those were load-bearing books," Sarah says unnecessarily.

We clean up the mess, placate The Professor with cashews, and move all the books to the window to build the castle bigger and better than before. Sarah directs the design, creating a stunning gold and pink and ivory castle surrounded by a moat of blue and peopled with the dashing, bare-chested heroes and desperate, clutching heroines of old romance novel cover art. When it's all done, we stand on the sidewalk and gaze in at our beautiful creation.

"I should have had you doing my displays all along."

"You're absolutely right," she says. "Maybe you could get someone from the paper to come down here and take a picture and get a little free advertising."

I nod despite my distaste for members of the news media. "That's a good idea." I reach for the door, but Sarah grabs my arm.

"Oh, Robin! I know how we can save your store."

12

then

S arah should be coming back to school soon."
Though I never asked about her, Peter faithfully updated me on Sarah Kukla's progress. We
were strolling through downtown River City
on an unseasonably warm and sunny December
afternoon, shopping for the few people in our
lives to whom we owed Christmas presents,
people neither of us actually knew very well.

"She'll be walking soon."

I was glad for her recovery, but I didn't want to
talk about her. She was on Peter's mind entirely
too much. When he visited her, did he talk about
me?

"What did you think of *The Yellow Wallpaper*?"
I asked.

It took Peter a moment to switch gears. "I
thought it was pretty good. Kind of creepy, in a
good way." He put a hand out to stop my forward
motion. "Let's go in here."

We stepped through the fake snow–encrusted
door of St. Macarius & Sons candy shop. The
smell of roasting nuts filled the air. The shelves

were lined with every kind of chocolate and candy known to man. If I found nothing else for her, I could at least get my grandmother some chocolate turtles and gourmet jelly beans. We drifted down the colorful rows of gummy fruit shapes, butterscotch, black licorice, and lemon drops. I thought of the mayhem The Professor could spread were he let loose in such a colorful, textural place.

Peter bent over and snagged a bag of burnt peanuts from a low shelf. "Why is it that there are so many crazy women in these books?" he asked. "Aren't there normal, happy women in the world that don't do completely irrational things?"

I was impressed that he had noticed that particular trend in the books we had been reading of late. His mother had obviously noticed it. In any book that included a woman who appeared depressed or insane, Emily Flynt had underlined, double underlined, and scribbled little notes that seemed to me to indicate some level of solidarity.

"The story tells you why," I said.

He picked up a bag of gummy orange slices, then put it back down. "What, because she couldn't write? That's what drove her crazy?"

"No. Not just that. Isn't it pretty obvious? *Their Eyes Were Watching God, The Handmaid's Tale, The Bluest Eye, The Color Purple, The Bell Jar*—they all tell stories of women controlled by men or circumstance or society's expectations. Everyone is telling them to act or look a certain way, and they don't fit the mold. At some point everyone breaks, I guess. They want to be in control of their own lives. When things are out of your control, sometimes you do dumb things, just to show yourself you can do *something*."

Peter shook his head. "I don't buy that. I don't know any women who are oppressed or controlled by men. That doesn't happen anymore. Women can do everything a man can do."

"I'm not so sure about that," I said under my breath. I didn't really want to get into this. I'd already had some of these gender conversations in English class, and they always turned ugly. I thought of my own mother, of Grandma's insistence that she had been tricked into helping my dad cover up his crimes and coerced into pleading guilty. I hadn't wanted to talk about it before, but the more I read Emily Flynt's books, the more I thought about it. What other options did my mother have, after all? Had she simply been boxed in by expectations? Had she snapped like the narrator in *The Yellow Wallpaper*? I wondered if maybe I wasn't being fair to her by refusing to read her letters, which Grandma had kept in an ever-growing stack on the kitchen counter until I told her I didn't want to look at them. Would it drive my mother mad if I never responded?

"Anyway," Peter went on, "it happens to guys too."

"What?"

"Being controlled."

I picked up a big box of jelly beans and headed for the counter. "Can I get half a pound of chocolate turtles? The ones with the pecans? And a bag of unsalted peanuts in the shells."

"Ew. Unsalted?" Peter said.

"For the bird."

He plopped his candies down by the cash register. "Geez, it's hot in here. Why do they have to turn the heat up so high? Everyone's dressed for winter weather and then you come in here and sweat to death."

"Will that be all?" droned a girl who obviously didn't want to be at work.

Peter paid up, took his brown paper sack full of candy, and waited outside for me to finish up. A few minutes later I was out with my own paper bag, larger than his. A crisp breeze cooled the sweat that had begun to gather at my hairline.

"Where to now?" Peter said.

I looked out across the gray-brown river. "What's on the other side?"

"Not much, I don't think. Bars and boats, mostly. A few stores."

"Let's go over there. We've already been almost everywhere on this side."

"Not the antique shop." He pointed across the

124

street to the sprawling antique mall that took up nearly half a city block.

I gave him a doubtful look. "You really think you're going to find your dad something in there?"

"Maybe. They've got lots of cool stuff. And there's always something my grandparents would like. They've got books there. Why don't we do that first and then we'll go to the west side."

"Yeah, okay."

"I'll run our bags to my car and meet you in there."

He trotted off down the sun-dried sidewalk. I crossed the street, entered the antique mall, and found myself hopelessly lost in its labyrinth of junk within moments. I spied a few things here and there that were likely worth something, but much of the inventory looked like it should be inserted into the deep recesses of a landfill, never to be seen again. Even a cursory scan of the books on offer revealed little of interest.

People got so sentimental about old things. The homes I had frequented when I lived in Amherst usually sported an impressive collection of high-end antiques and expensive paintings, some of which had been in the same families since before the founding of the nation. I grew up knowing that I was not to put a glass directly on wood, I was not to play with toys on the sideboard, and I was never to drink grape juice over the carpets. But of all the items I had seen thus far in the antique mall, none of them looked like they required any amount of special care beyond fumigation.

Peter finally caught up with me beside an endless row of porcelain sinks and toilets in the basement.

"So, are you thinking about getting your dad an antique john?" I quipped.

"Those are for restorations, smart aleck. Let's go look at the records."

I stood by as Peter thumbed through hundreds of LPs. "What are you looking for? I'll help you find it."

"I'm not really sure. I'll know it when I see it."

But he apparently didn't see it, because ten minutes later we were back upstairs. I was getting antsy and hot and tremendously bored.

"What does your dad like?"

"Oh, you know, football, beer, fishing, hunting—stuff like that."

I started to search for stuff like that. I wanted to get out of there. My grandma had enough old stuff. What she needed was some new stuff. Or less stuff.

Finally Peter found a lighted Miller Lite sign—an antique only in the very loosest sense of the word—and paid the cashier. We got into his car and headed for the Columbus Bridge. As we approached, the light on the bridge turned red. A bell began to ding as the red and white arms dropped down to block our path.

"Wanna see if we can make it to Cortez Bridge?" Peter asked with palpable excitement.

Racing bridges, I had learned, was one of the things the locals did for fun. It was safer than racing trains and it gave one a story to tell, albeit not a terribly unique one. Everyone raced bridges. When I first heard of it, it didn't seem like it would be all that hard to beat a freighter laden with cargo in a race. But the bridges opened so early for these giant ships and there were so many traffic lights on the roads between them that it was actually a fair contest.

"Let's do it."

Peter made a sharp U-turn on Chippewa, bent on making it down the twenty-five-mile-per-hour street through six lights and over Cortez Bridge before it opened for the oncoming ship. But traffic was thick, and too many people were either pulling out of a parking spot along the road or waiting for one to open up.

"Stupid holiday crowds!" Peter said as he hit the steering wheel at a red light. "We're never gonna make it. At this point it would take less time to turn around and go back."

"It's no big deal," I said.

"My dad always beats these things. So does Alex."

The light turned green and he gunned it, then braked hard at the next light.

"Who's Alex?"

"My brother."

"I didn't know you had a brother."

"Alex Flynt, class of 1997, star quarterback at Kennedy High. And now he's a starting quarterback for Michigan State."

"So football runs in the family. Is that what you plan to do as well?"

"We'll see." He made the turn onto Cortez Bridge, which was already beginning to rise, and let out a frustrated grunt. "I won't be going to State, though."

"Why not?"

"Dad thinks Alex is wasting his talent at MSU because he would get better offers from the pro teams if he was in a winning program like the University of Michigan—that's where my dad went. But Alex wanted to go to MSU because that's where his girlfriend was going."

The bridge was straight up in the air now, an impenetrable wall of gray. The big freighter came creeping in from the north, heading upriver to drop its load on trains or trucks that would disperse it all over the country. Probably one of the last of such deliveries until spring. In not too long, the river would ice over.

"You seem like you really care a lot about what your dad thinks," I observed.

"What does that mean?"

"Just what I said. You seem to really care about his opinion."

"Yeah?" Peter prompted.

"I mean, do *you* want to go to the University of Michigan and play football?"

"I could do a lot worse."

"Are you planning on being a pro football player then?"

Peter shrugged. "Maybe. I don't know. Maybe."

"Maybe."

"What?"

"It just seems like people who become pros in a sport have a lot more drive. Like they don't have any *maybes*, you know? So *maybe* you were meant to do something else."

Peter didn't speak again until the ship had passed and the bridge had lowered enough that we could see the cars waiting on the other side. "What was your father like?" he asked.

I didn't care for this turnaround. But if I was going to be critical of Peter's relationship with his father, perhaps I ought to be more open about mine.

"Is."

"Is?"

"What *is* my father like. He's still alive."

The red and white arms went up, the dinging bell fell silent, and the red lights switched to green.

"Okay, then what *is* your father like?"

"Ruthless."

His head swiveled toward me. "What do you mean?"

Cars honked behind us.

"I think they want you to go," I said.

Peter threw the car back in drive, and we crossed the bridge over the rolling wake the freighter had left lapping at the rivershore. On the other side he parked in a video store lot and turned to face me. "What do you mean, 'ruthless'?"

"You know, cruel, brutal, merciless. That sort of thing." I smiled. "I'm pretty sure that's a vocab word you should be familiar with by your senior year of high school."

"Did he hurt you? Is that why you're living here with your cousin?"

"He never hurt *me*."

"Your mom?"

"Not that I know of."

I savored the bewildered expression on Peter's face. It might be the last time he looked at me without pity or disgust. For all the wild stories I'd spread about myself, I'd noticed that there, hidden among the lies, the truth had already seeped out. Peter had included it in his list of rumors about me back in October. The only reason it didn't get much attention was that there were so many other stories floating around that were just as outrageous. Of all of them, though,

130

it really was the most plausible. Maybe Peter wouldn't be all that surprised to find it was true. He was my best friend. He deserved to know. Anyway, secrets want to be told, otherwise they wouldn't be so hard to keep.

"My father is Norman Windsor."

He looked like he couldn't place the name, so I helped him out.

"He's a senator—was a senator. He killed three people to cover up embezzling money from arms sales. My mom was arrested as an accessory or something a few months after my dad. His trial is going on right now. She pleaded guilty, so she's already in prison."

I paused, waiting for him to react, but his face was a frozen mask of confusion.

"So, maybe your dad's not so bad compared to some," I quipped. "But it still seems like he's pushing you to do something more for him than for you."

It took another moment for Peter to find his voice. "Are you serious?"

I nodded.

"You're criticizing my dad for wanting me to go to a particular college when your dad *killed* three people?"

"See, this is why I didn't want to talk about it before. It's not my fault my dad is a monster."

Peter stared at me. "You're making this up. Like all the other crap?"

I looked into his perfect blue eyes. He didn't want to believe this. I could take it back easy as that, push the reset button. Everything would go back to what it was. Sweet anonymity.

I forced a breezy smirk across my face. "Yeah. I'm screwing with you."

He rolled his eyes. "Geez, Robin. You're insane."

We drove in silence a few shabby blocks to a street that sloped toward the river. I felt as run-down as the houses we passed.

"This side of town is where people settled first," Peter informed me, "before the lumber boom and all those mansions got built up over on Centerline Road on the east side. Now it's mostly bars. This is the place to be if you want to get smashed."

Despite its seedy reputation, Midway Street was beautiful. Brick and stone buildings with tall, skinny second-story windows lined the street. It resembled the streets on the other side of the river, but there was something different about the west side. Something older, earthier, a bit unfashionable. It felt like an undiscovered country. Like a juicy little secret you wanted to share with people.

We parked and walked until we found a store-front that wasn't a bar. Mystic Rhythms Aroma-therapy Shop.

"Let's go in there," I said. "I need something

to cover up the smell of old cigarette smoke. I'm living in an ashtray."

When the door shut behind us, we were immediately assaulted by the thick odor of sandalwood incense and something that reminded me of the stoners smoking out on the corner during lunch hour.

"Oy," Peter said. "I think I'd rather smell like cigarette smoke than this."

I walked over to a shelf lined with scented candles and essential oils. A heavyset woman with long curly hair streaked with gray and about thirty filmy scarves around her neck drifted out from behind the counter. She wore a long skirt in shades of turquoise and jade, a flowing white top, and chunky brown sandals despite it being December. Her toenails were far too long. She looked to be in her forties—or maybe her sixties. It was hard to say.

"Is there anything I can help you with?" Her voice was like feathers.

"I'm looking for a gift for an older lady. Something to make the house smell nice."

She escorted me around the store, explaining the origin and properties of every product and making wild claims about how much each would change the recipient's life. I wanted to ask her if she had anything that would change my life.

Peter excused himself to wait outside. "This place is giving me a headache."

After twenty minutes I finally convinced the woman that I had made my choice. I assured her that I did not need Sensual Touch Massage Oil or healing crystals or a gold statue of Buddha, and walked out into the crisp air.

Peter was leaning against the wall, hands in his coat pockets, breath fogging. "I was wondering if I would have to send in a search party to extract you."

We started down the road.

"She talked *so slow.*"

Peter laughed. "Do you have everything you need for Martha?"

"I have enough. I hardly know the woman."

He gave me a sidelong glance. "So how did you really end up out here living with a woman you hardly know? For real."

"Peter, you wouldn't believe me if I told you."

"Whatever. I bet it's so boring and vanilla that no one would care, and that's why you won't tell the truth."

"Believe whatever you want." I put my hand out to stop him. "Wait."

"What?"

"Look at this place."

The yellow-brick building at the corner of Midway and Chestnut was empty. It sported a large front display window, a heavy wooden framed door fitted with leaded glass panels, and a large black-and-yellow-striped awning, torn and faded and filthy.

"That is so cool."

When I looked to Peter for confirmation of my assessment, he raised his eyebrows doubtfully. I ignored him and pressed my face against the window. Inside, the remains of some doomed business sat silently beneath a patina of dust. A chair lay on its side. Old candy machines stood waiting for small, sticky hands to insert quarters. A few tables and shelves sat empty. It was beautiful, abandoned, and full of possibility.

"What would you put there if you owned it?" Peter asked.

I didn't even have to think about it. "A bookstore."

He nodded and stuck out his bottom lip. "With a coffee shop?"

I screwed up my face. "Nah. All the walls would be floor-to-ceiling shelves, and a ton of shelves all throughout so you can hardly fit down each aisle. Like a rabbit warren."

"Sounds dark and claustrophobic."

"I think the word you're looking for is *cozy.*"

"But Barnes & Noble is really open, you know? With lots of space and lots of light. And a coffee shop."

"Then why would my bookstore need to be that way? There's already a Barnes & Noble in Saginaw. My store wouldn't be like that."

"But that's what people like."

"Not me. My store would be more like an old library, I think. I would have lots of used books. Ones people had written in, like your mom's."

"No one wants to buy books with stuff written in them."

"Why not? It gives them character. It gives them a life of their own. I like that all your mom's books are written in. It's like I can talk to her even though I never got a chance to get to know her."

"I guess you could sell those books in your store then. Look at that. Already have a start on your new business venture."

"Never. I'd never sell those books. They're friends."

Peter gave me a look. "You're so odd."

"I'll take that as a compliment."

"Take it however you like."

We walked on down the street toward the river. I wished Peter would put his arm around my shoulders, but he didn't. Ever since our interrupted kiss on the night of the accident, he'd kept me at arm's length, as though to get too close might have ill effects on the lives of others.

"Does your dad know you're giving away all of your mom's books?"

"I told you, he already got rid of most of her stuff anyway. Plus I'm not giving them away, am I? I'm selling them."

"For bad poetry."

"I think it's good. They're short, which is good for me. It's kind of turned into a fun game."

"A game?"

"It's like a treasure map. If I read closely and put all the pieces together, it should lead me to the real you, right?"

We stepped out onto a wooden dock devoid of boats. They were all in storage. Ice gripped the pylons where they met the still water of the empty marina.

"I guess that all depends on you," I said. "How well did your English teachers do teaching you to interpret poetry?"

"I don't know. Mom was always trying to get me to take more of an interest in it." He kicked a stone into the water. It broke through the thin layer of ice and sank to the bottom. "I think I must have disappointed her as much as my brother disappointed my dad."

"Why do you say that?"

"I dunno. Just a feeling. She never smiled anymore. I didn't realize it at the time, but the more I thought about it later . . . Anyway, your poems are good."

I wasn't really surprised to hear that Emily Flynt didn't smile. If my poems were a map to the real me, the notes she'd made in her books told the story of someone who was in a far darker place than her former students might have assumed. Whenever her name came up at Kennedy High, students and teachers alike painted a picture of a bubbly woman with endless energy and creativity. But the passages she underlined in her books told another story altogether. It wasn't hard to see that Mrs. Flynt might not have been the effervescent woman she so successfully projected.

I just wondered why I seemed to be the only one who could read between the lines.

13

now

As I explain Sarah's plan to save Brick & Mortar Books to Dawt Pi, I can't help but feel utterly ridiculous, especially as we click through the photos of past ArtPrize entries online. There were plenty of pieces constructed of random items—bizarre fabrications one might loosely term "art"—but none of those pieces seemed to have won either the juried prize or the people's choice. People's choice winners tended to be enormous and highly realistic drawings and paintings of people or animals or landscapes. Stuff that took a lot of time and talent but didn't always get a lot of love from the fine art community. The juried winners seemed closer to what Sarah might dream up—often strange and very artsy and not really made with the masses in mind. I couldn't envision someone putting any of the pieces in a foyer or living room. But people who knew something about art apparently thought they were pretty impressive.

"So it is a dinosaur?" Dawt Pi says.

"Yes, made entirely of books. It's art, but it's

also a metaphor for the printed book and the local independent bookstore in general. It's actually extremely clever."

"But where do we get the books?" Dawt Pi asks.

"From the store. We have a ton of used mass market books that have been here for years. No one's ever going to buy those, and selling them doesn't make us any money. We may as well use them as materials for the sculpture."

"So we use up the books to save the store."

I nod.

"And then what do we sell?"

"The rest of them. It won't use up all the books. We use them to make our ArtPrize entry, and then we'll have more shelf space for new inventory that might sell better. I'm thinking we should expand our cookbooks—people love big, glossy, photo-filled cookbooks, and they have a higher profit margin than used mystery novels from the nineties anyway."

Cookbooks? Has it really come to that? Next thing I know I'll be facing celebrity memoirs and self-help gurus.

Dawt Pi nods. "Dinosaurs were big."

"Some of them. But some were small."

"So we will make a small dinosaur?"

"Well . . ." I hesitate. "It can't be too small, or it won't have enough of an impact. We need people to be wowed when they see it—overwhelmed.

It has to be big enough to do that. Sarah said it should be life-size, but it's not like we could do like a brachiosaurus or a diplodocus or anything. Maybe a stegosaurus?"

A quick perusal of an old set of *World Book* encyclopedias that have been on a high shelf for at least five years reveals some handy charts showing the relative sizes of some of the more commonly known dinosaurs, comparing them to a six-foot man. Even the stegosaurus seems prohibitively large.

"You are crazy." Dawt Pi laughs. "How can we make one of those? How do we get up that high? How do we keep the books together? This is not like the castle in the window."

"Well, yeah, there are some technical considerations. We can't stack books without somehow securing them in place. We would have to construct some sort of skeleton out of wood or metal. And we would have to make it so that it could be partially dismantled so we could move it in a truck to Grand Rapids."

"Who will pay for the wood or the metal? And who will pay for the truck? Who will pay for the glue?"

"Let's not get ahead of ourselves here. We're in the early stages of development. Sarah had the initial idea, so maybe we should ask her if she's thought any of these details through."

But Sarah has never been one to think things

through. Not in high school when she climbed into the car with a drunken Brad Ellis and got in that terrible crash. Not when she cheated on her husband and ended up pregnant and then divorced and raising the kid on her own with only her mom to help her. Not when she goes out drinking every weekend at the bars down the street, drunk-texts her boss, and goes home with guys who only want one thing from her. But no matter how many bad decisions she makes, Sarah Kukla has been a friend to me for the past seven years—years when I really needed one. She may not be a detail person, but she is passionate about art, and if some of that passion and excitement can come my way and benefit the store, I am all for it.

"Let's see what she has to say," I suggest.

"Where will we build this thing?"

"We'll figure it out," I assure her.

"Americans always think there is an answer to everything."

"That's because there is. That's how we do things. You dream big and work hard and make it happen."

"I work hard." She doesn't need to say more.

"I know you do. Believe me, I know. Sometimes it takes longer than you want it to, but if you keep trying, eventually you succeed."

She looks like she wants to believe me. And truthfully, I wish I were not such a hypocrite.

Because no matter how much I try to convince myself that I can make this life everything I want it to be, I haven't really believed it, deep down believed it, since my father was taken away in handcuffs.

Dawt Pi nods and shrugs. "We will try it."

With that, we get back to work. As I look at the shelves of books now, I don't see stories or immortal authors or steadfast friends or conduits of some mysterious life-giving force. I see raw materials—bricks.

Late that night I meet up with Sarah at The Den. I had wanted to meet in my apartment, but she flatly refused.

"It's Ultimate Darts Tournament Night. Come on. It will be fun."

It will not be fun. It will be loud, crowded, and on the unintelligible side. But I give in, knowing that she often has better ideas when she's slightly inebriated. At a high-top table beneath an enormous TV showing the winning keno numbers, Sarah considers my questions. I try to ignore the bodies that brush my shoulder as other people attempt to mingle.

"So what will hold all the books together? What's inside?"

"Yeah, I'm not so sure about that," Sarah says slowly. "I'm more of the big-idea person. But if you want help with actually making the thing work, we should ask Caleb. He's great with that sort of thing."

"Caleb is fifteen."

"So? He's in Science Olympiad. They build stuff all the time. He could probably make it so you could move its head and its tail with your mind if you wanted."

"Let's not get crazy. Did you have any ideas about where we could put this thing together? Does anyone have an empty pole barn?"

"I did think about that," she says, clearly pleased with herself for this unnatural turn of responsibility. "What about one of the big buildings at the marina where they store all the sailboats during the winter? It's got to be empty in the summertime. You wouldn't have to transport materials too far, and you'd be able to walk down there any time to see how it's going."

"See how it's going? Am I not building this thing?"

Sarah stifles a laugh but cannot stop a mist of gin and tonic from escaping her lips and landing on my arm. I wipe it off with the damp napkin from beneath my water glass.

"You can't build a dinosaur by yourself. You need a crew. You'll need scaffolding and, I don't know, cables and stuff. You're going to need some people who know how to build stuff."

"And who would you suggest? Caleb?"

"Sure! His whole Science Olympiad team could

do it. Oh! I'm gonna text Coach Ryan." She picks up her phone and I place my hand on it.

"Do you really think you should be texting right now?"

She mock glares at me. "I'll thank you for not telling me when I'm drunk. I know when I'm drunk. And this"—she gesticulates wildly around her head and torso—"is not drunk. This is me at the top of my game, sweetie."

I back off, but I've seen Sarah this way enough times to know that she is already over the edge. "Okay," I say. "But you have to explain clearly that this is a volunteer thing. If there's any prize money, I'll make a donation to the Science Olympiad program, but we're not splitting anything evenly. If I win I want to have enough money to pay my bills, restock the store, and get Dawt Pi's family over from Myanmar."

"Really?"

"But she doesn't know," I rush on, "and I don't want her to know because I probably won't win, and frankly, I don't even know if their paperwork has come through."

Sarah draws her fingers across her lips to zip them. "I can keep a secret."

I give her a doubtful look.

"I can! I have all kinds of secrets."

"Is that so?"

She nods emphatically and begins to count things out on her fingers. "I never told my sister

145

that her best friend stole her diary and then showed it to everyone in their Girl Scout troop, and that's why they all called her Hairy Hannah. I never told anyone that I caught Miss Carter and Mr. Billings making out in the janitor's closet my sophomore year. I never told anyone that Jenni Garczynski peed her pants at my house in sixth grade—sixth grade!"

"Except you just told me all those things."

For just a moment she is speechless as she tries to understand what I'm saying. "So what?" she finally says. "You don't know half those people, and the other half moved out of town so you'll never see them. And Mr. Billings is dead."

"So you wouldn't spill a secret about someone I did know then?"

She points a finger vaguely in my direction. "Right. Like I would never tell you that Brad Ellis didn't actually cause that car accident senior year."

"What?"

"And I would never tell you that Peter Flynt is still in love with you."

"But—wait. What did you say?"

She puts her head down on the table and says into her arm, "You know you're what we fought about most? More than we did about the thing with Mark." She turns tired eyes upon me. "He never really got over you. You cracked him."

I hardly know what to say. "You told me you hadn't talked to him in years."

"Oh, Robin," she says like I'm an idiot. "Peter and I talk all the time."

I forget the store, forget the dinosaur made of books, forget even the incredible statement that Brad Ellis hadn't caused the car crash that took his life and forever altered Sarah's. I forget it all and zero in on Peter Flynt.

"When was the last time you spoke to him?" I demand.

My intensity seems to alert Sarah to her mistake. Her eyes search the room as though she will find a rewind button hidden somewhere between the bottles. "Shoot. No. No. I haven't. I didn't say that right."

"You have. It's obvious you have. Were you two talking about me? What did he say? Why is he sending me all these books?"

She switches into damage-control mode. "I don't know why he's sending you the books."

"Then what did you talk about? When did you last speak to him?"

"It was a while ago. Honest. I mean, we don't talk *all* the time. Just every once in a while. Like we talked a lot when he came back from his second tour in Iraq. But now I think the last time was like, I don't know, a while ago."

"He was in Iraq?"

"Robin! Don't you ever come out of your cave?

Don't you ever pick up a newspaper? He was in Iraq on his first tour when I got pregnant. That's when the whole thing happened. See, this is the problem with you!" Sarah is practically shouting at me. "You only think of yourself. You're always in your precious store with your precious books, and you never come out to the real world and participate. You're selfish. There are people out here, Robin. People who need you to make an effort sometimes."

"Sarah, I—"

"I'm not done." But she seems to have lost her train of thought.

I jump on the silence. "Look, I'm sorry about the way I am. Really. I wish I could be someone else. I've tried. But you have no idea what it's like."

She stands up over her seat. "Are you serious? You can't be serious. I had to finish high school the year after my class already graduated. I had to walk—no, lurch—around those halls with everyone believing some horrible rumor that Brad crashed into the ditch because I was doing all sorts of nasty stuff to him while he was driving drunk at ninety miles per hour. I know what it's like to want to hide."

I stand up too, but I can't match her in height. "You got into that car that night, Sarah. No one forced you to do it. I had no control over what my father did. I had no idea what was going on.

148

And yet somehow the rest of my life I have to be the one who's on display. They're both safe behind bars, and I'm out here having to deal with the aftermath."

"Well, safe for now, anyway."

Reality strikes me broadside. My father is not dead yet. But a stay of execution is not a pardon. It is a procrastination tactic. The majority of people polled—they actually polled people—are still crying out for his blood, still believe he had been colluding with al-Qaeda, still believe that lethal injection is too good for him, that the government should bring back hanging or the firing squad or erect a guillotine on the Capitol steps. The man I'd laughed with at the dinner table. The man who always told me how beautiful I looked. The man who taught me how to read. They all wanted him dead.

"I thought we were friends," I say, a little breathless. "I thought you were one of the people I could trust. I let you into my life—"

"Ha!" Sarah pounces. "You let me into your life? Are you kidding me? You let me into your *apartment,* Robin. Once. You've never let anyone into your life."

"That's not true."

"Oh, please. Where are all your friends then? Why do you have no one but me and some poor refugee who latched on to the first American who had time to teach her English?"

My eyes are burning to release the tears that are building up. "I let Peter into my life. I told him everything. And look where it got me."

By this time everyone in the bar is staring at us. I don't care. I stick a finger in Sarah's smug face. "If you ever compare getting in a drunk driving accident to my entire life being destroyed again, I'll—"

I can't think of anything I'll do. Instead, I rush out the door and into the night. I automatically turn to go back to the store, back to my apartment, back to my sanctuary. But there's no comfort for me there tonight. I turn the other way, toward the cold, rushing spring flow of the river. I want it to take me out into the bay, into the lake, into the deepest waters where a tow truck could never recover me. I want to step onto one of those pretentious little sailboats, catch the wind, and leave all of this behind. To run again. It seems so easy and so impossible all at once.

I stride north along the riverwalk toward the bay, propelled forward by some interior furnace, like the rumblings of a long-dormant volcano coming to life. I haven't felt this out of control in years. I rush beneath the Columbus Bridge and set my sights on the Magellan Bridge a mile away. I know the bay is there somewhere beyond it, waiting for me. But it's cold and windy and I forgot my jacket at the bar. Forgot my purse and my cell phone. Forgot my good sense.

I can feel a headache forming behind my eyes.

I wish I could take it all back. Take back the shouting, the anger, the bitterness. I wish I hadn't stormed away from a friend who was keeping me sane. I know I'm not only thinking of Sarah. I'm thinking of Peter. Of the moment it all ended. His betrayal. My revenge. I wish it could have been different. I wish I hadn't thrown it all away over one infraction, however serious. I wish I hadn't been so ruthless. But I had. And nothing could change that.

I turn toward home. Slower, colder. The space behind my eyes is beginning to throb. I will crawl back into my hole and stay there until it crumbles in around me. I don't need a dinosaur made of books. I can't save the store. I will accept the inevitable and sell the place. Dawt Pi will find another job. I can move again, start over as someone else in some other place.

Before I reach home, I can hear someone in the alleyway pounding on the metal door and cursing.

"Sarah?"

"You left this stuff at the bar." She presses my coat and purse into my arms and looks about to leave. "I drank too much, Robin. Don't listen to anything I said back there. About Peter, Dawt Pi. I didn't mean that stuff. Everything will be back to normal in the morning."

How can it be? I want to ask her, but instead

I say, "You could have let yourself in. My keys are in my purse." I don't tell her about the spare key I keep hidden in the alley, though her face is mere inches from it.

"Oh," she says.

I try on a little smile and she offers one in return.

"Robin, you're doing great. Most people? In your shoes? They would have snapped a long time ago. Like, bigger snapped. Like, rampage snapped. And here you are with your little dream, trying to make it happen."

I throw my coat over my shoulders to stave off the shivering and dig in my purse for my keys. "Why don't you come up and sleep here tonight. You can't drive home like that."

"Jeff said he'd give me a ride."

"Who's Jeff?"

"He's from Kennedy. Class of '98."

"He hasn't been drinking?"

"Not much. He's big."

I am not her mother. She is not my project.

"If you think that's best."

"It'll be fine. Look, I'll talk to Caleb's coach tomorrow and stop by to let you know what he says, okay?"

"Okay."

She starts to walk around me back out to Chestnut Street, but I redirect her into my arms for a hug. I think it catches us both off guard.

152

But after a moment it feels right. In fact, it feels like something I've been missing for a very long time.

I release her to the dubious custody of Jeff and unlock my door. Upstairs I watch her weavy steps through the window. A man in jeans and a big Carhartt jacket stands by a black pickup truck. He guides her around to the passenger side and opens her door for her.

At my computer, I close the tragic Brick & Mortar balance sheet and open a new Word document. Despite my growing headache, I stare at the blank, bright whiteness. A clean, empty world. I want to fill it with a poem. But I'm no poet anymore.

I type the first words of the new draft of my terrible novel.

When I married Austin Dickinson I had no idea that I was really marrying his sister.

Then I delete them.

14

then

"When are we going to visit your mother?" Grandma asked for the hundredth time. She shoveled another bite of whatever-it-was into her mouth.

"We're not."

"Robin, you need to see her."

I stifled my gag reflex as a string of spittle danced between her lips, and deftly changed the subject. "What did you say you call this stuff?"

"It's a pasty," she said around her food.

I stared at the lump of browned pie crust covered with ketchup and mused about the fact that *pasty* rhymed with *nasty*.

"Try it. You'll like it."

"What's in it?"

"Meat, potatoes, carrots, onions, rutabaga. It's the perfect food for winter. Miners up in the UP used to keep them in their pockets to warm their hands, and then they'd eat them for lunch."

"What's the UP?"

She gave me a disappointed look and then said,

"Upper Peninsula. It's the part of Michigan that's north of the Mackinac Bridge."

The answer didn't make the meal look any more appetizing. It looked like something they might be forcing my mom to eat in prison—Lindy Windsor, the woman who used to cater in posh parties people talked about for years afterward. But Grandma had been so excited to bring a cooler full of these frozen meat pies home from Mass that I cut into the shapeless lump, releasing a plume of steam. I took an exploratory bite and shrugged. It wasn't terrible. It wasn't anything.

"Probably needs salt," she suggested. She leaned across the table and liberally salted my food for me.

The next bite was better. I gave her a little nod of approval. We ate a couple more bites in silence before she resumed the line of questioning I thought I had successfully deflected again.

"When are we going out to see your mother?"

I sighed and The Professor mimicked me perfectly.

"We need to get something on the calendar," Grandma said. "And you need to at least write her a letter in the meantime. It would be nice if you'd get off your high horse and read one from her too."

I poked at my food. "I don't know what to say to her."

"Tell her about school. Tell her about your

friends. Tell her you miss her. She just wants to hear from you."

It wasn't true that I didn't know what I wanted to say to her. There were plenty of things I could say. I wanted to ask her what in the world she had been thinking. I wanted to know what had made her and Dad so selfish. I wanted to know why *their* stupid choices ruined *my* life. I wanted to know why I didn't even know who they were.

"How did my parents meet? I mean, how did Mom get from *here* to Amherst?"

Thankfully my grandmother took a moment to swallow her food before answering. "Your mother wanted to get out of Sussex since the minute she realized there was a bigger world out there. She met your father at Boston College her second semester. They had the same class— American history or something."

"Did you like my dad?"

"I didn't have a long time to get to know him. Like I said, I was only invited to the wedding. But far as I can tell, everyone liked your dad. He was very charming and obviously smart. I was sure Lindy would have a great life—a better life than I had. I was sorry she was going to be staying out east. And it took some time to get used to the idea of her marrying a Protestant, but I was happy for her because she was happy. I was as shocked as you were when everything came to light. I knew from the start that your mother had nothing to do with it."

I wasn't so sure. Mom had married him. She protected him. She let him do this to our family, and now I was orphaned and stuck forever in Sucky, Michigan.

"She should have stopped him," I said. "Or left him and taken me with her. She shouldn't have stuck around. It's pathetic."

Grandma frowned. "You should have a little compassion. Most women will put up with an awful lot to keep the men in their lives happy."

"Not me. I wouldn't have stood for that."

She nodded and said, "Sure."

"What?"

"Sure."

The smirk on her face sent me into a rage. "I guess you're the one who taught her to just roll over and take it when your husband's a terrible person. Nice job, Grandma. Great legacy you're leaving."

I wished I could take the words back the minute they were out of my mouth. Grandma's eyes glistened and her frown lines cut deep into her face. I should have said I was sorry. Instead, I started yelling.

"I don't want to see her! And I won't write her any letters. My life is none of her business anymore, and it's none of yours either!"

I stalked off to my room and locked the door.

I knew it was childish. None of this was my grandma's fault.

Eventually I could hear the sounds of cleaning up, of Grandma tearing off a piece of plastic wrap to cover the uneaten portion of my pasty and washing the dishes. When I heard her turn on the TV, I opened my door and crept behind the couch. The Professor watched me crawl to the kitchen but said nothing, just tilted his head to keep one beady eye on me. When I silently took the phone handset from the cradle, he let out the sound of the ringing phone at the top of his infernal little lungs.

"Shut up, Professor!" Grandma snapped. "I'm trying to hear the TV."

I quickly dialed Peter's number. He picked up on the third ring.

"Meet me in the cemetery," I whispered.

"Robin?"

"Yeah."

A pause. "I'll be there in five minutes."

I gently placed the phone back on the cradle, timing the motion with the applause of the *Wheel of Fortune* audience. I crawled on the floor under The Professor's watchful eye as the big wheel was spinning and everyone was clapping, hoping it would stop at a large sum or a special prize. Something they thought would make their lives better. I slipped my boots on. Vanna spun the big lighted blocks around to reveal the letters.

Another spin. More clapping. I waited. *Ding*. Vanna spun the letters.

Grandma bellowed at the TV, "The truth shall set you free!"

The Professor screeched.

I had my coat down from the peg by the door and on in a second. Grandma shouted out her answer again, hoping the slack-jawed contestant would hear her. "How can you not see that?" she moaned.

I slipped outside, shutting the door quietly behind me, and jumped off the porch into the new-fallen snow. Through the closed window I heard The Professor shout, "I'd like to buy a vowel!"

The moon lit my way through the trees to Emily Flynt's black stone. The snow had piled up, partially obscuring the day she died. Down the road Peter's headlights swung into view, passed the trailer, slowed, and turned into the little gravel lot. I trotted across the frozen dead and opened the passenger door.

"What happened?" Peter said as I plopped down into the seat.

"I had a fight with my—Martha."

"I figured that. So what happened?"

I took a long breath. "It doesn't matter."

"Where are we going?"

Snow danced in the headlights like a cloud of gnats in a beam of summer sunshine. The car was warm. Too warm. Peter must have been driving it not long before I called him. Had he been visiting Sarah? I shut every vent I could reach.

"I don't know. Where's there to go?"

"Nowhere," Peter admitted.

I sighed.

Peter turned off the headlights and put the car in park. "You know, I should be finishing a paper right now. What's going on? Why are we out here sitting in the dark when I should be home finishing a paper?"

I slumped in my seat. "It doesn't matter. You never believe me anyway."

I could feel him staring at the side of my face.

"I'll believe you. Whatever you say, I promise I'll believe you."

He was in his winter jacket, but like me, he had no gloves, no hat, no scarf. He must have left his house quickly to come rescue me.

"My mom wants to see me."

"You don't want to see her?"

"No."

"Why not?"

I stared out the windshield at the rows of gravestones standing black against the snow. "Because she should have left with me right when she found out about my dad. Then I would at least have a mom. Now I have nothing."

"Okay, so what really happened then?" There was an edge of frustration in his voice.

A cloud slipped in front of the moon and the graves disappeared. I focused on the snow-flakes falling on the windshield and melting into droplets.

"My dad really is Norman Windsor. You didn't believe me, but I was telling the truth. I could show you my birth certificate. My dad is Norman Windsor and he's on trial for killing three people. He might get the death penalty. My mom is Lindy Windsor and she's in prison for twenty-five years as an accessory and for obstruction of justice. While she should have been protecting me and getting us the heck out of there, she was busy trying to make it so that my father wouldn't get caught, and when he did get caught, she was busy trying to make sure they couldn't convict him. And in the meantime she forgot she had a daughter, and maybe she should have been more concerned with an innocent kid instead of a guilty grown man who deserves whatever punishment he gets."

Peter was quiet for a moment. I could see out of the corner of my eye that he watched me intently. "Okay," he finally said. "I believe you."

The anxiety left my body in a turgid black stream.

"I'm sorry I didn't before," he went on. "But you have to admit you made it hard with all the lies."

"Can you blame me?"

161

"No."

"And you're not going to tell anyone, right?"

"Of course not. But how do you know he did it?"

I scoffed. "The FBI doesn't come pick you up if you didn't do it."

"I guess."

"Oh, and Martha's not my fourth cousin. She's my grandma."

We sat in silence a moment more, getting comfortable with the reality of who I was. The cloud that had blackened the moon drifted on, and I let my eyes roam over the tops of the gravestones, hop, hop, hop, all the way to the last row. Then I saw the dead house.

"You have a flashlight in here?"

"I think so."

I opened the car door. "Come on."

Peter turned the car off, rattled around in the glove box, and emerged with a flashlight. "Where are we going?"

"I want to check out the old house."

"The Doll House?"

"It's called the Doll House?"

"That's what I've always heard it called."

We started across the cemetery.

"Why?"

"In one of the upstairs windows there's an old, creepy doll looking out with these empty eyes. Plus, you know, it kind of looks like a doll house, I guess."

We walked through the fog of our own breath, following the jumping flashlight beam. Snow squeaked beneath our boots. The thin, sharp air filled my lungs, and I was thankful that my grandmother didn't live in Florida or Texas. The cold put everything else on pause—the trees, the rivers, the flowers—so you could deal with the bones of life. It changed everything to blacks and whites, throwing the world into clear relief, separating the good from the bad, the true from the false, the beautiful from the ugly. Winter made the rest of life's ambiguities somehow bearable for a while.

We cleared the graves and stood before the massive old house. The foundation was crumbling, the front porch lurched to the left, every window had been broken. But even in the dim glow at the edge of Peter's flashlight it was easy to see that the place had once been beautiful. Beneath the chipped paint were charming architectural details adorning every angle and corner, curlicues and flowers carved from wood, making it look like a life-size gingerbread house. It must have been like a fairy tale once. Now it looked like some frozen witch had come along and cursed it.

"My mom grew up here."

"In this house?"

"That's what my grandma said."

"It's been empty as long as I can remember."

"Grandma got the trailer when the house was condemned and they wouldn't let her live in it anymore."

Peter swept the flashlight over the second-floor windows. "I think the doll is on one of the sides."

"Think we can get in there?"

"Why would you want to? It's half eaten by termites and dry rot. There are probably bats and raccoons living in it."

"Let's go in."

Peter hesitated. The sagging front porch leaned away from the house like it wanted to disassociate itself from the place. The bottom step was gone, completely rotted away. I slid my bare fingers into the snow on the handrail and put an experimental foot on the second step. The porch let out a shrieking crack that echoed against every quivering snowflake falling through the black sky.

I snatched my foot back and looked at Peter. "Maybe there's a back door."

We walked through drifts up to our knees and located the back door, which wasn't a door at all anymore, only a gaping rectangular hole in the wall, like an open grave. We stepped into the yawning darkness within, and Peter moved the light slowly along the walls. The yellowed wallpaper had been torn into jagged strips like sickly icicles. A gust of wind through the doorway sent a few curled-up strips of paper skittering along the floor like oak leaves across crusted snow.

For every step we took, the house answered back. Creaks and groans, voices of anger and sorrow. I thought of my own house back in Amherst. Had the people of my town given it a nickname? Did teenagers drive past it slowly, telling the sad story of its former inhabitants? Did little children walking home from school quicken their steps when they reached it or cross over to the other side of the street, afraid of the murderous ghosts that might dwell within?

I suddenly felt bad for being in this house as a gawker. I was about to suggest we leave when Peter pointed his flashlight at a staircase and started his ascent. I followed close behind as the walls and ceiling pressed in around me.

At the top, Peter shone his light at one of three half-closed doors. "I think it must be this one." He pushed it the rest of the way open.

The flashlight beam tracked across a bed, a chair, a chest of drawers, pictures of horses on the walls, until it stopped upon a doll seated at the window, looking out, looking for the girl who once hid under that bed when her father was in a rage—my mother. This doll had waited for Lindy Gray for more than thirty years. How long would I wait for her?

I didn't touch her, in the same way you would not touch an artifact at a museum or the host upon an altar. But as Peter came up behind me and adjusted the beam of the flashlight, I saw her dusty, sun-bleached face and unblinking eyes. They looked dry and desperate, as if they belonged to someone who had been buried alive.

"Let's go," I whispered.

"We just got here."

"I'm cold."

I closed the door on my mother's childhood and followed Peter down the stairs. At the bottom, the light danced across the wall of what used to be the living room. Above the fireplace, hanging crooked but intact and covered with a thick layer of dust, was a family portrait. I walked through the room around the old furniture, Peter on my heels. Four people, jaundiced from whatever chemical they used to process photos back then. Two smiling children—a boy and a girl—a rather blank-faced father, and a mother who looked as if she had a headache.

"See anyone you know?" Peter asked.

No, I didn't know any of these people. Not really. I studied the faces. "That must be my mom and my grandma. I've never met my grandfather or my uncle."

I stared at the little girl. Despite the dust and discoloration, I thought she looked a bit like me. Or maybe like I did when I was six years old. Were all bad people once beautiful children? Would I turn out just like my mother or father? At that moment, I was sure I would. At some point in the future—I couldn't know exactly when—something in my brain would twist out of place and I would become a bad person, someone who thought only of her own gain, someone whose every action would be turned inward in selfish ambition and self-preservation. And I would drive away anyone who had ever cared about me. The thought terrified me—but at the same time it seemed inevitable.

I swallowed down my fear and turned away from the family on the wall. They were all as dead as the house in which they hung. Whoever they had been then, they were now something else. My grandfather was presumably in the ground somewhere, though I hadn't found the family name in the Methodist cemetery in my Catholic grandmother's backyard. Grandma wasn't the overworked matriarch of this sad little kingdom. When she wasn't volunteering at the church's resale shop, she was lost in TV land, shouting at game show hosts who never listened to her. My uncle was no longer a rosy-cheeked little boy. He was off in Alaska, prospecting for oil or something and probably sporting a bushy beard and a receding hairline. And my mother—well, I knew exactly what she was.

When I walked back through the hallway into the snowy dark, the torn wallpaper had morphed from icicles to bars. I couldn't get out of there fast enough. Despite his athleticism and longer legs, Peter had to work to keep up with me as I strode back across the cemetery to the trailer. When I finally stopped at the porch, he put his hands on my shoulders.

"You okay?"

"Sure."

"I'm serious. I know what it's like to lose a parent, and it's terrible. But you lost two, and in a way I really can't imagine. I'm worried about you."

"I'm exactly the same person I was before you knew."

He bit his lower lip. "Are you going to go see your mom?"

I was shaking my head without even meaning to. "I don't want to see her. And I sure don't want to spend that long in a car with my grand-mother."

"I'd take you." His face was serious, his eyes full of kindness.

"You'd drive all day to take me to visit my mom?"

"Sure. Why not? We could go on spring break."

I grimaced.

"Road trip," he added in a singsong voice accompanied by a mischievous smile.

"I guess. But I really don't want to see her. So thanks for offering—it really means a lot—but I'll have to pass."

He looked down for a moment. "What about your dad? Would you want to see him?"

"No. Anyway, I doubt they'd let me talk to him while he's on trial."

"Maybe. It's not really any of my business, I guess, but you might regret it if you didn't take the opportunity to talk to him before . . . I mean, you know. I'd give almost anything to be able to talk to my mom again."

The falling snow piled up like powdered sugar on his hair and shoulders.

"What would you say?"

"I don't know. I guess I'd tell her how much I love her and how much she taught me. How she made me into the man I am now." He glanced up at the sky a moment. "I'd tell her that even though it seemed like we took for granted all the meals she cooked and all the work she did around the house, once she was gone we realized how much she did. I'd tell her how much all her students loved her, how much she's missed. I don't want to tell you what to do, Robin, but most people don't know what kind of time they have left with someone. You might. So maybe you should see your dad, tell him what you feel."

I shifted my weight to the other leg. "It wouldn't be all that nice stuff you just said. Anyway, no one's really going to sentence a senator to death. That's what my grandma said. And even if they did, I've got time. Death sentences go through years of appeals."

"Okay. But the offer stands. If you ever want to see either of them."

I put a hand on his arm in lieu of what I really wanted to do, which was to bury my face in his chest and feel his arms around me. I had gone months without a hug. "Thanks."

I could barely see his half smile in the glow cast by the porch light. Then it vanished. He leaned toward me, put an ice-cold hand to my cheek, and pulled me in for a kiss. I winced, remembering the car crash. But as his lips gently touched mine, I couldn't hear a thing.

"I better get inside," I said when he pulled back.

"Hopefully she hasn't locked you out."

"If she did I deserved it. I wasn't very nice to her tonight. Anyway, there's a key under Mary. Grandma figures no one would be so sacrilegious as to employ the mother of our Lord as an accessory to breaking and entering."

Peter snickered. It reminded me of the way I'd heard him laugh with his friends at school.

"Peter, you can't tell anyone."

"Why would I tell anyone where your grandma hides her extra key?"

"No, about my parents, or my grandma. You can't tell anyone. You know that, right? I'm Robin Dickinson, not Robin Windsor."

"Of course."

"Because if you did, that would be it. That would be the end of our friendship—no questions asked, just gone, done. You understand?"

He grasped my hand. "I promise I won't tell a soul. You can trust me, Robin Dickinson."

"Okay."

I let go of his hand and tried the door. Locked. Grandma must have gone to bed without realizing I wasn't in my room. I shuffled through the snow in front of the trailer where Mary and her gnome attendants stood watch. I tipped her forward and felt around. The key was frozen to the ground. I pried it up, opened the door, and stepped out of the snow globe night.

"Good night, Peter."

" 'Night, Robin."

I sloughed out of my coat and boots and tiptoed back to my room. I could hear the car driving away as I pulled the covers over my snow-dampened head. I touched my lips where Peter's had touched them. Then I thought of the doll in the window, of the tiny, cold lips that my mother had probably kissed hundreds of times before she left, never to return. And I thought maybe I should go see her after all—if only to be sure she understood exactly what she had stolen from me.

15

now

I sit across from Science Olympiad coach Ryan Miller and sip dreadful coffee. Underneath the table, I check the time again on my phone.

"Why don't we order and let Sarah catch up to us later," he says. "I'm sure she wouldn't mind."

He flags down the waitress and motions for me to go first. I order poached eggs, bacon, and an English muffin. Ryan opts for eggs over easy, hash browns, and white toast. Then he retrieves a large pad of drawing paper from the seat beside him, flips open the cover, and slides it my way.

"Now, this first page is what the exterior will look like; that's Sarah's drawing. Next couple pages are interior. Those are mine. We've got a tough, lightweight metal skeleton—same sort of material as tent poles—that we fit with these wheel-like plastic collars at all these points in order to build the skeleton out and give you something to connect the books to. Those go from head to tail and down the legs. If you turn to the next page you see the different sections that we'll build separately, then you snap and twist and they're securely fastened to one another, like in an action movie when someone assembles one of those big guns that has to be carried around in a suitcase."

I let the pages fall back into place and look up to him. "This is a brontosaurus."

"Actually, brontosauruses never existed. They've known that since like 1903, really. I blame reruns of *The Flintstones* for the continued misinformation. It's a *Dreadnoughtus*. They found one of these in Argentina not too long ago. They were probably the biggest dinosaur, when you combine height and weight, that ever walked the earth. It was heavier than a Boeing 737 or a herd of African elephants or seven T. rexes!"

He's entirely too excited about a subject that most boys outgrow by the time they're eight years old.

"Whatever it's called, that's the point," I say. "It's huge."

"Sarah said it had to be big."

"How long is it?"

"A little over eighty-five feet from nose to tail."

I almost spit out my coffee. "Sarah chose this?"

"No, her son Caleb did," he says. "It's very clever when you think about it. The word *read* is right there in its name—*D-read-noughtus*—so there's probably something a wordsmith could come up with there for the name of the piece. Plus it literally means 'fearer of nothing.' Which, considering your situation, seems to be the name you might need to claim for yourself."

I keep my face impassive. Sarah didn't need to blab about my "situation" to tell this man that I needed some help with an ArtPrize entry.

The waitress arrives and begins to fill the table with steaming plates. Ryan thanks her and then looks back to me with the sparkling eyes of an eager child. I place the sketchpad beside me on the torn vinyl-covered seat to keep it safe from grease stains and pick up my fork.

"I don't see how I'll have enough books to cover it. I don't think there are enough books in my whole store for that. I appreciate all the time and thought you've put into this, but I think it's going to have to be a smaller dinosaur. Maybe one with some interesting features, like sails or body armor. Like a stegosaurus, or what are those things with the clubs on their tails?"

"Ankylosaurus," he supplies effortlessly.

"One of those. Then we can showcase the books more. Don't you think that would offer a little more opportunity to be artsy about it?"

"Well, sure, I guess. You would get admirers for that. But you might not stop anyone in their tracks. Sarah said it had to be something that left people awestruck."

"Sarah's not in charge."

The minute the words leave my lips I wish I hadn't said them. Sarah is just trying to help. And frankly, she is probably right. She's the one with the experience in wowing people, not me.

"I mean, I just don't think it can be done. I'm sure you and the kids on your team can build it. But I don't know where to get the books. And all this high-tech lightweight metal and all the parts? Where are you going to get that and how much will it cost me?"

"Robin, you're looking at this all wrong. Big projects are not the work of one person. They might start out as the vision of one, but they are never completed by one. You've got your technical advisors—that's me. Your construction team—that's the Science Olympiad kids and maybe a few of their parents. And your corporate sponsors—that's who is going to provide either the funds to make the skeleton or the materials themselves. I've already got a few calls out to companies that manufacture this kind of thing. You have their name somewhere to show that they sponsored you. Big companies do things like that all the time. It's good PR. They've all got philanthropy in their budgets."

"Okay, so that takes care of the skeleton, but we still have the problem of enough books. Where do those come from?"

He leans back against the booth. A moment later he's leaning forward again with bright eyes. "You do a book drive!" He takes a triumphant bite of toast.

"A book drive." I let it sink in a moment. It could work.

"You do it in May or June when everyone is cleaning out their basements for garage sales. Make it a big event, get the *River City Times* down there and a couple local news stations. You could even go door-to-door with a truck to do pickups for people who can't get to the drive. Old people have a lot of books. Then all those people have a stake in the project and in supporting your store."

I'm beginning to catch some of Ryan's enthusiasm. *Dreadnoughtus*. Fearer of nothing. I need more of that fearless spirit. Sarah has it. Dawt Pi has it. Ryan seems to have it. Maybe they could rub off on me a little.

As if she knew I was thinking of her, my phone buzzes.

"Hang on. It's Sarah. Let me take this." I slide out of the booth and answer the phone at the same time. "Hey." I walk to the foyer at the front of the restaurant. "Where are you? I'm all alone eating breakfast with a stranger."

"Sorry, my alarm didn't go off."

I suddenly begin to worry that Dawt Pi's alarm might not have gone off, that maybe she didn't open the store this morning as we had arranged.

"Anyway, Ryan's a nice guy. Did he show you the plans?"

"Of course he showed me the plans. What do

you think, we've just been getting to know each other over bad diner coffee and burnt toast?"

"You should get to know each other. He's a nice guy."

"You already said that."

"He's single."

"Don't do that."

"What?"

"You know exactly what. So are you coming?"

"Did you already order?"

I glance back to the table where Ryan is mopping up egg yolk with his last piece of toast. "We're practically finished."

"Then no. I'll catch up with you later. You like the plans, though? He's got it all figured out."

"It's so big."

"Caleb picked it out. I think it's awesome."

"It's starting to grow on me. But we'll need to do a book drive to cover this thing."

"Perfect! Ooh! I'll get started on posters today. Text me the dates when you have it figured out. And Robin? Ryan's a really nice guy."

"I believe you."

I hang up, then sit back down in the hollow of the old booth that indicates where thousands of breakfast-loving people have sat before. "Her alarm malfunctioned. She's not going to be able to make it."

"Bummer." He looks like he really means it. Like every other guy in this town, he's probably in love with Sarah Kukla. But he's definitely not her type. He's smallish and smart and wearing a sweater vest over a sharp button-up shirt and vintage tie. He's clean-shaven, shaggy-haired, and wearing hipster glasses. His pants are corduroy. I can almost guarantee he drives a hybrid car. Or perhaps a bike. He's a nice guy.

I wash down a bite of cold poached eggs with cold coffee like a guy slamming a shot to get up the courage to hit on Sarah. She will not save me from this conversation. I have to be sociable. Fearer of nothing.

"So, Ryan . . . tell me a bit about yourself."

16

then

It's hard to know someone—to really know them—when they're dead before you meet them. But as winter eased up that year in Sussex, I found that, along with falling for her son, I wanted desperately to know Emily Rose Flynt. With each book that Peter gave me, I felt sure that I was getting closer and closer to the real Emily. Every book revealed another layer, like pulling the outer petals from a rose, ever narrowing and bringing into focus what was inside.

As the volumes mounted and sprawled beneath my bed, I began to have visions of the dwindling stash in Peter's basement. Someday the boxes would be empty and my font of knowledge about my new obsession would run dry. No more clues to follow, no more codes to decipher. I began to despair of how quickly Peter breezed through the books, inserting them into my locker with the regularity of a tray of food sliding through a slot to a prisoner in solitary.

In January and February I read no fewer than a dozen books, including all seven of Jane Austen's novels and a good deal of Virginia Woolf's. When Peter asked if it was okay if he skipped reading Woolf's abridged diaries and simply passed them on to me, I acquiesced and dutifully scratched out a poem in payment. Late into the nights, I scoured the pages for Woolf's incisive wisdom and dry wit. Emily's markings seemed more insistent here than they had been in any other book, with whole paragraphs and sometimes entire pages of text underlined. Was it simply because Woolf's wandering sentences were difficult to excerpt? Or was there more to it?

Already knowing the end of Virginia's story, that she would drown herself in a river to silence the voices inside and release her loved ones from her madness, I read slower than normal in order to savor her voice as long as possible. With each turn of the page the water rose a little, as did my suspicions regarding Emily's sudden death. I had been waiting for Peter to see it in the other books, where his mother had made careful note of the emotional chaos that seemed to over-come so many female characters. He'd certainly noticed that there were a fair number of crazy women, but it was obvious that he accepted his father's explanation of his mother's death—that she'd died of an aneurysm, without warning and without lingering.

I'd seen Jack Flynt at football games in the fall. He stood grim-faced at the chain-link fence that separated the fans from the field, his eyes critical, his mouth sour. It was hard to envision him with everyone's favorite English teacher, who seemed in every story to be graciously lending a hand and a smile to anyone in need of one.

There were vestiges of Emily and Jack all over school: names on trophies and plaques, faces reaching across time from black-and-white photographs. They'd been high school sweethearts at Kennedy, attended the University of Michigan, married before they graduated, had two handsome and talented boys. They seemed like a fairy tale.

I was staring at one of these artifacts in a glass case as the halls were emptying out for spring break when Peter came up beside me.

"What are you looking at?"

"Your parents."

He squinted at a photo of the court at the 1972 senior prom, part of a display the student council had arranged to drum up interest in the 2001 senior prom. "Good-looking couple. But you know, I think we have them beat."

"Pardon me? Are we a couple? I thought you only wanted to steal kisses from me when I was feeling vulnerable. You've hardly let yourself be seen with me here at school."

Peter clutched his chest. "Ouch."

"The truth hurts, my friend."

"I haven't been avoiding you. We just don't

cross paths all that much. I'm a senior. You're a freshman. Never the twain shall meet in the halls. I don't see you coming down to the senior islands anymore."

I poked him in the chest. "I only do that when I want to throw books at you. I like a good spectacle now and then."

"Well, what do you say we make a big spectacle of ourselves and rock the prom together? Or do you still think dances are lame?"

I rolled my eyes. "Dances are never like they are in movies, at fancy hotels with amazing live bands. In junior high they were always in the cafeteria, reeking of yesterday's tuna salad, with a crappy DJ playing the Chicken Dance every sixth song."

Peter put his hands on my upper arms and turned me to face him. "Does that mean you're turning me down a second time? Because seniors don't get turned down by freshmen. Not twice. We don't have to spend much time at the dance. Enough to get our picture taken and to show off how incredible you look." He pulled me closer, put his face to the top of my head, and breathed deeply. "And maybe we'll have time for some slow dances so I can smell your hair."

"Weirdo," I said, pushing him away. "You know, I was standing here thinking that maybe my mom went to Kennedy at the same time as your parents."

"Maybe. There are school yearbooks in the library."

"Want to help me look?"

He checked the clock on the wall. "Doubt it's open now. Spring break. We're probably the last ones left. We better leave so we don't get locked in here all week with nothing to eat but ketchup packets."

"Can't we just look?"

"Why don't you ask your mom? That's still happening, right?"

I spun around and groaned as I walked away from Peter and the Proms of Years Past. "I don't know."

"If we don't go this week, we won't have another chance until June."

"And if we don't go check the library this moment, we won't have another chance until next week, so come on."

I skipped off and knew that Peter followed. He caught up with me down the next hall and overtook me to try the door. "See, it's locked."

I tugged on the library door and it opened easily.

"You don't trust me!" he exclaimed.

I laughed. "And obviously I shouldn't."

Inside, the fluorescent lights were already off. I glanced around for Mrs. Dabrowski, the librarian, but she was nowhere to be seen.

"So where are the yearbooks?"

Peter led the way to a dusty back corner shelf of local history books. I ran my finger along the spines and pulled out the yearbooks from 1968 through 1972. I gave two to Peter, sat down on the floor, and started flipping pages.

"What's your mom's name?" Peter said from above.

"Her maiden name is Lindy Gray. Well, Linda Gray, I guess."

"Why don't we take these with us for now?"

"It says right on the shelf that you can't check these out. And anyway, I didn't see Mrs. Dabrowski at the desk."

"That's probably because she went home already and the janitor is about to lock up these doors and we're going to get stuck in here."

"What, are you afraid?"

He bent over and snatched the books out of my hand.

"Hey!"

"Come on, Robin. Let's go. We'll bring them back after spring break, and no one will miss them."

I tried to grab them back, but he started for the door.

"You big baby," I called after him.

He let out a loud laugh and burst through the door with me on his heels. When he suddenly stopped in his tracks, I ran hard into his back. "What the—"

"Can I help you two?" Principal Pietka stood with his hands on his narrow hips.

"Sorry, sir," Peter said. "Just getting some last-minute books for a paper I need to do over spring break. We're on our way out now."

"I see, and what is this paper about?"

"American youth culture during the Vietnam War," I supplied.

Mr. Pietka held out his hand and Peter handed him the yearbooks. "I didn't think we loaned out yearbooks."

Peter found his tongue. "You don't, normally."

"Mrs. Dabrowski said since the paper is due the day we come back from spring break that she'd make an exception," I said.

Mr. Pietka extended the books back toward Peter. "Have a safe spring break."

"You too. Thank you, sir."

We walked quickly down the hall and out to the back parking lot, where Peter's car was the only one left. The moment the doors closed behind us I burst out laughing. A second later Peter followed suit, though a little less boisterously.

"You should have seen the look on your face!" I guffawed.

"Hey, it took me off guard, okay? I'm not a natural-born liar like you are."

"Obviously." I swung my backpack off my back and shoved the yearbooks in.

"Want a ride home?" Peter asked.

"Yeah. Bus is long gone. I can't wait 'til it's warm enough to ride my bike again. I hate taking the bus."

Peter unlocked the passenger-side door and opened it for me. "Why don't you ever ask me for a ride?"

"I don't know." I sat down in the car and tucked my backpack at my feet. "You're a senior. I'm a freshman. Never the twain shall carpool for fear of what his friends will say."

"That's a load of bull and you know it. I don't care what my friends think." He shut the door hard and walked around the front of the car to the driver's side. He pulled out of the parking lot too fast.

"Well, I care," I said. "I don't want to be within twenty feet of your idiot friends."

"So what? Ignore them."

"Okay," I said, "you want to know what I really think it is?"

"Yes, I do."

"My parents."

"Your parents? That's completely irrational! I helped you steal yearbooks from the library to see if our moms might have been friends in high school! I'm taking you to Connecticut on spring break instead of going to my uncle's place in Arizona to sit by the pool! I don't understand you, Robin. I'm the one who's asking you out and giving you books and coming to get you in the

186

middle of the night when you've had a fight—and yet I'm supposedly the one who's avoiding you? That's insane. You're insane."

The rest of the drive was silent. Peter's face was a younger version of his dad's, staring grimly ahead. When he pulled up at my grandma's trailer I started to get out, but he put a hand on my knee.

"Wait. I'm sorry. I just don't know what I'm doing wrong here."

"Nothing."

He scoffed and shook his head.

"No really, nothing," I said. "You're right. You've been nothing but nice to me. You're perfect. I guess I just don't see why anyone would want to get involved with . . . all this."

"Look, I get it. Really. But I like you. And I want to take you to the prom. So say you'll go with me."

"Of course I'll go with you."

His face broke into a brilliant smile. "Great. So are we going out east this week or not?"

"Let me think about it." I leaned over to kiss him on the cheek, but he redirected me to his lips. When I could breathe again I said, "I'll call you tomorrow."

I got out and waved as Peter drove off. I watched the car until it disappeared and turned to go in. It was only then that I realized the door to the trailer wasn't shut.

17

now

Ryan, I didn't think when you said 'you' that you were talking about *me* specifically. I thought it was like a general 'you,' meaning 'the people involved in the project.' Wasn't that your whole point when you were talking about a team?"

"But it's your store, Robin. You need to be there. They don't want to talk to me; they want to talk to you."

Ryan takes a sip of red wine. I hadn't expected my uncharacteristic attempt at small talk to result in this man asking me out, especially to a place that serves wine. And I had so rarely allowed myself to be in a situation where a guy might propose a date that I stumbled into accepting. I used to be so good at lying. I had lived and breathed my own lies for so long that I guess I thought I didn't have to try very hard at it anymore. Apparently I was wrong.

"I think you and the kids would make a great story," I say. " 'Devoted teacher and coach challenges his ragtag group of young geniuses to put their considerable brainpower to work to save local bookstore.' How is that not a more interesting angle than 'Quite-possibly-washed-up old maid begging for your old books to save her business, even though this town has made it abundantly clear that it doesn't need a sweet, quirky used bookstore'?"

Ryan laughs. He looks like a different person when he laughs. Like a guy who drives a beat-up old Camaro instead of the Prius in which we drove to this restaurant.

"You're not an old maid."

"Maybe not by today's standards, but in Jane Austen's day I would have been."

"Well, we're not in Jane Austen's day, are we?" He refolds the cloth napkin he had placed on his lap. "Stay here. I'll be right back."

"Where are you going?"

"I have to run out to the car. Watch: the minute I leave, the food will come."

I sip my glass of water and watch him leave. Then the waiter comes in fast from the kitchen, tray high overhead, weaving through the crowded room like a carefully controlled tornado. He lowers the tray onto a stand and begins to populate the table in front of me with what is the prettiest food I've seen in years. Ryan is coming back in from the parking lot with an I-told-you-so grin on his face and a large cardboard box in his hands, even though this restaurant is not one into which a person would ever think to bring a large cardboard box.

"What is that?" I ask as he tucks it under the table.

"Oh, just a little something I got for you. But I'll show it to you after we eat. I'm starving."

Over our meals, Ryan and I pick up where we left off at breakfast last week. I know he teaches earth science and biology at Kennedy High School, so I keep my questions aimed in that direction. I ask him to explain all the different events at Science Olympiad. He asks about the bookstore and about what Kennedy was like back when Sarah and I went to school there. I almost tell him about the novel I have been working on most nights, but that revelation seems one level too deep for a first date.

Eventually the dirty plates are whisked away and nothing is left between us but space and silence and bread crumbs. Beneath the table I finger the copy of *Pride and Prejudice* in my purse and silently recite the poem I wrote for it.

Pinned and labeled, lit dimly to preserve
Put on display, I am observed
Yet watch as you pass.

Scrutinized—What specimen is this?
Whatever I was once, I am now less,
Immobilized by glass.

Or is it I who walks these echoed halls
While you hang—static—upon the wall?

"Okay," Ryan says, "I was out looking for a birthday gift for my nephew and I saw something I thought you'd like. So I got it, but then I thought maybe I could improve on it a bit. So . . . I made some modifications."

He reaches into the box and places the mystery object on the table between us. I am speechless for a moment. There in front of me, in miniature form, is a dinosaur that appears to be made out of tiny books.

"It's not a *Dreadnoughtus*, of course, since those are a fairly recent discovery," he says. "But I made the tail shorter with a knife and bulked it up a bit around the middle when I put the little books on it."

"How did you—"

"I sliced up a magazine in my crosscut shredder and then went to town with the glue while I was binge-watching old episodes of *Doctor Who*. It was more fun than I think I'd like to admit."

I carefully turn the dinosaur on the table. It's about a foot tall and a foot long, and every micron of it is covered in tiny squares of colorful paper representing books.

"I figured it would give you some inspiration, and it would be something to have in the store—kind of a mascot and an in-joke—that people around here would come to know and recognize as representative of the big chance you took and the spirit you need to have in order to succeed."

"All that?" I joke, a little uncomfortable at the thought that I might not actually have the spirit it takes to succeed.

"Plus now you have a 3-D model to show to people at the book drive. You could easily show it on the news."

There it is again. The news.

"This is really sweet, Ryan. But I'm not sure I can talk to a reporter. Sarah could do it. Or maybe even Dawt Pi."

"Well, yeah. They can both be there, but Robin, it's *your store*. You need to be the face of it."

I'm shaking my head.

"Why are you so afraid of reporters?"

"Don't you watch the news?"

Ryan smiles. "Yeah. Robin, look, I know all about the thing with your father. Everyone knows. You have to get over that. You have to stop hiding. It is what it is. And you have a life to live. Don't let some scummy tabloid jerks determine your future. *Dreadnoughtus*—fearer of nothing. You need to be like this little guy here." He turns the dinosaur to face me. "You need to show those punk predators that you are not someone to be messed with. You're *Dreadnoughtus*! You don't run away and you don't hide. You're too big to hide! You stand there eating your leaves, and when you feel one of these reporters gnawing on your leg, trying to bring you down, you stomp the stuffing out of them, okay? You knock down a whole row of them with your tail! Then you go on doing your thing, living your life. Doesn't that sound better than always worrying about what people are saying about you?"

It's hard not to get pulled in by a pep talk like that. The guy must be a great teacher and coach. But I don't feel like I'm more massive than a Boeing 737. I feel like I'm a foot tall and a foot long and I'm stuck in a fixed position where I can't move my feet to stomp on anything or move my tail to knock anything down.

The tornado waiter comes up with our desserts high atop his perfectly balanced tray. He lowers it to the table, sets the plates in front of us, and disappears. Ryan picks up his fork and digs into his carrot cake.

I stare at the dinosaur on the table. "Do you think we could make it move?"

"What?"

"The dinosaur. The big one. Do you think we could make it move? The head and the tail, a little bit? So it looks alive instead of looking like it's an exhibit at a museum? This whole time something about this project has been bothering me. I think the dinosaur image is clever, but it's extinct. And that's not really the message I want to send about my bookstore or bookstores in general.

What if we could make it so it looks alive? Sure it's old, but it's still alive. It's a survivor."

"It would cost more. And we'd have to get another company involved to help with the parts needed for the robotics."

"But it could be done?"

Ryan picks up the little dinosaur and slowly spins it in his hands. "Anything's possible."

I take a bite of gelato as Ryan puts the dinosaur back on the table facing me. "So," he says, "are you going to be at the book drive or not?"

I breathe deeply. Sometimes you do things you don't want to do in order to please your friends.

"I'll be there."

18

then

Faced with that unlatched door, I couldn't breathe, couldn't move, couldn't think. In a nearby tree, a robin let loose an alarm call. The first robin of spring. Time began again. I crept up the stairs and, hands shaking, pushed the door open, but something stopped it. Panic fluttered in my stomach.

"Grandma?"

At the sound of my voice, The Professor started screeching. I squeezed through the half-open door into the trailer. Everything that had been in the front closet—coats and shoes, an oscillating fan, the twisted hose of the vacuum cleaner—was piled on the small square of linoleum that served as the entryway.

"Grandma?"

In the kitchen, every drawer had been pulled and dumped, every cupboard opened and ransacked. Broken plates and glasses, silverware, pots and pans—all scattered across the floor. My eyes swept the living room. A chair overturned. Cushions everywhere, slashed and bleeding stuffing. A cigarette moldering on the carpet. I stomped it into oblivion. The Professor screamed and leaped in his cage amid a cloud of feathers. My chest was caving in.

"Grandma! Are you there?"

I tiptoed to her room. I wouldn't find her. She was out at the store or at a friend's house or at the church. She would come home soon and be as horrified as I was at the state of the house. But she'd be okay. She'd put her arm around me and we'd sit together in the mess as we waited for the police. She'd get that stupid bird to calm down.

But I did find her, stuffed between her bed and the wall, two viscous trails of blood running down her face from somewhere on her skull. Her bedside lamp was in pieces, her dresser drawers had been emptied all over the room, and the mattress had been pulled off the box spring and both slashed to ribbons. I threw off my backpack. I felt her wrist for a pulse, but I couldn't be sure if the heartbeat I felt was hers or my own throbbing in my fingers. I snatched up the phone receiver. No dial tone. I slammed it on the cradle and tried again. I couldn't see the buttons through the tears. It took three tries to dial those three magical numbers.

I could hardly hear the 911 dispatcher over The Professor. I wanted to wring his rotten little neck—anything to stop the shrieking. I thought

I might let him out of his cage, open the door, shove him outside so he would fly away. Then I remembered his clipped wings.

It took forever for help to arrive. Why did she have to live in the middle of nowhere? Finally the ambulance came. The police asked their questions. They wanted an inventory of what was stolen, but there was little I could say. Nothing she owned was really worth anything. The old TV and VCR were still in the living room. In my bedroom, Emily Flynt's books were scattered all over the floor. My eyes darted around at the titles. All there. As far as I could tell, the intruders had taken nothing at all. But they had obviously been looking for something.

"Jewelry?" a cop shouted over The Professor's histrionics.

"I don't know. My grandma will have to look through things once she's released from the hospital."

I didn't like the way the cop looked at me then. It was the same look I'd gotten from the social worker when I told her I could stay at my house alone because the police had made a mistake and my mom would be back the next day. I never saw my house again.

The EMTs loaded Grandma up in the ambulance and invited me to ride along. I wanted a minute to call Peter, but things were moving so fast. I threw the black sheet over The Professor's cage to calm him down. I was not conflicted about shutting the door on his screams.

After several long hours in the ER, Grandma was moved to ICU with cracked ribs, a broken collarbone, and a concussion from a blow to her head. The steady beeping from the machines and monitors they'd hooked to her sounded like trucks backing up. Her swollen eyes fluttered open once, but she was hopped up on so many painkillers and anti-inflammatories that I couldn't ask her anything about what had happened. I sat in an uncomfortable chair in the corner, relieved that I'd had the presence of mind to grab my backpack on the way out of the trailer.

In the dim light of a lamp, I flipped slowly through the yearbooks, looking for the young Emily and for the Lindy Gray my poor battered grandmother believed was as innocent as the day she was born. I found Peter's mother easily, her blonde hair stylishly flipped and her light eyes sparkling even in black and white. My own mother was harder to track, but I finally found her portrait in the 1972 yearbook. Peter's parents were seniors that year and seemed to infuse every other page with their perfectly happy glow. Lindy Gray was a freshman. In her long dark hair, deep eyes, and serious expression, I saw a near mirror image of myself. My eyes were my dad's hazel and my hair was more auburn than brunette, but in every other way I looked exactly like her.

I flipped through team photos and candid shots, my eyes drifting slowly down every page, following each line of text with my finger, looking for more Lindy. Finally I found her name in a caption about making a homecoming float. Emily stood beside her.

The faces were small and a little blurry, the photographer having framed the photo so that the large float was wholly visible. A few other girls stood alongside, their straight backs and broad smiles showing how proud they were of their accomplishment. The float was impressive, a large Viking ship covered in tissue paper flowers and sporting a banner that read "Vikings Take No Prisoners."

But what really caught my eye was the house in the background. The distinctive ornamentation along the roofline and between each column on the large front porch was utterly familiar. I struggled to lift its importance from the sloshing pool of information in my mind. Then all at once it came bobbing to the surface like pieces of a shipwreck. It was the Doll House, my mother's house, the dead house that still slouched behind the cemetery.

I took the yearbook into the blinding, buzzing fluorescent lights of the hallway and shut the door behind me.

"You need something, sweetie?" a nurse asked.

"Is there a phone I can use?"

"There's one in the room."

"I don't want to wake up my grandma."

She gave me the same look as the police officer and the social worker—a pitying smile and a slight shake of the head.

"There's a pay phone in the waiting area."

"Thanks."

The nurse went on her way. I didn't have any change, so I began a slow stroll down the hallway. At the end I found a room that was unoccupied, slipped in, and closed the door. I set the yearbook on the bed and dialed Peter's number. He answered on the third ring.

"Peter, I found a photo of our moms together at the Doll House. I think they may have been friends."

He yawned. "You do realize it's one in the morning, right?"

"Oh, crap. No. I didn't. Sorry. I've been at the hospital and I lost track of time."

"The hospital?" He sounded fully awake now.

I told him about the break-in and how I found my grandmother beaten and unconscious, about the destruction, about the odd fact that nothing seemed to be missing. As the story unfolded, I felt like I was living it again. Though I was surrounded by machines that were supposed to keep people's hearts beating steadily and their lungs puffing in and out in rhythm, my heartbeat raced and my breath came in gulps. Once I got to the part about the hospital I calmed down. Hospitals fixed things. Everything would be okay.

"So, I guess this is my answer about whether or not we're going to see my mom this week," I said.

"Yeah, no kidding. Do you want me to come to the hospital?"

"No. But maybe you could stop by and check on my grandma's parrot? Make sure he has food and water? He's freaking out."

"Sure." He sounded dubious. "Does he bite?"

"Viciously. But you can fill his food and water from outside the cage. You could swing by in the morning. He's probably fine for tonight."

"Why don't I pick you up and bring you home?"

"Are you kidding? I can't go back there. Anyway, I'm not sure I should leave. She might wake up."

We said our goodbyes and I went back to the cool dark of Grandma's room. The machines still beeped and hissed. I traded the yearbook for *Moby-Dick*. I had to finish it soon because I already had the next book in hand.

"It took me so long to read that beast, I wanted to follow it up with something short and sweet," Peter had said when I complained he'd given me the next book too fast.

"The next one may be short, but I don't know that I'd call it sweet," I said.

"Well, no. I guess not."

"You better read something by Dickens or Tolstoy next, or I'll never catch up."

"Deal."

I finished *Moby-Dick* in some nameless hour in the night and quickly wrote my payment poem while it was still fresh in my mind. Then I turned the page in my notebook and wrote the next poem. I didn't need to read the short and not-so-sweet book to write about it. Everyone knew that story. And anyway, it was practically poetry itself.

The next morning, Grandma was sitting up in bed. It would have been a heartening sight if she had looked anything like herself, but her face was more purple than peach and the normally sagging skin around her eyes was taut and puffy.

"How are you feeling?"

"Like a truck hit me."

"I think the police need you to go down to the station once you've figured out what all was taken so you can give them a full list. Do you remember anything about the guy who attacked you?" I asked.

She closed her eyes and didn't answer.

"It didn't look like he took anything," I continued.

"Who?"

"The person who broke into your house."

A look of concern settled on her brow. "Some-one broke into my house?"

"You don't remember? There was stuff thrown all over the place."

"You were in my house?"

"What? Yes. Why wouldn't I be?"

"You're too young to be a police officer."

"I'm your granddaughter. Robin."

She squinted and slowly shook her head. "I don't have a granddaughter."

I felt like I had swallowed a nest of baby snakes. I got to my feet and swung open the door. "Nurse!"

Peter carried my suitcase into the foyer of his house. The place looked like Jack Flynt—serious, no-nonsense, and a little bit empty. Whereas my grandma's trailer was packed with decades of kitschy, cutesy knickknacks—Hummel dolls, Precious Moments figurines, limited-edition plates with state capitol buildings painted on them—Jack Flynt's house was clean, linear, masculine, and stalwart. The tables and shelves were mostly bare, the occasional blown-glass vase or bronze casting the only decoration. Two empty nails in the wall reminded me of Peter's comment about his father erasing all evidence of Emily Flynt after her death. What had hung there? The beer sign Peter had bought his father for Christmas was nowhere in sight.

The nurses had told me to go home and get some rest, but there was no way I could stay in that ransacked trailer all alone with an apoplectic parrot. Peter picked me up at the hospital. We stopped at the trailer so I could pack a bag, but I could hardly get my feet to take me inside. Peter went first and I followed close behind, my fingers curled around his belt.

I fed and watered The Professor and changed out the newspaper at the bottom of the cage. He had plucked out all of the feathers from his breast to his feet so that now he looked like a fat little naked man in a gray cape and hood. Careless in my overtired state, I let the tip of my pinky slip between the bars as I put the water bottle back in place. The Professor sped across his perch and clamped down on it with his beak before I even realized what was happening. I couldn't find the antibiotic ointment or the bandages in the pile of junk on the bathroom floor, so I wrapped my finger in toilet paper and squeezed it with my other hand as Peter took my suitcase to the car.

I locked the door out of habit, as Grandma had insisted.

Once we were out of sight of the trailer and I could breathe normally, I pulled two folded pieces of paper from my back pocket and handed them to Peter. "Before I forget."

"You read them both?"

"I finished *Moby-Dick*."

"You have to read the other one before you write the poem."

"Just take it. Things are so crazy, if I don't give it to you now it might get lost and your collection will be forever incomplete. And anyway, I've read it before."

Peter had acquiesced and covered the rest of the distance to his house. He left me standing in the foyer while he deposited my suitcase in a room down a dark hall, then emerged a moment later with a small first aid kit. He led me to the kitchen and doctored my finger.

"Dad's probably in the den," he said. "We should go say hello."

I followed Peter down a short hall to a closed door. He knocked lightly, and a voice from the other side granted us access. When the door opened, all I could see were bookshelves, an entire wall of them. All empty. They shrank back like a woman stripped of her clothes in front of a crowd. I wanted to turn off the lights, to clothe them in darkness. A rustle of paper drew my attention to the corner of the room where Jack Flynt sat calmly in a brown leather chair, reading the newspaper, as if nothing scandalous was happening, as if he was not to blame for the bare bookshelves.

"Dad, this is Robin Dickinson."

Mr. Flynt looked up from his paper. "The breaking and entering?"

"Yeah."

"I'm sorry to hear about your cousin, Robin. Please make yourself at home. I'm afraid two men make for poor hosts, but we'll do our best."

He was already focused back on the newspaper when I managed a small thank-you.

Peter steered me out. "I can make eggs," he said.

I watched him at the stove and listened to the symphony of the kitchen. The ticking of the toaster, the smack of the eggshells against the pan, the sizzle of butter, the various taps and clinks of spatulas and plates and glasses of orange juice. But somehow it all rang hollow, like the cellos were missing. I felt the losses in our lives compound and expand until they filled the room. Lost parents, lost innocence, lost homes, lost security. When Peter slid a plate in front of me, a tear tumbled down my cheek and betrayed me.

"What's wrong?"

I wasn't going to cry here. I wasn't going to be some hysterical female in this cold male house. I kept my feelings locked deep within my chest where, despite my practiced indifference, they had been slowly poisoning me for months.

"Robin, she's going to be fine."

I shook my head.

"She will," he said.

Couldn't he see? Didn't those naked shelves gnaw at him? Didn't the empty nails snag him as he walked through these rooms? How had he managed to continue living here when the life of this house was gone? Why didn't he leave, abandon this place like the Grays had abandoned the old house beyond the cemetery one by one?

When things are out of your control, sometimes you do dumb things, just to show yourself you can do *something*.

I stood up. "Where's my suitcase?"

"It's in the guest room. Why?"

"We're going to see my mom."

19

now

The morning of the book drive is the first time
I've been back to Kennedy High School since
I left Sussex. Even after I moved back to River
City and started the store, I rarely crossed the
river and never went within a mile of the school.
To do so seemed dangerous somehow, like ice
fishing in March. Virginia Woolf had drowned
herself in March 1941 in the River Ouse after
returning to her own Sussex in England, having
been driven from two separate homes by Nazi
bombs and driven mad—by what? A childhood
trauma? The loss of so many dear friends? The
deaths of her parents?

When I step out of Sarah's car onto the
cracked blacktop parking lot, nostalgia and
fear grumble in my stomach like the river in
springtime. The asphalt seems solid enough,
but that's probably what the guy with the blue
pickup had thought about the ice. It's a warm
morning. Perhaps the present is only a thin crust
that might break apart beneath my feet at any
moment, allowing the river beneath to sweep

me inescapably back into the past. If I walked to the football field right now, those boys might be there in dirty red practice jerseys, Peter among them. He would look up and notice me as he did then, and we would start over and I would be fourteen again.

"Why are you just standing there?" Sarah says. "Come on. We only have an hour to get everything in place before this thing starts."

I follow her across the parking lot to a patch of lawn north of the main entrance. She snaps out the card table legs, flips it over, and affixes a poster to the front with masking tape. I stand dumbly, staring at the red mites running across the Spam bricks, waiting for orders.

Ryan eases a small rental truck parallel to the sidewalk and jumps down from the driver's seat. "Balloons are in back." He rolls open the back door of the truck to reveal dozens of helium balloons attached to weights. Grabbing a few, he trots off to place them at the entrance of the parking lot.

Sarah positions some more around the table and on either side of the truck, then puts some in her car. "I'm going to go put some of these at a few strategic corners. You and Ryan get the sign on the truck. There's duct tape in that bag."

Happy for a clear task, I scramble onto the hood of the truck, then the cab, then the box. Ryan tosses a folded sheet up to me. The sign is secured too quickly and I'm back on the ground with nothing to do. A little breeze sneaks behind the sheet, rippling the painted dinosaur and the words, "BOOK DRIVE! Build Our d*READ*noughtus! Save Our Bookstore!"

"Did she really need that many exclamation points?" I ask.

Ryan laughs. "You know Sarah. Did you bring your little dinosaur?"

I pull the model out and place him on the table between a box for monetary donations and a stack of informational flyers Sarah had picked up from the copy shop this morning. On one side they explained the struggle of the independent bookstore, the symbolism of the dinosaur we had chosen to build for our ArtPrize entry, and how we would use the prize money if we won. On the other side was a coupon for 25 percent off at Brick & Mortar Books. I had put the flyers infoside up. Sarah had flipped them over to show the coupon.

Dawt Pi arrives in a car driven by her pastor's wife, the back seat stacked with boxes of donuts, the trunk full of collapsed cardboard boxes she has spent the last week begging off of every business in town. Sarah returns from her balloon errand, and we all get busy putting the boxes together. Now all we need are books, which start to roll in a few minutes after nine o'clock.

"I've had these for years," one woman says.

"I've put them in every garage sale I've had and they never seem to sell."

I can immediately see why. Most of them seem to be her college textbooks, outdated psychology books, touchy-feely counseling pamphlets, and books on guided meditation. The covers are all typical of the late 1970s. I thank her, hand her a flyer, and offer her a donut.

"My daughter read all these," a man says of a box of well-loved romance novels.

"She doesn't want them?" I ask.

"I've been telling her to get these out of the basement for eight years. She's had her chance." He gratefully accepts a powdered donut and walks a few steps away to read the flyer I've pressed into his hand.

Several more cars roll in, most bearing at least one box or paper grocery bag full of books, a few with half a trunk load. I sift through them all, looking for gems I might want to save from use in the *Dreadnoughtus*, but find little worth keeping aside. Most of these books are not alive. They have not stood the passage of time. They do not still burn in the hearts of those who have read them. It's unlikely any of those readers could pull the names of the protagonists from memory. They are merely inert paper and ink, and I doubt very much they could live again. Like old Farley. Like the frog we dissected in eighth-grade science. Like Emily Flynt.

How much time does my father have left? Stays of execution don't last forever. Some last only a day, some last a few months, but almost all are simply buying time. Most of those convicted are executed anyway. Peter's long-ago words trip through my mind. *You might regret it if you didn't take the opportunity to talk to him before . . .*

We've collected from perhaps a dozen people when the remote news crew from WRST rolls in and starts getting their equipment set up. My palms are already sweating. The reporter who alights from the van is the same woman Dawt Pi pushed out of the store a few months ago. I can tell by the way Dawt Pi looks at her that she recognizes her too. I take a slow, deep breath. Let it out. Ignore the damp feeling under my arms and at my hairline. I force my feet to move and approach the woman with a pleasant smile arranged on my face. I'll pretend that I have never seen her before in my life, and because I pretend, she'll pretend. And that's how we'll both get through this.

"Hi, I'm Robin Dickinson of Brick & Mortar Books." I hold out my moist hand to her.

The woman pauses a moment before she decides to play along. She grips my hand in a firm shake and smiles broadly. "Winnie Myers, WRST. Thanks for inviting us out today." She wipes my sweat off her hand on the back of her skirt. "We'll be live this morning on the eleven o'clock show, so no second takes, okay?"

I nod my understanding, though the blood coursing through my ears muffles her voice. A few more fake pleasantries are exchanged before the camera is turned on me and Winnie Myers, standing by the truck. The cameraman says, "And we're on in five, four," and silently finishes the countdown with his fingers. Winnie's anticipatory smile looks more and more like a grimace the closer he gets to *one*. Then he points at her.

"This is Winnie Myers on location in the Kennedy High School parking lot in Sussex, where Robin Windsor, owner and operator of River City's Brick & Mortar Bookstore, is running a book drive for a project of 'literary' proportions. Robin, tell us what you're doing out here today."

Winnie turns the microphone and her bright white teeth on me. She said Windsor. I am Robin Windsor. I am exposed. I am standing before an oncoming train, unable to lift my leaden feet.

I see Sarah's upraised thumbs and urging eyes, Dawt Pi's calm smile, Ryan's relaxed posture and nodding head. I focus my mind on the talking points I spent the past week memorizing and hear myself speak.

"Today we're collecting used books from people around the area to be used in a special project for Brick & Mortar Books. We're entering a very large piece of art in the ArtPrize contest that's held in Grand Rapids, and we're asking residents to be a part of that by donating their used books, which we'll be using to build an animatronic dinosaur called a *Dreadnoughtus*."

"Wow! And can you give us an idea of what this dinosaur looks like?"

I hold up the prototype that Ryan created for me. "This model gives you an idea of how it will look, only we intend to make it full size, which is about eighty-five feet from nose to tail."

"Amazing. Obviously you're not doing this on your own. Tell us about your team."

"I'm grateful to have the support and expertise of local artist Sarah Kukla, my friend and coworker Dawt Pi Lian, and Ryan Miller, who is a teacher at Kennedy High and coaches the Science Olympiad team, which is playing an integral role in designing and building the inner skeletal structure. We're also the happy recipients of building materials from Neometallum Incorporated, which is providing the high-tech lightweight metal tubing for the skeleton, and Mid-Michigan Robotics Corporation, which has agreed to provide the materials necessary to bring this dinosaur to life."

"I see. And what will you do with the money if you win?"

"The bulk of the money will be used to pay bills and back taxes at Brick & Mortar Books, make some building improvements and renovations, and refresh our stock. We're the only remaining independent used bookstore in the area, and times have been tough over the past several years. In order to keep operating and keep serving River City readers, we need more resources. I'll also be making a donation to the Kennedy High School Science Olympiad team."

Winnie turns away from me to address the camera. "Okay, folks, get into your basements and attics and bring your old books to Kennedy High School in Sussex today before four o'clock or tomorrow from noon to four. And then get out to Brick & Mortar Books at 1433 Midway Street on River City's west side. I'm Winnie Myers with this Round About Town report."

"And cut," says the cameraman.

Winnie finally sheaths her teeth. "I think that went well. We'll also run it at six and eight."

"You got my name wrong."

Winnie pastes a surprised look on her face. "Did I?" She walks back to the news van.

Ryan puts his arm around my shoulders, pats twice, and lets it drop back to his side. "Nice job, Robin."

"Thanks." I let out a long breath, dizzy from the soliloquy. "I'm glad that's over."

Winnie emerges from the back of the news van with a big box of books. "We took up a donation at the station and managed to get a few boxes."

"Thank you," I struggle to say. "That was thoughtful."

"Unfortunately there are some kind of smutty ones in here. I don't know who put them in—I have my suspicions—but I figured you could put them on the top where no one would see them. There are two more boxes in the van."

"Let me help," Ryan says as he trots off.

All day the stream of books ebbs and flows, flush one moment, dry the next, and by four o'clock we're all done in. We've made a decent haul, but it doesn't look to me like it could possibly begin to cover such a large dinosaur. Still, it's a start. By five we're packed and ready to go to Ryan's house to watch ourselves on the six o'clock news.

As Kennedy High School recedes in the side-view mirror, I feel as though I accomplished something far more important today than simply gathering building materials. I survived. I dipped my toe into the raging river of the past and some-how managed not to get swept away.

"What's the weirdest book you saw today?" Sarah asks as she arranges pizza and chips on Ryan's coffee table.

"*Knitting with Dog Hair*," Ryan says.

"Ew!" Sarah says. "Mine was *Psi High*. The cover had a hand that had an eyeball in it, and three of the fingers were chunky naked people."

"I don't know," I say. "There was so much to choose from. I think we're doing the world a favor by getting some of these out of circulation."

We look to Dawt Pi for her answer.

"I saw a book of fat babies dressed like bugs and cabbages and things. It was cute. But strange. You know?"

"Yeah, we know." Ryan chuckles.

"Shh! Here it comes," Sarah says, waving her hand at us and turning up the sound on the TV.

"Now we go to Winnie Myers with a story about a local business in crisis and the gargantuan effort one woman is making in order to save it."

The interview appears on screen, and I am happy to see that my hair looks fairly under control, there are no sweat marks showing through my shirt, and I'm not stumbling over my words, though I probably should have put on some makeup as Sarah kept insisting on the drive there. I'm chagrined to see that I winced visibly when Winnie said my real name.

It finishes far quicker than I remember it taking to film. Back in the newsroom, the anchor says, "If you missed the book drive today, never fear. As Winnie said, you can donate your books tomorrow between noon and four o'clock. And if you can't make it out then, you can still do your part to build that massive dinosaur by dropping your used books off at Brick & Mortar Books at 1433 Midway Street in River City."

A shot of the store appears on screen. There. That wasn't so bad.

"Regular viewers may remember the store from our coverage of the River City connection to the case of former senator Norman Windsor, whose bizarre saga continues as calls to reopen the case are being made. Brick & Mortar Books owner Robin Windsor is the senator's daughter. Now we turn to Steve Bartkowski for weather."

All the breath leaves my body. Ryan flips off the TV. No one says anything for a moment.

"All publicity is good publicity," Sarah says. "It'll bring more people in and it'll bring more books in."

Sarah and Dawt Pi help Ryan clean up the plates and cups as I stare into space, wondering what Monday will bring. They say their goodbyes and head out to the car.

I turn to Ryan at the door. "Thanks again. For everything you're doing. If it weren't for you . . . well, I think we both know it wouldn't happen."

He gives me a melancholy smile. "No problem."

"So, Fred says we can start moving materials into the marina. I can help you unload all the books tomorrow after the drive."

"Sure." He puts his hand on the door, almost around me. "See you tomorrow."

I don't know why I wish he would actually touch my shoulder. Maybe so I could be present in this moment rather than obsessing about the moments that have passed and those still to come. But he doesn't. I walk into the still-bright evening sun and get into the car. I look back to the house. In the place where Ryan stood is a closed door.

20

then

D o you think your dad saw the note yet?"
Peter gripped the wheel and stared straight
ahead. "Probably."

We had entered the stream of traffic on I-75 as
the sun was breaking over the eastern horizon
and hit the Ohio border before I normally got out
of bed on a weekend.

"Are you going to get in trouble for this?"

"Probably."

"Sorry."

"Forget about it. He's never happy anyway."

"I thought when you had offered to take me that
it was something you'd checked out with him."

"Not exactly."

We drove on in silence for a while until finally
he exclaimed, "Gah, I hate Ohio!"

"Why?"

He glanced at me. "You're really not from
Michigan, are you?"

"Duh."

"Well, what do people in Massachusetts hate?"

I thought about that a moment. "Mediocrity."

Peter rolled his eyes. "I'm talking sports teams."

"Oh, I don't know. I don't do sports. I guess New York."

"Okay, Ohio State is Michigan's Yankees, then. And their speed limits are too slow. And the toll roads. And honestly, we've already been driving here for a year!"

It did feel like it took forever to get out of Peter's least favorite state, but when we stopped for lunch and gas in Pennsylvania, I was surprised to see that it was only 1:30. The next hundred and fifty miles were some of the most beautiful country I'd ever seen. Greening hills sprinkled with trees and adorned with the big red barns of bucolic farms.

"Man, what I wouldn't give to drive all day every day," Peter said.

"As long as it wasn't through Ohio."

"Right."

"Maybe you should be a long-haul trucker."

"Yeah, Dad would love that. 'This is Alex, the NFL sensation, and this is his brother Peter, the trucker.' Anyway, all they see is the highway and the backs of warehouses. I'd want to stop and walk around the woods and hike in the mountains. There's nothing like this back home. Everything's so flat in mid-Michigan, nothing but farms."

"There are farms out here."

"Yeah, and they're not growing corn as far as

the eye can see. There are sheep out here and horses and weird people in hats."

"They're called Amish."

"Whatever they are. It's beautiful."

I did agree. Why did my grandmother have to live in boring old Sussex? Why couldn't I have been sent to live in Montana or Colorado or even here?

"So you basically want to be a park ranger," I said.

Peter stuck out his bottom lip and nodded. "Yeah, I can see that. What about you?"

"I don't know. All I want to do is read."

"I don't think people pay you to read."

"Maybe a writer?"

He nodded. "I can see that."

"Or maybe I could teach English."

"If you were a writer you could live anywhere, travel."

A part of me liked that idea—picking up, leaving everything behind, driving off to discover the world beyond the horizon. But then where was home? I'd already been uprooted and it had hurt. Months later I was finally feeling like the place I lived was home. Could I really stand that kind of dislocation again? Without its root, a plant dies.

"Oh my gosh."

"What?" Peter said.

"Yesterday was my birthday."

"What?"

My birthday. I had missed it. Because my parents had missed it. They were the ones who bought cakes and presents, who sent invitations and threw parties. Birthdays were their job. They hadn't even managed to send a card. They'd forgotten me.

"I'm fifteen." I barely got the words out.

"Yesterday was your birthday? Aw, man, that sucks! That's it. We're going out tonight. We'll find a decent restaurant and get you cake for dessert."

He put a hand on my knee and drove with the other down the curving highway. We came down out of the mountains, whooshed through rich valleys, and crossed the Susquehanna River. The highway turned north, then south, then east into New York. Not long after we crossed the Hudson, we entered Connecticut. Our destination was north of Danbury. One hundred miles or so from there was my old house in Amherst.

It was seven o'clock by the time we walked into the reception area at the Federal Corrections Institute. At my paralyzed stare, Peter took the lead. "Linda Windsor's daughter Robin is here to see her."

The woman behind the desk gave me a sympathetic look. "I'm sorry, but visiting hours end at three o'clock on Sundays. You can come back tomorrow after 8:30 a.m."

The breath left my body, and relief over this temporary reprieve replaced it. Despite having months to think about it, I still had no idea what to say to my mother.

"Thank you." I turned around and we made our way outside. In the parking lot I looked at Peter. "I believe you owe me a birthday dinner."

In town we found a little out-of-the-way restaurant that didn't look too fancy. Peter used the pay phone in the entryway to let his dad know we weren't dead on the side of the road. When he came back he was a little pale.

"Everything okay?"

"Not really. But it can't be helped now."

I ordered clam chowder, something I'd missed since moving to the Midwest. Peter ordered fish and chips. I was three bites in before I thought to ask, "So where are we going to sleep tonight?"

"I asked the hostess about motels when you were in the bathroom. She gave me kind of a dirty look, but she gave me directions to a couple. I think you'll have to stay in the car while I get a room."

"Why?"

"Do you really have to ask that?"

"Oh . . . Are we going to get in trouble for this?"

"Not if we're careful."

Dinner and dessert were over too soon, and we followed the hostess's directions to the first motel. It looked like a scene out of a movie, one designed to show you how down on their luck and desperate the characters were. Peter vetoed it on sight. The second motel was clean and well-lit—at least on the outside. I chose to see this as a good sign. Peter secured a room for one with the emergency credit card his dad had given him when he got his driver's license. He removed our two suitcases and brought them inside, instructing me to keep my head down until he came to get me. The car got colder and colder. A full twenty minutes later he opened my door from a crouched position. We both crept to the end of the car and made a dash for it.

We sat inside with the blinds drawn and the TV on a rerun of *Friends* and avoided talking about the sleeping situation. I fiddled endlessly with a motel matchbook, flipping it through my fingers until the edges were soft and worn. Peter put his arm around me and I settled into the crook of his elbow, my head on his beating heart.

Eventually—miraculously—I fell asleep on top of the covers. When I woke in the early morning light I was beneath them, still fully clothed, Peter asleep beside me, his warm fingers laced in mine. Had I gripped his hand in my sleep? Or had he simply known I needed something to hold on to? I didn't want to let go, but I had somewhere to be. I slipped from the bed and into the tiny bathroom to shower and change. By the time I came out, Peter was up and dressed.

"It's nine o'clock. We better get going."

I nodded, but I didn't want to go to the prison anymore. I didn't want to speak to my mother. I didn't want to ask about her old doll or her old friends. I didn't want to yell at her for failing me. All I wanted was to keep on driving. If we left now, we could be at the Atlantic in just a few hours. I could stand with my heels on the sand of Cape Cod and my toes in the ocean, as I had every summer of my life—until this last one. Maybe for that moment, as the salt wind tangled my hair, I would feel like me again. Maybe the wind would blow me out of this story and set me down inside a new one, one that didn't include prison as a setting.

Instead I waited at the window for Peter's all-clear signal, dashed into the car, and let him drive me to the prison that would be my mom's home for the next twenty-some-odd years. The same woman was at the desk. I filled out a form and read the long list of rules and restrictions for visitors. I emptied my pockets into Peter's hand—a few coins, a ChapStick, and the motel matchbook. Then I left him sitting in a plastic chair while a guard wanded me and escorted me to the visiting area.

The room was spare and unadorned. A few round tables with built-in backless seats were bolted to the floor in no particular pattern. A couple other visitors were already waiting, and more came in behind me. When everyone was seated, I heard a buzz and the clicking of a lock being released, and the prisoners were led in.

She was third in the line, and I saw her before she saw me. Her hair was a little longer, unstyled, looking far less silky than it had seven months ago. She wore no makeup, her pale lips disappearing into the surrounding skin on her flat cheeks. The dull gray of her prison jumpsuit and the harsh fluorescent lights gave her whole face an ashen cast. I could tell when she spotted me. A slight hitch in her breath, a sudden slackness to her hard jaw that morphed into a smile—that brilliant smile that transformed a room.

She sat down across the table from me, never breaking eye contact. "Robin. I can't believe you're here. You're finally here." Tears formed in her eyes. "Happy birthday, baby."

She hadn't forgotten.

I wanted to go to her, to hug her, to crush the distance between us in an embrace. But the rules were clear on physical contact—there would be none if I wanted to continue this conversation. And now that I saw her, I did. Desperately. I didn't want to talk about what had happened back in Amherst or tell her what a terrible mother she'd turned out to be. I only wanted to rewind my life and have a mom again.

"I've missed you, sweetie," she said.

I pulled back the tears that wanted to fall. "I've missed you too."

"Is your grandmother here?"

"No."

I wouldn't tell her about the break-in. Not yet. There was nothing she could do, so why worry her? When I got back to Sussex and things got back to normal, I would write to her.

"Who brought you here?"

"A friend from school."

She smiled. "You're going to Kennedy, aren't you?"

"Yes."

She began asking all about Sussex. How was The Professor doing? Was this restaurant still there? Had Mr. So-and-So retired from Kennedy? We talked about Emily Flynt. I told her about meeting Peter in the graveyard. For some reason, I didn't tell her about all of the books beneath my bed. Those were just for me.

"It's a bummer your mom had to move out of that cool old house and into some dumpy trailer," I said.

She frowned a little and looked at her hands. The guard in the corner of the room gave a ten-minute warning.

"You know, my grandfather built that house. Every stick of it was nailed together with his own hands."

"Why did Grandma leave everything behind?"

"What do you mean?"

"A bunch of furniture, the pictures on the wall, your doll."

"My doll?"

While I described the dilapidated house and the doll in the window with the ever-watching eyes, my mother seemed lost in memories. It was then that I realized that her childhood was gone too. And now her adult life was as well. If my life had been disrupted by my parents' bad choices, hers had been utterly destroyed.

"Your grandmother has a lot of bad memories of things that happened in that house," she finally said. "I don't blame her for wanting to start fresh."

"Time's up," bellowed the guard from the corner of the room.

Already used to following orders, my mother stood up at once. But time couldn't be up. It had barely started.

"I love you, Robin." She leaned closer and winked a teary eye at me. "Keep your eyes open. Your grandmother's hiding something. Something for you."

For a moment all I could hear was the sound of slippers scuffling across linoleum. Mom was directed into a line and shuffled out a door with the other prisoners. I was directed into another line and shuffled out another door.

Back in the lobby Peter stood and frowned. "What's wrong?"

"Nothing. It's just—let's go."

In the car I replayed the conversation for Peter as best I could, ending with my mother's bizarre non sequitur about my grandmother. Had Mom somehow managed to send me a birthday gift from prison?

"Weird," Peter said. "She said your grandma is hiding something from you?"

"No, *for* me."

"That's not what you said."

"It isn't? I said *from?*"

"I'm pretty sure."

Had I? Which was it?

21

now

W hat do you mean you got a job?"
Dawt Pi furrows her brow. "You told me
look for a job. So I did."

I can't argue with her. But now that there is
some slim chance of saving Brick & Mortar
Books, I can't quite picture its future without her.

"Yes, of course, that's great."

"It is just on the other side of the river, at a
salon."

"But don't you need a license to cut hair in
Michigan?"

Dawt Pi rolls her eyes. "Anyone can cut hair. I
cut my own hair since I was ten. I cut my sisters'
hair, my brothers' hair, my parents' hair, my
aunts' hair. But it does not matter for now. I will
be the receptionist, and the owner says she will
help me get my license."

I try to imagine the permed old ladies of River
City attempting to make appointments with
someone with such a heavy accent. Will they
think her name is Dorothy like the postal worker
does?

"When do you start?"

"Wednesday."

"This Wednesday? That's only two days."

"It's okay, Robin. I will still come by the store. I promise. But you don't need me. Anne's salon is very busy. She needs me."

"Who will I talk to?"

Dawt Pi is unable to stifle a little laugh. "The better I speak English, the less we talk." She puts a hand on my arm. "Talk to your customers. There are more since the book drive. You talk to them, okay? Talk to Sarah. And Ryan. Ryan is nice."

We go about the day as normal. Only it's not normal anymore. Every action takes on new significance as I count it among the last of such things. The last time Dawt Pi will straighten that book, the last time she will sweep that corner, the last time she will get the mail. I hardly acknowledge today's fat, padded manila envelope. It sits unopened behind the counter until closing time when Dawt Pi flips the sign and locks the door.

"Are you ever going to look at this?"

I sigh and pick it up. It feels like my heart—large and hard and heavy. I already know what it is, and I don't even have to open it to remember the poem I wrote after reading it that fateful week when everything I was building in Sussex—everything I was building with Peter—fell apart.

I chase my death upon the waves of Fate,
Thinking it a trophy for my shelf
And, triumphing, I leap into my grave
And pull the tender dirt upon myself.
In bless'd oblivion beneath the ground
My peace with vengeful rancor I have
    found.
I knew, despite my hunting faithfully,
Death was always in pursuit of me.

I put the package down again and start to count down the register. "You can open it."

"Kentucky," she says, followed by the dry hiss of paper fibers breaking apart as she pulls the red tab. "*Mobby-Deek.*"

"*Moby-Dick.*"

I don't need to give her a summary of the plot, because it is spelled out in oil paints on the cover. A small boat, an angry monster from the ocean depths, a crew of terrified men on the brink of drowning, and one defiant captain looking into the great eye of the creature that will destroy him.

"Looks exciting."

"It is. But it's a tragedy."

"What is that?"

"A story that ends badly with no one getting what they want. Often lots of people die."

She examines the books that have taken over the shelves behind the register. They fill every inch of space and flow like water onto the

233

floor. A few hand-scrawled notes proclaim their unavailability for the curious customer. Dawt Pi has been on me for weeks to box them up and take them to my apartment.

"Most of these books are tragedies?" she says.

I make my own perusal. Do any of these books end happily? As I scan the spines I begin a defense a few times, only to have memory cut me short. For the most part no one gets what they seek, or if they do it's not what they thought it would be. People die, love is lost, lovers are destroyed, lives go on empty of meaning. So much heartache and pain. So little hope. Sometimes there is justice. Sometimes not. They don't all fit the textbook definition of a tragedy, but most come close. Then at the bottom of one stack I spy a series of spines that lift my spirits.

"Jane Austen's books end well. Those aren't tragedies. They're comedies. Comedies of manners. They poke fun at the way people act—their misunderstandings and mistakes—but the hero and heroine turn out okay in the end." My smile fades. "Maybe that's why they're not always taken as seriously."

"Is tragedy better?"

"I don't know." I take *Moby-Dick* from her hands. "Maybe it's truer."

An hour later I find myself alone in my apartment, bathed in the glow of my laptop, staring at the novel I am attempting to rewrite. Is it a tragedy? It's certainly not a comedy. Are those my only options for this story? Are those the only options in life?

These questions swirl around in my head for the next few days as my own little tragedy unfolds. Dawt Pi's last day. Then a quiet, gnawing emptiness, until at last it is Independence Day, the only day in this town that's bigger than St. Pat's.

Evidence of the impending celebration has been popping up all week. The carnival being erected on the east side by chain-smoking nomads who roam the country tightening and loosening bolts and taking tickets. Signs touting prices to park at churches and businesses. Municipal workers trimming grass and installing battalions of extra trash cans. Trucks laden with porta-potties rumbling over the bridges. Close to one hundred thousand people visit the city during the Independence Day weekend, triple the population.

The river is already getting crowded by midday as people take their boats out and claim the best spots to watch the fireworks. The wind sends whiffs of fried food and carnival-ride screams and snippets of songs from the long string of concerts being held in the park across the river. By late afternoon, the streets on both sides of the river are jammed with honking cars, every spot of green grass is covered with picnic blankets, and parking lot attendants are dragging sawhorses in front of their full lots.

A little before twilight, I head up to the roof with a lawn chair. I am about to sit down when I hear my name from the roof across Chestnut Street, where the bar crowd has gathered. Sarah is waving frantically. Glittery red, white, and blue stars wobble about at the end of springs a few inches above her head.

"Come join us!" she bellows, red plastic cup in hand.

I shake my head and sit down.

"Come on!"

"No thanks!"

She makes a face. "I'm coming over!"

"The door is locked."

"So unlock it!"

"Go to the back."

A few minutes later, Sarah appears at the alley door in a tiny patriotic halter top and cutoff shorts that would be considered underwear if they weren't made out of denim. The crescent-shaped scar from the long-ago surgery on her shattered knee shines white against her otherwise tan legs. She's still gripping her red plastic cup.

"Come on, Robin. Come over there with me. You'll have a good time."

"I'm pretty sure I won't. Go have fun and I'll be peachy over here."

I head back up to my own roof, Sarah following, determined as always to get her own way.

I sit down in my lawn chair. "Sorry I don't have two. I could grab a chair from the kitchen table."

"No need." Sarah plops down sideways on my lap, and her beer sloshes over the side of her cup and onto my chest.

"Sarah!" I push her off of me, and she lands on her backside on the hot black roof. "Now I'm going to smell like the bottle return room at the grocery store."

I head back down to my apartment, Sarah on my heels like a fox running down a rabbit.

"Why won't you come hang out with me? I haven't seen you in weeks. I know Dawt Pi is gone. I saw her at the salon when I had this done." She points to the red and blue streaks in her peroxided hair.

"I don't want to be stuck on a roof with *fifty* people spilling beer on me. I'd sooner jump off it." I hurry into my bedroom.

"Fine, then let's go down to the river."

"There are even *more* people down there."

"Ryan texted me he's at Dockside tonight. Let's find him."

"Dockside's on the other side of the river. I am not driving anywhere tonight. I'll be stuck in traffic for an hour before I can get home, even though it's probably less than half a mile away.

Why can't we just watch the fireworks from my roof in peace?"

"He told me you haven't been down to the marina in a few days."

I throw up my hands. "Why were you guys talking about me? Why is my life always everyone else's business?" I search my closet for a new, beerless shirt.

"Wear this." Sarah pulls out a filmy white spaghetti-strap tank top I bought to wear under other practically see-through white shirts. "And this." She hands me a red pencil skirt from a suit I had bought online a year ago at her relentless badgering and then never worn.

"My shorts are fine."

"Not with this shirt."

"That's not even a shirt. That's an undershirt."

"It's sexy."

"I don't need a sexy shirt to watch the fireworks."

"We're wasting time. We're going to miss the start of the show. It's getting dark. No one will see you anyway."

I do as Sarah commands, if only to get her off my back. "I'm not going up on the roof over there."

"Fine. Get your shoes on."

I slip my bare feet into some old flip-flops.

"No! Gross! Not those."

Sarah rummages around the bottom of my

closet and comes up with a pair of strappy high heel sandals she gave me last summer, right after she saw me wearing the very same old flip-flops she's just rejected. I roll my eyes and put them on. As I struggle with the tiny buckles on the side, Sarah takes out my braid and fluffs my hair with her fingers. I make a move to stop her, then reconsider. At least I'll be able to cover my chest with my hair now.

"Perfect," she says. "Now let's go."

I head for the roof, but Sarah easily pulls me downstairs instead. Sitting on my butt in a bookstore for years is no match for her thrice-weekly gym attendance, and the ludicrous shoes have made me clumsier than usual.

"Where are we going?"

"To the river. We're going across to find Ryan."

I stumble along behind her. "What, are you going to swim? How long have you been at that bar?"

"We'll get a ride."

"On a boat? Have you seen the river? It's packed."

"Fine, then we're walking across."

We push our way past hordes of people, and I somehow navigate the decline down to the river in the unnaturally tall sandals without twisting my ankle. Across the river I can clearly see the strings of lights outlining Dockside's large out-door patio.

"The bridge is that way," I say.

"We don't need a bridge."

We pick our way down the packed dock to the sounds of appreciative whistling. At the end of the dock, I arrange my hair back over my chest. The closest boat is ten feet away.

"Yoo-hoo!" Sarah calls sweetly. "We're trying to get to the other side. Can we walk across your boat?"

It doesn't look to me like there is room for even one more person on board. But the guys seem to appreciate Sarah's attire and spunk. One throws a rope onto the dock and Sarah loops it around a cleat. Hand over hand, the man draws the boat close enough, and two other men reach out for Sarah to help her onto the deck. Then they turn to me with beckoning hands and hopeful grins. I feel their hands on my arms. Then I am floating above the river for a moment before they set me down on the deck. I make my way to the other side of the boat where Sarah is busily flirting her way across the river.

"Now what?" I ask.

She scans the water a moment and picks out our next stepping stone. "That one."

"You got it," the man next to her says.

The first firework screams into the sky and explodes overhead. A loud whoop goes up from the crowd, followed by more fireworks. After much shouting and many hand motions, the man with the rope has managed to draw close enough to the next boat for us to move ahead on this insane errand. We alight on the deck of a pontoon strung with blinking white lights and crawling with baby boomers. A couple gray-haired men tear their eyes away from the sky to ogle us. A woman scowls.

Head down, I make for the side rail. If I were not in this restrictive skirt and these impractical shoes I could leap to the next boat. But as it stands, a couple of inches seems to be the farthest apart my knees can go.

Another set of shouted instructions and a rope bring us close enough to bridge the gap. The next boat is one of five already latched together, a group of quite obviously wealthy friends who seem to be split on their opinions of our escapade, one half bemused and ready to join us, the other half suspicious and hugging their purses. The air is thick with smoke and chatter. Reflections of the ongoing fireworks sparkle in eyeglasses and wine glasses.

We pick our way across the group of boats with the help of plenty of willing hands until we are on the last one. Up on her tiptoes, Sarah searches for the next step.

"Hey, down in front," says a voice from the distant past.

Sarah doesn't notice it. It's not from her past. It's from mine. I look in the direction of the voice.

The reds and greens and blues of the fireworks alternately cast eerie light and deep shadow on its source. A man sits alone on a bench seat at the back of the boat.

"Here we go!" Sarah says as the next boat is drawn closer.

I move toward the man to get a better look. Why do I know that voice? I can feel the hairs on my arms shift and stiffen. A flash of bright white as several fireworks blast into pieces at once. I see him clearly. And it all comes back in a rush of moments. That face—in doorways, turning back from the front seat of a black sedan, at funerals, at backyard barbecues. Always serious, yet always with a wink in my direction.

This man worked for my father.

22

then

Pointless. This trip had been utterly pointless. All it did was make me ache for something that could never be and churn out questions about what had been. Exhausted and bitter and confused, I turned away from Peter in the car and watched the landscape fall away behind us in a blur.

I don't know how long we had been driving when he finally touched my leg and said, "I'm stopping for lunch."

The car slowed as Peter steered onto the exit ramp, pulled into a parking lot, and killed the engine. "Let's go."

"I'm not hungry."

He got out of the car. A few minutes later he came back with a bag of food and two drinks. He handed me a burger and a sleeve of fries. "You know where I want to go right now?" he said after a few bites. "Niagara Falls."

I sat up straighter. It hadn't occurred to me that I could go anywhere but back to Sussex, back to the nightmarish trailer, back to the hospital where my grandmother didn't remember who I was. What if she never remembered? What would I do? No, I could not go back into that mess right now. I needed a break. Just a break.

"Really?"

"Why not? It's still spring break."

I knew it was wrong, knew it was irresponsible. But I was fifteen. This was the time to be irresponsible. Maybe that was what was wrong with my parents. Maybe they had done everything right when they were kids. Maybe they had followed every rule, kept every law, suppressed all their irresponsible leanings until they were adults, when being irresponsible had far greater consequences. Wouldn't it be better to get it out now? Wouldn't it be better to ignore my problems a little while longer if it meant that I might be a better adult because of it?

We finished eating and gassed up. Then we were back on the open road. Conversation for the next six hours was minimal and restricted to what we saw out the window, which, while pleasant enough, was nothing like the lazy rolling expanse of the Appalachians. I didn't know what occupied Peter's thoughts during the quiet times. I thought of Amherst. About my old school and my old friends and my old life. I thought of Grandma in the hospital. Of her hiding something from me. But then maybe she wasn't hiding some *thing* for me or from me or whatever. Maybe she just had a secret. Would her mind be in any shape to remember it?

The sun was hanging low in the sky when we reached Niagara, and I had to shade my eyes. I felt the falls before I saw them, a low thundering in my ears and a shivering beneath my feet, like the entire world was trembling. It wasn't a fearful trembling, like what I felt as I searched the ransacked trailer for my grandmother. It felt like a release.

The crowd of tourists parted like curtains in front of us as we approached the rail, and I looked out into the watery cauldron. While the people around me sought to defend themselves against the spray with hoods and umbrellas and arms clasped around their own bodies, I welcomed the storm. Tiny bullets of icy water assaulted my cheeks and my eyes. Meltwater from the winter snows fed the insatiable river and barreled on down into Lake Ontario, eventually emptying out into the ocean I longed for. There it joined powerful currents and raced off to the far reaches of the globe, where no one had ever heard of Norman Windsor.

In the deepening twilight, the shouts of men and women and the squeals of children dropped away behind me until I could hear only the voice of the falls. Then it was not one voice but many, thousands upon thousands of murmuring, grumbling tones, flinging themselves off the cliff to merge with the swirling mass below. If I leaned forward a little more, I might fall in and join them.

Peter took my hand in his.

"I can't believe you could start right here and float all the way out to the ocean," I said.

"You could start in Chicago or Minnesota and do the same thing, going through the Great Lakes."

A few minutes later, a cheer went up from the crowd as the colorful spotlights were turned on the falls. We stayed a little longer, but I didn't care for the lights. I would rather have stood there until the sky blackened into night and the people all left for their beds and only the roar was left in the darkness.

Back in the parking lot I leaned on the car. "Are they really all that big?"

"What?"

"The Great Lakes."

Peter laughed. "You've never seen any of them?"

"I grew up near the *ocean*. Lakes just don't seem all that impressive."

We got in the car.

"You'd change your mind if you saw them."

"What's the best one?"

"I can tell you the worst one—Lake Erie."

"Why's that the worst?"

"It's filthy. The water's been on fire before. Think of that. *On fire.*"

I laughed. It felt good.

"The best one for beaches and sunsets is Lake Michigan. But we usually took vacations along Lake Huron since it was closer. I've never been to Lake Ontario. Superior's the coldest, but it's the cleanest and there's some amazing scenery up there. I guess it all depends on what you're looking for." Peter yawned and started the engine. "I think we need to find a place to stay for the night. I'm beat and it's still five hours to home, plus time at the border crossings."

"Border crossings?"

"Only makes sense to go through Canada from here."

"I don't have a passport."

"It's just Canada. You don't need a passport."

I turned on the overhead light, pulled out the atlas, and examined the US map. My finger traced a wavering line through Ontario and into Michigan. I looked at the big blobs of blue surrounding the state and followed the yellow lines of highways across the map. It seemed possible. And why not?

"Okay, Mr. Michigan. Let's see the Great Lakes tomorrow. All of them."

"All of them? In one day?"

"Yeah."

"Why be in such a hurry? Just see them one at a time."

"No, that's no fun. The *point* is to see them all in one day. I bet no one has ever done it."

"That's because when people go to the lake they actually want to spend time *at the lake,* not stuck in the car. I've been driving practically nonstop for two days. I don't know that I want to make the trip any longer."

"I do."

Peter looked at me with kindness in his eyes.

"Peter, I don't want to go back to that place."

He put his arm around me. "You can stay with me."

"For how long? I can't live at your house."

"Either way, we're not starting home tonight so we need a place to stay. We can decide tomorrow." He pulled the atlas from my lap and flipped over to New York. "How about we stay in Buffalo? That way, even if we don't see all the Great Lakes, you can at least see Lake Erie."

"The worst one."

Peter laughed. "Yeah. And we can swing by Lake Ontario too. We'll be driving right by it on this road here."

It took some searching to find another motel that would rent a room to an eighteen-year-old, and it wasn't nearly as clcan as the last one. Exhausted from the past couple days of travel, Peter immediately fell asleep on the concave bed while I lingered in the waking world, listening to the mice in the walls and parsing my mother's every word and expression. Morning was long in coming, and when Peter tapped me on the shoulder I thought it was still night for how dark it was.

"Hey, Robin, get your stuff. We're doing this."

"It's too early."

"Gotta get going or we won't get to Lake Superior until after dark."

I was instantly awake then. "Really?"

"Why not? When are we going to get this chance again? Anyway, it'll give you a story to tell people—a true story."

We packed quickly and walked through the chill air to the car as night was still considering whether it would yield to morning. As Peter drove toward downtown Buffalo, the streets slowly filled with men and women on their way to work. He parked at a small patch of grass near a factory, and we walked out to the edge of gray water that was beginning to take on a morning hue.

"Okay, it's pretty big," I admitted.

"It's not even the biggest one. Wait until tonight."

"If you can't see across any of them, they'll all seem like the same size."

"No they won't. You'll see."

We stood at the edge of the shore until our

shadows were thrown ahead of us in the rising sun. I turned to tell Peter I was ready to go and saw he was staring at me. I gathered my unbrushed hair in my hands. I'd never worried about what I looked like to him before, but I did then. There was something about sunrise. Something about the sleepy look on Peter's face. He was more to me than books, more than a friend. I knew then that even if Erie was the worst of the Great Lakes, it would always be special to me. Because that was the moment I realized I loved him.

I brushed my tangled hair as we headed north on I-190. We crossed into Canada with the rush hour traffic, and Peter took a coastal road along the shore of Lake Ontario for several miles, allowing me to stare out the window at the glittering mass of water set alight by the brilliant morning sun. It looked as though all of the stars of last night had dropped into the water to await the next evening, when they would shoot back up into the velvet sky.

We stopped for breakfast and got directions back to the highway from two large and congenial men slurping down coffee in the booth next to ours.

"Wow, those guys couldn't have been more Canadian," Peter said as he pulled out onto the road. " 'It's aboot five miles down da road, ya know, eh?' "

"You know that's what you sound like, right?"

"No I don't. People from Michigan don't have an accent."

"Yes you do. You sound almost exactly like them."

"No we don't. Are you kidding?"

"You have an accent."

"Haven't you ever watched national news? Newscasters all sound exactly like me, no matter where they're from. Which means they're coached to sound like me. They're not coached to sound like you. *You* have an accent." He gave my arm a playful push.

I flicked his ear in retribution. "And you sound like a Canadian."

Canada slipped by over the next couple hours, but I was largely unaware. My restless night had caught up with me. Peter had to nudge me awake when he eased the car into line at the next border crossing. The Canadian guard that morning had been pleasant, looking over our IDs and telling us that he could only let us into his country if we could name one Backstreet Boy. We managed to answer to his satisfaction, and he opened the gate. Now on the way back into our own country, the humorless American guard analyzed our IDs with a frown and quizzed us about what we were doing in Canada and why we weren't in school.

"You went to Canada on your spring break?" he said doubtfully at Peter's explanation.

"Not exactly, sir," Peter said. "We're driving through it because it's faster."

The guard examined the ID that had come in the fat envelope from the social worker when I changed my name, and narrowed his eyes. For a moment I panicked, wondering if it was real or if maybe she had gotten it made by some counterfeiter like in the movies. What if the guard didn't let me back in?

"You two related?"

"No."

"Your parents know where you are?"

"Yes," Peter said.

"I'm talking to her."

"Y-yes, sir. Well, no. I mean, I live with my grandmother."

"Her parents are dead," Peter said.

The officer pressed his lips together and seemed to be deciding whether or not he believed that. "Pop the trunk," he commanded.

He walked around to the back of the car and was gone so long I was sure I would soon be hauled off to a tiny interrogation room somewhere. Maybe the entire Windsor family would end up in jail.

Peter leaned over and kissed my cheek. "Hey, it's fine. Relax."

"I thought you said you were from Michigan,"

the officer said when he appeared back at the open window. "Your luggage tag has a Massachusetts address."

"I'm originally from there," I managed to say. "I moved to Sussex, Michigan, last summer. When my parents died."

"It's near River City," Peter supplied.

"I know where it is. You should change your luggage tags."

"Yes, sir."

The guard looked us both up and down once more and then zeroed in on me. "I'm sorry about your folks."

"Thank you, sir."

He waved us on but looked doubtful that it was the right thing to do.

At some point I began breathing normally again. On I-75, Peter said, "Last chance to call it quits and go home."

"Do you want to go home?"

He let loose an enormous yawn. "I sure don't want to face my dad."

"Keep driving."

We were ravenous by the time we found a McDonald's. We ate quickly and were back on the road by four o'clock. For a hundred miles or more, we passed only farmland and windbreaks, the flat, featureless expanse of fields Peter was so tired of. I followed our progress on the map, ticking off mile markers and mouthing the names of all the little towns we didn't have time to explore. We raced the sun as it made its relentless journey across the sky. Clouds drifted in from the west. Fields gave way to trees, and the earth began to flex and roll. It was after six o'clock when the towers of the Mackinac Bridge finally came into view.

"Think we'll make it to Lake Superior before sunset?"

"If we count the Straits as both Lake Michigan and Lake Huron we might."

For a moment at the top of a hill I could see forever in both directions, green and brown land hemmed in by vast blue inland seas. "That's technically both of them anyway, right?"

"Yeah. And you'll see more of Lake Michigan when we get to the UP."

"Oh! Upper Peninsula. They eat pasties there."

Peter stared at me for a moment.

"What?" I said. "They do. My grandma told me."

He looked back to the road. "How do you think she's doing?"

I'd been trying not to think of her as we slipped down the gray ribbon of highway. It wasn't working, of course. I'd been imagining every scenario and what I would do. If she never got back her memory of me, if she was brain damaged for life, if she couldn't make dinner or go to the bathroom by herself. Would I have to drop out of school to care for her? Would we have to have a live-in nurse? Where would I go if she never recovered and had to live in a nursing home?

"She's in a hospital. I'm sure she's doing fine." Only I wasn't sure at all.

At the base of the enormous suspension bridge, Peter slowed and took the middle lane. The bridge was five miles long, the wind stiff, the buzzing sound of the tires unnerving. For several minutes we were suspended almost two hundred feet above the churning waves below. These waters were not the near mirror of Lake Erie before the morning's boat traffic disturbed the surface. They did not have the starlight glow of Lake Ontario, which called people to leave their responsibilities on shore and hop on a sailboat. These waters were surly, still edged with winter's ice, battering the ferries that were busily traversing the space between the mainland and a far-off island like ants following a trail.

When we reached the other side of the bridge I had almost the same feeling of relief I'd had when we finally made it through the border crossing back into Michigan. We paid the toll and then Peter aimed the car toward the setting sun.

I pulled down my visor and examined the map. "Isn't the lake north?"

"If you go straight north from the bridge you'll end up at the Soo Locks. You can't say you've seen Lake Superior until you've at least seen it from somewhere like Grand Marais. So I'm bringing you up there. There's a spot that's easy to park at where you can see the Grand Sable Dunes on one side and cliffs on the other. It's gorgeous at sunset."

I found Grand Marais on the map at the eastern end of something called Pictured Rocks National Lakeshore. "What's Pictured Rocks?"

"It's a national park. There are hiking trails there, gorgeous beaches, and all sorts of cliffs and arches and caves along the water. Some of them look like things—like an Indian head or a fleet of ships—and some of them have waterfalls that go into the lake, and minerals leach from the rocks and stain the cliffs with stripes of all different colors. We took a family vacation up there a year before Mom died. Alex was home from school. The whole family was together. Well, mostly together. Dad stayed at the hotel and got some work done while Mom and Alex and I did a boat tour of the cliffs and then went to the sand dunes."

I rolled my eyes. Didn't he see it? It was plain as day if you just paid an ounce of attention.

"Did you ever talk to any doctors about how your mom died?" I asked.

"My dad did. Why?"

"I didn't know if you had been at the hospital with her or anything."

"No. It happened when I was visiting Alex at MSU. By the time Dad got ahold of us and we got home, her body was already at the funeral parlor."

I nodded silently.

"Why?"

There are moments in life when everything pivots, where your trajectory changes and the future you were headed toward dissolves and is replaced by another. This was one of those moments, though I didn't know it then. The moment when everything twisted out of place. The beginning of the end. The water over the fall. I could have stopped it if I'd just kept my mouth shut. But I didn't. I never did back then.

"Did you ever wonder if maybe it wasn't an aneurysm?"

23

now

B illy."
It comes out as a whisper the same
moment the report of an explosion reaches my
ear. He can't have heard me. I'm not even sure
he sees me as he picks a bit of loose tobacco
from the wet end of his cigar. I forget about my
unconventional trip across the river and stare
at the man in the back of the boat. How can
he be here? I'm mistaken. It's not him. It can't
be him.

I step carefully across a couple of life pre-
servers and sit in the opposite corner of the bench
seat. I tousle my hair so it covers more of my
face, though even if this really is my father's
former chief of staff, I doubt he'd recognize me
after all these years.

"This your boat?" I ask between explosions.

"Nah. Mine's a thirty-footer. Left her in the bay
and caught a ride upriver with these fellows."

"Friends of yours?"

"Just met them." He leans forward. "What's
your name, sweetheart?"

I look around for Sarah, but she is nowhere to be seen. "Emily."

"I'm Billy," he says. Or did he repeat "Emily"?

We're quiet for a moment as the sky explodes above us.

"Where are you from?" I say in a pocket of silence.

"Everywhere. Live on my boat." More explosions. He leans a little closer, clearly happy that a younger woman seems interested in him. "I winter in the Caribbean and the Gulf of Mexico. Head up the West Coast some years and summer off Washington or British Columbia. Other years I come up the East Coast and summer in Maine. First time I've come down the Saint Lawrence Seaway, though. Tomorrow I'm bound for Lake Superior. Want to come along?"

I ignore the suggestive invitation and shout to be heard over the fireworks. "First time in Michigan?"

"I've been here before. Long time ago."

"Sounds like an interesting life."

"It's great. Never feel tied down." He takes a long draw on his cigar. "Meet lots of interesting—and beautiful—people along the way."

I fight back my gag reflex. "I assume you're retired?" I risk a sidelong glance at him and see that he's frowning.

"Kind of nosy, aren't you, Emily?"

The sky goes silent for the space of a breath. The finale is coming.

"This is the best part," I say, pointing at the sky, pointing away from my inquiries.

The fireworks begin again, three times as big and loud, a constant barrage of booming explosions. The cheers and whistles of more than one hundred thousand people rise up from below and seem to blow the lingering smoke across the sky.

After fifteen minutes of nonstop detonation, my chest is rattling and I can hardly take any more. Then the bottom drops out. Silence. The crowd erupts. After the aural bombardment, their screams and whoops sound like they're coming from inside a refrigerator. I forget myself and join the standing ovation. If there's one thing my adopted city does better than anyone else, it's fireworks.

The older man beside me takes the opportunity of being in a boisterous, largely drunken crowd to press his advantage. "God bless America!" he shouts, then he grabs me around the waist and plants a disgusting kiss on my lips. After a moment he releases his hold and finally looks me full in the face.

"Lindy?" he says in disbelief—or is that fear in his eyes? He takes a step back. His heels connect with the bench and he sits down hard.

Sarah descends upon me. "There you are! I've

been looking all over for you! Took me three boats to figure out you were gone!"

I extract my arm from her grip. "Stop it." I turn to the man. "I'm not Lindy."

He nods slightly, but it takes a moment for his expression to change.

"Come on, Robin. Ryan's waiting for us."

I swat at Sarah like a mosquito. "So go without me."

"Look, these guys are not going to be happy if I have to come back for you again."

"I said go without me."

"Why? You know this guy?" Then to him, "Who're you?"

I speak close to her ear. "I can't leave now. This man . . . is a family friend. You go on. Give Ryan my regrets. Take a cab home."

She lets out an angry huff. "Fine. But you're missing out." She wags a finger in my face, then heads to the front of the boat.

For a moment I worry about her stumbling into the river, but then I think of all the men out here who'd love to be on the receiving end of her gratitude for saving her life.

Billy is leaning toward me, elbows on his knees, studying my features, schooling his. "Robin. Wow. I don't think I've seen you in—"

"Almost twenty years," I supply.

Something flashes across his expression, but whatever it is, he draws the blinds so quickly

261

I can't even be sure I saw it. The casual, cigar-chomping sailor is back.

"So, what have you been up to?"

"What is anyone up to? Working."

He nods. "I got out of politics. Bought the boat. I thought it would be best to keep moving. When you're in one place too long, people start recognizing you, calling up the local news. Maybe you know what that's like."

I feel a tightening in my stomach, like the cinching of the belt on a bathrobe to keep it from falling open.

"Couldn't really get regular work with my . . . associations anyway," he continues. "Your parents managed to make enemies all over. Especially your mother. Turns my blood cold to think of her getting out soon. If you knew the truth . . ."

I struggle to get the words past my clenched teeth. "What's the truth?"

He squares his shoulders and looks me straight in the eye.

"The truth is your dad didn't kill those people."

24

then

There are many types of quiet. The quiet after the last dying note of a symphony. The quiet of your bedroom when you've woken suddenly in the night with a nameless anxiety. The quiet of the doll in the window of my mother's decaying childhood home.

Peter's quiet hung in the air between us like a slowly circling mist. I was tempted to break it apart, wave it away like Grandma's cigarette smoke, and go on talking to fill the silence. Instead I waited. I'd said what I thought he needed to hear. Now it was his turn.

"I'm not sure what you mean," he finally said.

"I don't know, only . . . you had to take your dad's word for it that an aneurysm was what she died of."

"And?"

"Well, do you think your dad told the truth?"

Peter shifted in his seat and glanced from me to the road several times in rapid succession. "What possible reason could he have for *not* telling the truth?"

I hesitated. I don't know what I expected, but it wasn't the combative tone I was hearing. "I don't know. Parents lie sometimes. I always trusted my parents, and look what happened to me."

"Yeah, and I'll ask again: what possible reason could my father have for lying about how my mom—his wife—died? Just because your parents turned out to be lowlife criminals doesn't mean all adults everywhere are hiding some deep dark secret, okay? I know it's hard to come to grips with what happened with your parents, but you can't take that out on other people."

I wanted to grab the wheel and run Peter off the road for saying that. Visions of Sarah Kukla's bloodied and broken body flashed through my mind.

"Sorry," I said instead. "You're right. I don't know what I'm even thinking anymore."

He put a hand on the back of my neck and squeezed it gently. "You've been through a lot lately. Don't worry about it. Just . . . get out of your head, okay? It's kind of messed up in there."

He was smiling as he said it, and I laughed it off. But I couldn't escape from the cyclone of my mind. I was always in there, swirling around among the debris. What had I been thinking? Did it really matter how Emily Flynt had died? Wouldn't it be better for Peter to believe she'd died at the cruel hand of fate rather than at her own desperate hand? Who's to say I was even remotely close to being right anyway? Maybe I was seeing a pattern that existed not on the page but in my own "messed up" psyche. Maybe the wallpaper was simply wallpaper and there were no prison bars, no grotesque bulging eyes or gaping mouths taunting me from beneath the acanthus leaves. Maybe I was going mad.

In the deepening silence, we stopped at a dinky gas station where patrons could fill their tanks and buy the pelt of a skunk, coyote, or bear, then headed north on an empty road. There was still snow this far north, but the road was clear and we flew down it, trying to beat the sun. Peter passed an empty visitor station, still closed for the season, and an inland lake ringed with ice. It was nearly 7:30 by the time we pried our butts off the seats in a small, deserted parking lot. Peter took the flashlight from the glove box and a plaid wool blanket from the trunk, and we walked along a snowy, paved path until it disappeared into snow-streaked sand.

A sign covered with dire warnings in bold type seemed to indicate that we would be in need of emergency assistance should we choose to go down the steep dune called the Log Slide to the water's edge, but I had no desire to do anything of the sort. There was some menacing force down there. I could hear it. We crept over the crest of sand and dead vegetation, and my breath was swept from my body by an arctic blast of wind.

Then I realized that I could see nothing but water and sky.

A deep and ominous gray-blue, frosted with whitecaps breaking on snow-crusted blocks of ice that had been thrown to shore, the lake stretched out to the horizon where it merged with the darkening sky. To the left were craggy cliffs reaching along the shore for miles until they touched the setting sun, which was at that moment painting the underside of a cloud bank in brilliant pinks and corals and purples. To the right were the dunes, glowing like endless mounds of orange sherbet.

"Wow."

"See?"

"I'm glad we didn't start here and end with Lake Erie."

Peter's laugh flew away on the wind. He stood behind me, enclosed me in his arms, and wrapped the blanket around me like a mother bat wraps her wings around her baby. I gripped the edges, but the bottom corner still flapped with every gust.

We stood, bodies warm against each other, faces stinging from the cold wind, until the burning orb of the sun dropped into the pine forest and the steady blinking eye of a distant lighthouse could be seen through the murky dark. Peter extracted himself from the blanket and turned on the flashlight. With his arm around me he guided me out of the gale to the dark path through the woods and back to the parking lot.

There was another car there now, with a man halfway in his trunk, rummaging around. He emerged with a large bag and something straight and shiny. He lifted his hand in greeting as our flashlight beams merged on the asphalt between us.

"Hey there, folks. Sunset?"

"Yeah," Peter answered. "What are you doing out here so late?"

"Star trails," the man said as he waved what I now assumed was a tripod. "And if I get lucky, maybe the aurora will be out tonight. You should stick around. Good chance of some fireworks."

"We have a long drive."

We parted ways, us to the warmth of the car, him to the endless black expanse of water and sky.

"Now what?" Peter asked. "We're not going to try to find a place to stay the night up here, are we?"

I held my hands to the heater. I didn't want to leave. I wanted to stay up here forever.

"I guess we have to face the music at some point. I need to check on my grandma and feed The Professor, and you need to talk to your dad."

He nodded, but he looked unconvinced. "It sucks to be eighteen. I'm not a kid, but I'm not an adult. Still answering to my father. I envy Alex. He can do whatever he wants."

"At least you're not fifteen. At least you can pick up and drive wherever whenever you want."

"Not sure I'll be able to after this." He put the car in reverse and then put it back in park. "Everything will be all right. It'll all work out, and the only thing we'll remember from this trip will be the good stuff—Niagara Falls and your crazy scheme to visit all the Great Lakes in one day. It won't be about your parents or my parents or your grandma or anything like that. It'll just be me and you." He seemed to be trying to convince himself as much as me.

Crossing the big bridge back into the Lower Peninsula was somehow less terrifying in the dark when I couldn't see how precariously I was perched between earth and sky. I made myself stay awake for the entire five-hour drive back to River City in solidarity with my dog-tired driver. According to the car's odometer, when we pulled up to my grandmother's trailer a bit after 1:00 a.m., we had driven over two thousand miles in the past three days.

"Give me a few minutes to check the messages and feed the bird."

The Professor cussed me out as I filled his bowls and changed out the water in his bottle. I tripped over all the junk that was still strewn across the floor and then had the sinking realization that no one was going to clean it up for me. I'd have to be the adult and do it.

The answering machine flashed the number thirteen in lurid red. Four messages were from the hospital. The rest were from Grandma's priest and various church members checking up on me. All insisted I call immediately upon receiving their message. But it was the middle of the night and I was about to collapse. It could wait.

Back out at the car I shook Peter awake. For a moment he looked like he didn't recognize me. He rallied long enough to drive to his house, unlock the door, and climb the stairs to his bedroom. A few minutes later, I was lying on the guest room bed, suddenly wide awake and wishing I'd grabbed a book. Where did Peter keep his mother's books anyway?

But no. I couldn't just take one. That wasn't our deal. Instead, I crept to the kitchen and found the phone book.

"River City Medical Center, how may I direct your call?"

"I'm checking in on Martha Gray. I've been out of town, and the nurses up there left a message on the answering machine that I should call."

The receptionist transferred me. It rang once. Twice. I fingered the motel matchbook in my pocket. Another person answered the phone. I explained my identity again. The voice on the other end of the line turned serious.

"Robin, I'm sorry to tell you that Mrs. Gray's case became critical. She was hemorrhaging in her brain and was rushed into surgery on Monday to try to alleviate the pressure. We tried to call you. I'm afraid she didn't make it. She died on the operating table."

25

now

I don't understand."

The dull ache in my stomach is spreading to my chest like smoke rising from a burning ember. The party is breaking up, and people are untethering the boats.

"We're heading back out," a man shouts.

"Come with me and I'll explain," Billy says.

I can still taste his cigar on my lips from the unwanted kiss. "I need to get back to shore."

He walks to the front of the boat and talks to a man with receding white hair in a navy golf shirt and madras plaid shorts. A moment later he is back. "He's going to take us to shore and drop you off."

"Thank you."

He stares at me a moment. "I can spend the night in the bay and come upriver in the morning. I don't think I'd feel right leaving without giving us a chance to talk. And I'd love to see what my little Robin has been up to all these years."

My gut twists at this overfamiliarity, but I manage to say, "I'd appreciate that."

"Where can I find you?"

I point to the western shore of the river. "You see that big blue building at the marina over there?"

"You work there?"

"No, I'm building—well, I'm working on a project there. It's a long story. I can tell you about it tomorrow. What time?"

"Ten?"

"Sure, that'll work."

A few minutes later the boat pulls up next to a dock. Billy gets out and gives me a hand up. His hand is warm, but touching it sends a chill up my arm.

"I'll see you tomorrow, Robin."

I watch them melt into the stream of boats heading back to the bay. Then I hear the music that must have been playing all along, and the sounds of voices intoxicated by independence and too much alcohol. I turn and for a moment I'm utterly disoriented. Then I hear my name.

"Robin! You made it!"

Sarah is squished into a four-person booth with six other people, including Ryan Miller, who waves.

I'm on the wrong side of the river.

From nine o'clock to ten the next morning, I am alone in the marina, sorting books according to size and color. Everyone else is home, sleeping off yesterday's celebration. It's just as well. I wouldn't be able to talk to anyone this morning with my thoughts so tangled.

By 10:15 I'm getting anxious. Did he change his mind? Haul in the anchor and skim away across Lake Huron, free from the past in a way I could only dream of?

Then the light from the doorway blinks, footsteps scratch across the floor, and that familiar voice calls out, "What's all this?"

"It's for a contest."

"Holy mackerel. You built this?"

"I have help. It's a very big project."

For the next few minutes I ignore the voice in my head that is screaming out for explanations and try to make a bit of polite conversation even though I'm no good at it. I describe the contest, show him the boxes of books, explain the construction.

"Two hundred thousand dollars, eh? What would you do with the money?"

"It's for my store. I own a bookstore up the street. With things going the way they have been, I can't make ends meet."

He furrows his brow. "You don't have any money socked away? Nothing for a rainy day?"

I shake my head.

He looks to the door. "I'd love to see the store. And I know we have a lot to talk about."

"Um, sure. I guess we could go up there. I'm closed on Sundays."

Though the walk is short, the day is already heating up and I'm sweating by the time we reach Brick & Mortar Books. Billy admires the window display as I unlock the front door.

"What a sweet little shop," he says.

I have never thought of my store as small, but it is. Long and narrow, the tall shelves like a hedge maze. I always liked the library feel I got from those shelves, which I kept packed tight with books. Until we started pulling books for the *Dreadnoughtus*, there was never any empty space. I hate the sight of an empty shelf.

"Hello?" comes the crackly old voice of The Professor from beyond the shelves.

"That's my bird," I say. "He's very ornery, but people like him, so I keep him in the store instead of up in my apartment."

"You live here too?"

"Upstairs."

I lead the way through the shelves and come around to where The Professor is hanging onto the inside of his large cage. He whistles when he sees me. Then he jumps back onto a perch and lets loose with high-pitched screaming.

My hands fly to my ears. "Oh! I'm sorry. He never does this."

We stride past the cage into the back room and

I shut the door on the screeching, but that only dampens the sound a little.

"Why don't we go upstairs?" Billy suggests.

There is no way I'm letting this man into my apartment. "He'll stop in a minute. I'm sorry. Birds are funny. You're a new face, and they just don't like some people. It makes no sense at all to me. If I'd had a choice I'd have gotten a fish."

"No problem." But he looks angry.

The squawking turns to grumbling, and I offer Billy an old wooden chair while I sit on the steps, blocking the way upstairs.

"I'm afraid I surprised you last night," Billy says.

"You looked kind of surprised yourself."

"Yes. Well, you look so much like your mother. Caught me off guard. How old were you the last time I saw you? Twelve?"

"Fourteen. That's how old I was when Dad was arrested." I take aim. "I never saw *you* after that."

But Billy doesn't seem flustered. "I would have liked to see you and your mother, to offer my support. But my lawyers thought it best to keep my distance. Rough times for everyone. I can't imagine being a kid and having to deal with all of that. Then after Lindy was arrested and you moved out here, I—"

"Look, Billy, I don't mean to be rude, but I'm not really interested in reminiscing. You said my dad didn't kill those people. How do you know that? Did you tell them that when you testified?"

He looks annoyed to be interrupted. "I tried. There was just too much evidence against him."

"But the first trial ended in a mistrial, so obviously whatever evidence there was wasn't enough for the jury to come to consensus."

"Enough to convict him later, though, wasn't it?"

"But how could there be all that evidence if he didn't do it?"

He lifts his palms in a shrug. "People plant evidence, Robin."

I'm sure my skepticism registers on my brow. "But who would do such a thing?"

He shakes his head. "Your mother."

I'm trying to remain focused on what Billy might say next, but my mind is already riffling through the files marked "Mom," looking for a way to reconcile this claim with what I have always thought to be true.

"Why would my mother plant evidence to get my father arrested, especially when that evidence would later implicate her somehow?"

"Just because someone tries to frame another person for a murder—or for three murders— doesn't mean they'll be completely successful. Your mother was smart, just not smart enough. She saw what Norman was doing and wanted a stop put to it. So she took matters into her own hands."

I am frantically flipping through the files,

searching for the folder that could make sense of this accusation. When had my mother been cruel or vengeful? When had she been conniving or sinister? I am coming up empty.

"I don't believe you."

Billy maintains his impassive expression. "It doesn't matter what you believe. What matters is your father is going to die for crimes he didn't commit. I mean, don't get me wrong, he committed plenty of crimes himself, but they don't execute men for embezzlement."

"He's being executed for treason."

"Not really. You know that. He's being executed for the sum total of all of those crimes. Judge couldn't state it that way, but that's what was going through his mind when he decided the sentence. He didn't have to go the route of capital punishment. If Lindy had stood trial for her own crimes, they would have both just gotten life in prison. But now she's going to get out and he's going to take the fall."

"How do you know this?"

I hear the ding of the front door, and The Professor squawks. Someone is in the store. I forgot to lock the door.

I get to my feet. "Excuse me."

A voice on the other side of the door calls out, "Robin? You in here?"

Billy stands as the back room door swings open.

"Ryan."

"Hey, I was just going to—oh, I'm sorry. I'm interrupting." He starts to back out of the room.

"No, you're fine. We were just finishing up."

He looks from Billy to me. "Everything all right?"

No.

"Yes. Mr. Ackerman was just leaving." I indicate the metal receiving door that leads to the alley behind the store. "Why don't you go out the back so you don't set the bird off again."

"It was good seeing you again, Robin," he says. He pulls me into another uncomfortable hug and says into my ear, "People are never who you think they are, are they?"

Then he is gone.

I sit back down on the stairs. "Ryan, will you lock the front door?"

He's only gone for a moment, but it's enough time for me to finish flipping through the file drawer of my mind. At the very back is a new folder marked "The Truth." It is empty.

Billy had to be lying. But what if he wasn't? The execution had been stayed, but why and for how long? Would they reopen my father's case? If he was found innocent after all these years, he might live. But did that mean my mother would be tried for those murders, that she could take his place on death row? All I have is the word of a man whose entire lifestyle is obviously designed to avoid detection. There's no new evidence in the cases, no reason to retry anyone. And what good could it possibly do? Wouldn't it be better to simply let it be? The charge of aiding and abetting America's enemies would stand. And shouldn't Norman Windsor be punished for that—even if he was my father?

"Hey, I wanted to stop by and see how everything was going," Ryan says as he reappears.

Terrible. Confusing. Worse than ever.

"Have you been down to the marina this morning?"

"I was a bit," I say. "I was the only one."

He rubs the back of his neck. "Yeah, sorry about that. I think we all had a bit too much fun last night. I'm hoping that we can start getting the books in place soon, once we get the kinks out of the movement. We're having some issues with the head, but the tail looks good. It will take a long time to cover the whole apparatus, and I don't want us to be scrambling near the end. Two months should be long enough."

He must notice that I'm hardly listening.

"Hey, are you okay? Who was that?"

In a dirty T-shirt and frayed cargo shorts that have obviously been worn while painting, he looks too young and irresponsible to be molding minds, too lazy to be building robotic structures approaching three stories tall. He looks a bit like Peter did on our hasty road trip, shaggy and disheveled. Maybe he's not the right person to ask for advice. But at the moment, he's the only one around.

"Can I ask you a question?"

He sits on the chair Billy vacated. "Sure."

"If you knew from experience that someone was untrustworthy, and someone else who you didn't know very well came along and told you something that seemed to indicate that the first person—"

"The untrustworthy one?"

"Yeah, that that person was even more of a liar than you thought, would you trust their story?"

"The person you don't know well? Would I trust them?"

"Yeah."

Ryan rubs his stubbled jaw. "I really don't know. What's going on?"

"You probably wouldn't believe me if I told you."

"Try me."

So I do. I tell Ryan about Billy's connection to my family, his declaration of my father's innocence, his accusations about my mother's part in it all. When I finish, it's a relief to have simply told someone. Like opening a release valve on my brain.

"Listen, Robin, I can't really give you any good advice on this," Ryan says when I finally run out of things to say. "It's too far outside of my own experience. But I will say that if I were you and had had that conversation with this Billy character, I'd talk to your mother about it. And I'd talk to a lawyer."

"Should I write her a letter?"

"Might be better to talk to her in person. Usually when someone's lying you can see it in their face—unless they're really good."

"I can't go to Connecticut. I'm a small business owner with no employees. Time off does not exist for me."

"Maybe you could get Dawt Pi to watch the store for a day."

"It's a three-day trip, minimum."

"Not if you fly."

"I can't be blowing money on plane tickets and car rentals. And even the thought of flying makes me nervous. All those people."

"Then you go over a weekend, and one of those days you're closed anyway."

"And the other?"

"If Dawt Pi can't help, I'm sure I could figure it out. I clerked my way through college. I know how to use a cash register."

With my excuses obliterated I can only agree. I see him out the front door and lock it behind him. He heads down to the marina. I wander back into the heart of the store, stand on the customer side of the counter, and rest my arms on the worn wood like Sarah might at a bar. At this moment

I sort of wish I did drink. The shelf is filled with all but one of the books Peter had given me when I was a girl, each one a bottle containing some intoxicating fictitious elixir that promises to take me away from this incomprehensible chaos of real life and into a carefully plotted story. A little Austen and a splash of Fitzgerald—a blend that starts smooth and bubbly, but with a fatalistic finish. A straight shot of Hemingway to help me face down the angry bull in the arena. Some Nabokov and Atwood and Huxley and Orwell, shaken with ice and garnished with Kafka, and I might end the night bleeding out in a filthy bathtub somewhere.

Isn't there some literary cocktail that will help me escape? And would that be enough? I used to think so. But now I am older, and for better or worse, the magic seems to be wearing off. Maybe these old paper-and-ink friends of mine can't help me anymore.

I pick up the phone and call Dawt Pi to ask her to sacrifice a day off. She's more than happy to help, declaring that she misses The Professor, and we set the date for the next available weekend.

In the intervening time, I scour the internet for every bit of news I can find on my parents' trials, and the first books are adhered to the *Dreadnoughtus* skeleton. But the books from Peter have ceased. I'd gotten so used to getting them that it's a shock when the flow stops—

especially since I know there is one more book. The last one. And after that . . . then what?

All I know for sure at this point is that I'm keeping the books and I should get them out of the store so Ryan or Dawt Pi don't accidentally sell any while I'm away. The night before I'm scheduled to leave for Connecticut, I carefully pack them into six boxes, stack them by the stairs in the back room, and place a note on the top that says "Not for Sale."

26

then

Sometimes death howls. Sometimes it whispers. Sometimes it chokes. I knew I must still be alive when I heard the nurse's words on the other end of the line—I was still breathing, my chest moving in shallow ripples like water around a sinking stone—but I felt as though the wind had been knocked out of me. She couldn't be dead. She was all I had.

I didn't know what else was said before I hung up the phone. I was alone in the dark in someone else's house. Somewhere upstairs Peter had collapsed into bed, probably fully clothed and still wearing his shoes. I couldn't wake him. But I couldn't sleep either.

I felt my way numbly through the dark, down the hall to the den where I had met Mr. Flynt a few days earlier. Illuminated by a small reading lamp, I shuffled through the stack of newspapers by his leather chair, looking for the obituaries, for some physical evidence to confirm the nurse's incomprehensible statement. A headline in the national section of last Sunday's paper caught my eye: "Mistrial in Norman Windsor Case."

Mistrial? What did that mean? Why hadn't Grandma mentioned it? I scanned the article. Jury deadlocked. New trial likely. Time for more evidence. Did that mean he might be released? That maybe he wasn't guilty after all? But he had to be. Because Mom was, or so she had told a judge. And if she was, then he was, because her crimes were all related to his. If he hadn't done it, she couldn't have aided and abetted; she couldn't have obstructed justice. So he had to be guilty. Didn't those idiots on the jury have even the common sense of a high school freshman?

I was still chewing on this when I found yesterday's obituaries. I scanned the list of the dead for Martha Gray. There was no photo and the text was scandalously brief—just a few lines giving her place and date of birth, the address of the church, the time of the service, and a list of relatives. Predeceased by her parents, a brother, and her husband. Leaving behind her daughter Linda and son Kevin. No mention of me. No last names that might indicate unwelcome connections to the corrupt senator who may now escape justice. Nothing of the attack or the injury that led to her death. Just another old lady gone. How many would even miss her? Some women from church who were probably getting used to burying their friends. Probably it was one of them who submitted the obituary to the paper.

Except for me, no one in Martha Gray's family had visited her for years, decades perhaps. And I only did because I'd been forced to.

I slumped in the big leather chair and let the paper fall to the floor. Outside the small cone of light cast by the reading lamp, I could just make out the shelves that covered the walls. If I didn't know they were empty, I might not believe it in this light. Only the edges shone in their burnished golden finish. If I reached out into one, wouldn't my hand touch the spine of a book rather than sinking into dark, empty air? No. The books that belonged on these shelves were all under my bed. How long would it even be my bed?

Where did I go now? Alaska, to live with an uncle I'd never met? Would the authorities have to search through my father's family tree to find a branch that might sustain me for a few years until I was eighteen? Would I get shunted into the foster care system? Or could my criminal father walk free and reclaim me? No matter what, I would have to move again. Away from Sussex. Away from Peter.

Life was defeating me. The cruel, gnarled hand of fate was grasping at what little I had left and ripping it away, piece by piece. I sat there in the dark and cried. When I had no more tears left, I reached to turn off the lamp and sent it crashing to the floor. I righted it and switched it off. I was about to tiptoe back to the guest bathroom to look for tissues when I sensed a presence in the doorway and let out an involuntary shriek.

"It's just me." Mr. Flynt flicked the switch on the wall, and the light on the ceiling blazed forth, spilling into the corners of those empty shelves. "So you made it back."

"Peter didn't tell you?"

"I was asleep. I heard something crash down here. Is everything all right? Have you been crying?"

Mr. Flynt wore athletic shorts and a white undershirt and stood upon bare feet. My father would never have been seen in such a state. Any time I had ever seen him in nightclothes, which was not often, he had worn pajamas and a robe of expensive silk and moccasin-style slippers. I don't think I'd ever seen his bare feet except on the shore of the Atlantic.

"I knocked over the lamp. It's not broken."

"What were you doing in here? I'd think you'd be asleep by now."

"I was just . . . The hospital told me my grandma died. I was looking for her obituary."

"I thought you lived with your cousin."

"She's my grandma!" I yelled. "My grandma!" And right then, in front of a man I didn't really know but disliked anyway, I started to cry again.

"Oh, uh, now, now," he said as he guided me back to the chair with one hand lightly touching my shoulder. He sat across from me on the ottoman. "It will be okay."

I sniffed loudly and dug the heels of my hands into my itching eyes.

Mr. Flynt popped up and left the room. He returned a moment later with a box of tissues. "I think you need to get some sleep. Things will look better in the morning."

"No!" I wailed. "They won't! I have nowhere to go!"

"I'm sure that's not true."

"It is!"

Mr. Flynt glanced at the door, as if he wanted to be sure it was still there for him to walk through once he could make good his escape. What did he care? I wasn't his problem. I wasn't anyone's problem anymore.

"Just calm down," he said. "There's no need to get hysterical."

"Hysterical? You think I'm hysterical? And just how would you be acting in my situation?"

He threw up his hands and turned to leave. Abandoning me just like he'd abandoned Emily.

"You ought to know better," I said.

"Pardon me?"

"She didn't have an aneurysm!"

Peter's dad flinched.

"I read her books and I know. She didn't die of a stupid aneurysm."

"What are you—"

"She died because she thought it was her only option, the only way to stop spiraling further down into depression. And you! You should have known better! You should have been there for her! But you weren't!"

"Hey!" he broke in, red-faced. "I will not have someone stand in my own house and accuse me of—"

"What is going on down here?" Peter burst through the doorway, more awake than I'd seen him in two days.

"Your friend is ready to go home," Mr. Flynt said sternly.

"Robin? What's going on?"

"Your mom didn't die of an aneurysm, Peter. She committed suicide."

"That's enough!" Mr. Flynt stormed. "I want you out of my house!"

Peter looked as though I'd kicked him in the gut.

"You read her books," I said. "How could you not see it? Every note, every underline was like a big, red, blinking sign screaming 'I'm dying inside!'"

He shook his head slowly, then vigorously. "You're reading stuff into it that isn't there."

"And I don't appreciate being accused of lying to my own son about what killed his mother," Mr. Flynt said.

"You're lying right now! I know you're lying.

Why else would you get rid of everything that reminded you of her? Why else would you completely erase her? Because everything she loved was there, pointing at how you failed her!"

"Robin, stop!" Peter put his hands on my shoulders. "You're just tired."

"And probably in shock," Mr. Flynt added. "She found out that her cous—her grandmother died at the hospital while you two were off on your joyride."

Peter looked at me. "Is that true?"

"That's not what this is about."

He pulled me into a hug. "Oh, Robin, I'm so sorry."

I pushed him away. "Take me home. Take me back to the trailer so someone can break in and beat me to death with a baseball bat. I'd rather that than stay here."

"Now hold on," Peter said. "I think we all need some sleep right now. Things will look better in the morning."

Hearing his dad's words come from his mouth, I let fly a disgusted scream and stomped from the room, Peter on my heels. I slammed the guest room door in his face, but he opened it immediately.

"Knock it off, Robin. You're acting insane."

"Maybe I am. Maybe I just snapped, like your mom."

I saw the movement in his right hand before

he could stifle it. He didn't strike me. But for the barest moment, he'd wanted to.

"I'm leaving," I said.

"You can't leave."

"I *am* leaving."

I grabbed my suitcase and headed for the front closet where I'd hung my coat. Peter tried to keep me from opening it, but his father tapped his shoulder.

"I'll take her home. You get back into bed."

Mr. Flynt was already dressed in jeans and a sweater, his feet now shod in boots.

"Whatever," Peter said. He stalked up the stairs.

The drive was dark and silent except for my curt directions. When Mr. Flynt pulled up in front of the trailer, I started to get out.

"Hey," came his sharp voice.

"What?"

"I don't want you anywhere near my son, you understand?"

I retrieved my suitcase from the back seat without a word and shut the car door.

He rolled down the window. "I mean it."

I turned my back to him and walked up the porch steps. Inside I locked the door and slid down into the mess that was still in the entryway. I thought I would cry again, but no tears came now. I was alone—really alone—for the first time in my life. No parents, no social workers, no grandmother, no friends.

I walked slowly through the ruined rooms and kicked at the junk covering the floor. What would happen to it all? Dumpster? Thrift store? Someone would have to deal with it.

The only someone around was me.

I picked up a vinyl raincoat and hung it back up in the empty closet. What had he been looking for? Something small. Something you could put in a closet or in a drawer. Otherwise, why empty them?

Keep your eyes open.

I poked through my grandmother's little jewelry box. Some of the stuff looked like it might be real. Why leave it behind?

Because it wasn't what he was looking for.

Your grandmother's hiding something.

But what? Had he found it, whatever it was? From the state of the place, whatever the intruder was searching for was either in his possession or wasn't here to find.

Back in the living room I looked at The Professor in his cage. He was uncharacteristically quiet. Watching me. What would happen to him now? He didn't squawk or growl or try to bite me when I changed out his newspapers and filled his food bowl. I replaced his water bottle and looked out the window to where the dead house stood silhouetted by moonlight. He had once lived in that house as my mother's pet. He'd known my mother before I did. I couldn't just leave him here.

He looked out the window too.

"You miss that house?"

He tilted his head like a dog.

"You miss your mom? You miss Lindy?"

At the name he let out a little parroty gurgle.

"Yeah, me too."

I looked at the clock—3:27. I didn't have much time. I found two old suitcases on the floor of my grandmother's closet, which I filled with every other scrap of clothing I owned. Then I found a flashlight on the kitchen floor.

"Come on," I said, opening The Professor's cage. "I have to go get something from your old house. You can come with me."

I tentatively offered him my hand. He edged along his perch, reached out with his beak, and bit me hard. When I didn't react, he kept moving, stretching out one gray foot then the other, and wrapped his toes around my first two fingers.

We walked out into the still-dark morning. He gripped my hand tightly and flapped his wings to steady himself, but he did not fly away. The dead house crouched beyond the cemetery. I stepped carefully through the forest of headstones. The closer we got, the more The Professor flapped.

"Big money, big money," he repeated again and again. "No whammies."

That was a new one.

I went around the house to where the back door yawned. Through the hall of shredded wallpaper, up the creaking stairs to the second floor and my mother's old bedroom, still filled with all her things. The moment we entered the room, The Professor flapped madly and wouldn't stop, so I put him down on the back of a chair.

"Big money, big money, no whammies. Big money, big money, no whammies."

"I get it," I said aloud. Only I didn't. What the heck was a whammy?

I shone the flashlight across the room. The doll was waiting for me where I had left her in January. When I slid her off the chair and tucked her under my arm, I heard the sound of tinkling metal, like a dropped coin. I caught The Professor in the flashlight beam, thinking he must be messing with stuff on the vanity, but he was still on the back of the chair.

"Big money, big money, no whammies."

I swept the floor with the light, stopping when something glinted back. A key. It must have been beneath the doll. Like the key beneath Mary that opened the trailer door. But what did this key open?

I picked it up and brought it over to The Professor. He tested it in his beak and dropped it on the floor.

"Big money, big money, no whammies."

I picked it back up and gave it to him again. "What do you suppose this opens, Professor?"

He manipulated it with one foot and dropped it

again. "Big money, big money, no whammies."

I put my hand out for him, but he didn't want it. He was trying to shimmy down the side of the chair. He hopped off and landed rather ungracefully on the floor, then scuttled off like a crab, his nails clicking along the hardwood. I picked up the key again and searched for him with the flashlight. He had stopped at my mother's pink bed.

"Big money, big money, no whammies."

I got down to my knees, lifted the bed skirt, and examined the spot in which my mother used to hide from her father. Her safe place. Tucked out of reach beneath the bed was a gray metal box. Lying on my stomach on the floor, I slid half under the bed, barely able to get a finger hold and drag it out. I sat back up, dusted myself off, and examined the box. There was a lock on the top. Like the box I'd once seen my father open when I'd asked to see his grandmother's immigration card.

I tried the key in the lock. It fit.

"Big money, big money, no whammies."

I turned the key, lifted the lid, and gasped. It was filled with banded stacks of hundred-dollar bills. I glanced at the windows and shut the box.

Your grandmother's hiding something.

Was this what the intruder had been looking for? But how would anyone know about it— unless it was someone my father had stolen from?

He'd embezzled millions. Perhaps not all of it was accounted for. I could turn this in. I should turn this in. Turn myself over to the authorities and be sent to live with a foster family. Maybe if it was returned, my parents . . . No. That was stupid. The crimes had still been committed. Giving it back would do nothing.

Something for you.

I reopened the box. In the shaky flashlight beam, I counted it up three times, sure I'd gotten it wrong. But each time the sum was the same. Five hundred thousand dollars.

"Big money, big money, no whammies."

I should call the police.

Something for you.

I locked the box and tucked the key in my pocket. With the lockbox under one arm, the doll under the other, and The Professor on my shoulder picking at my ear, I struggled back across the cemetery. The graying eastern horizon warned of dawn's impending arrival.

Grandma's purse and keys were on the floor by the kitchen counter. Leaving The Professor to his own devices outside the cage, I found another suitcase and put the lockbox in it, along with the envelope of documents the social worker had given me a scant nine months ago, covering them with towels, a blanket, and a pillow. I filled the back seat of Grandma's old burgundy Camry with all my suitcases, grocery bags stuffed with food from the pantry and the floor, and a big bag of parrot pellets. I found The Professor's travel cage by the closet, convinced him to get into it by means of some strategically placed grapes, and put the cage on the floor of the passenger seat. I was about to turn the key in the ignition and discover whether one could learn to drive from movies and TV alone when I remembered the books. I would need the books where I was going, even if I didn't know exactly where that was.

I gathered cardboard boxes from closets, the pantry, and under the bathroom sink and emptied them of their contents. I tucked each book into a box like stacks of cash. But there were too many. I filled three pillowcases and a Rubbermaid container my grandmother used to store yarn. I stuffed it all into the trunk and slammed it closed.

Fearing the growing daylight, I got into the car and set *The Complete Poems of Emily Dickinson* and my mother's doll on the passenger seat. I started the car and glanced out the window at Mary and her attendants. The gnomes grinned cheekily at me. *Go ahead,* they said. But Mary's eyes were downcast, her hands turned up slightly as if to ask, *Why?*

I looked away and tried to put the car in reverse, but the shifter wouldn't budge. I put my foot on a pedal and the engine roared. I yanked it up again. I put it on the other pedal, which resisted a little.

I tried shifting again. This time it worked. But as I was lifting my foot off the brake, someone knocked on the window next to my head.

I let out a yelp and turned to find a woman smiling at me beneath big blonde bangs. I almost bolted. But for some reason, I rolled down my window. If it was someone from the church, Mary would be even more upset if I blew her off.

"Yes?"

"Hi there," she chirped. "How are you this morning?"

"In a bit of a hurry. Can I help you?"

"Gosh, I hope so." Her smile remained fixed in place. "I'm looking for Robin Windsor."

Bolt.

"Why's that?"

"Are you Robin Windsor?"

Bolt.

"Why?" I said slowly.

"Is your father Norman Windsor?"

Then I saw a little notebook in her hand. I took my foot off the brake and stepped on the gas. The woman leapt away as the car shot backward faster than I thought it would go. I slammed on the brakes. I cranked the wheel and shifted into drive and tore toward the little driveway over the deep ditch. Smoke and broken glass and Sarah Kukla's bloodied homecoming dress flashed through my mind, and I braked hard again. With a lighter touch on the gas pedal, I managed to jerk my way over the culvert. I pulled onto the road and aimed the car toward Peter's house.

27

now

Early on Friday morning I leave an envelope of cash on the counter for Dawt Pi with a note directing her to take the money from any sales that day as well. Ryan may be watching the store Saturday as a friend, but it only feels right to pay Dawt Pi for time lost at her new job. I pack my suitcase, the same one I packed the last time I traveled to Connecticut to see my mother, the same one that has traveled with me since the day I left Amherst. It's battered around the edges now and the tag is gone, lost somewhere along the twisted way. I think of the border guard who almost didn't let me back into Michigan all those years ago because of this suitcase. I can't take the Canadian route this time now that you're required to have a passport. I've never gotten one.

The hours tick by as I cross through the interminable state of Ohio into Pennsylvania and then New York. Every mile I drive toward the Eastern Seaboard brings me closer to Peter—or at least closer to where he recently was, according to the padded manila envelopes. I imagine him driving past some of the same farms, the same horses, the same billboards a few weeks prior when he mailed out his mother's copies of *My Ántonia* and *The Bell Jar*. If I saw him now, at a gas station or a rest stop, would I even recognize him? When I picture him it's as he was then, face shadowed by a couple days' growth of beard, hair unkempt, clothes rumpled, driving his old bronze Dodge Charger to the ends of the earth for me. His eyes are kind and bright and filled with the sheen of love that only exists between two young people off on an adventure for which they never got permission. I can't imagine him now—a war veteran, probably clean-cut, sitting up straight, and driving a sensible car.

I hope he's driving alone as I am.

When I finally arrive at a cheap motel in Connecticut and step out into the lingering heat of an August sun, I am struck by how familiar the long, low building looks. I guess it looks like most motels—old and tired and kind of sad. But there's something else beneath all of that that I know deep in my bones. The man with the long white nose hairs at the front desk takes my cash and hands me a key hanging from a large plastic diamond key ring with the number seven on it. I park my car by the corresponding door, turn the key in the lock, and step into the past.

It is the same motel, the same room, right

down to the faded bedspread and the carpet compacted by decades of feet. The same bad hotel art in imitation brass frames. The same now hopelessly out-of-date tube TV with built-in VCR. This room has remained fixed in place while the world has spun through time around it. It's clean, and in fact it seems cleaner now than it did back then. The stale cigarette smell has finally drifted away or been painted over. But other than that, it is exactly where I spent the night with Peter eighteen years ago. Memory has chosen it for me without my rational mind's consent.

I brush my teeth and slip neatly into the shallow depression in the old bed where thousands of other people have slept. The twin depression next to me, the spot where Peter had once lain, his fingers woven into mine, is empty.

Somehow I fall asleep, and I remember no dreams when I reemerge in the waking world the next morning. I drop the key off at the front desk, eat breakfast as slowly as possible, then face the fact that I must perform the task for which this trip has been taken.

In the prison parking lot, it's hard to get myself out of the car. Too much time has passed. Too much unspoken grief. All the letters I never wrote. But I can't go home with nothing to show for the miles this time. I can't keep going on this way, swept along by the winds of rumor and regret. Time moves in only one direction. I can't get back the time I've squandered. I can only move forward.

I make it through the door and the paperwork and am ushered into the visiting room of the new facility. It's not unlike the old one, and both guards and prisoners seem to be wearing the same uniforms. But when I see the woman being led toward my table, I feel at first there must be some mistake. She is most certainly not the same. Hair streaked liberally with gray, pale skin in the middle of summer, wrinkles that betray more frowns than those conversation-stopping smiles. A striking timidity, like a wild horse that has been broken. She is me in another twenty or thirty years.

Or perhaps I am already her, caught in a prison of my own making.

I push the thought away as she sits down and looks at me with tired eyes. She waits for me to talk. The burden is on me. I'm the one who abandoned her.

"Hey," I say.

"Hello, Robin."

I can't tell if she is happy to see me or if she's angry that it's been so long since I visited her. Her face is blank. Empty.

"Mom"—the word sounds foreign on my lips—"what would you say if I told you I ran into Billy Ackerman?"

303

"I'd say I'd rather have heard that you ran *over* him."

I take a breath. "I need to know what happened. What really happened. There's no jury here, no judge—just your daughter, who I think you know deserves some real answers after all these years."

She lets out a tired sigh. "I don't know what you want me to say, Robin."

"Was Billy lying to me when he told me that Dad never killed any of those people?"

She snatches a sidelong glance at the nearest guard. "No. In that one thing in his entire sorry life, Billy was not lying."

I am stunned to hear the admission. "But, then why—"

"I'm not going to discuss this with you, Robin."

"You owe me an explanation." I lace my fingers together to keep from shaking one in her face. "I'm trying to get on with my life, but every time I think I'm past all of this, somehow I get dragged back into this pit you guys dug for me. Don't you want me to live? Don't you want me to get married and have a family and have a real life? Don't you want me to be happy?"

"I hardly think I can affect all those things from a thousand miles away."

"Are you kidding? I don't trust anyone. I've only been able to trust one person since I was a teenager, and he's been gone for years. Do you know what that does to a person?"

"Yes, I do. I know exactly what it does to a person. I know what it's like to lose faith in someone." She's quiet a moment as she seems to reach for what to say. "Power is corrosive. It tempts people to do things they wouldn't otherwise. It lured your father into illegal activity to make more money than we needed. Norman gave me everything I wanted—a beautiful home, an important position, connections, first-class travel anywhere I wanted to go. It was convenient and I never questioned it."

She shifts in her seat.

"It also lured him into liaisons with other women wherever he traveled—flight attendants and waitresses and interns. Or that's what Billy told me. I guess I'll never really know for sure. Norman was gone a lot and Billy was . . . there. He told me everything and was always there to comfort me."

My gut twists at the memory of his unwanted embraces, that wet cigar kiss.

"He made me feel special again, how your father used to make me feel. So we left things as they were for a while. Norman wasn't hurting anyone but me, and my relationship with Billy took the moral high ground out from under my feet. But after the bombings in Kenya and more and more news about terrorism against the West, I knew that I couldn't be complicit in it. People were threatening to talk, and I didn't want to go down with the ship. Billy said he could eliminate the problem. To protect me—to protect you. I never questioned how until it was too late."

"Wait, Billy killed those men?" A shiver races down my spine. How long had I been alone with him in the bookstore? What if Ryan hadn't shown up? "He told me you killed them."

"Well, obviously he wouldn't admit it to you when it was your father who was sentenced for it."

"But why tell me anything at all? Why even bring it up? Why not let me go on believing my dad had done it? What does he stand to gain by trying to get me to believe you had?"

She shakes her head. "I'll be up for parole soon. Maybe he thought you'd tell someone and I'd be charged. I'm sure he doesn't like the idea of me running free with what I know."

"But how was there any evidence to link Dad to the killings if it was really Billy?"

Billy's words rush back to me before she can answer. *People plant evidence.*

"The FBI found material from the murder sites on the soles of your father's shoes. They found fibers from his suits and strands of his hair. Billy always had full access to our house. He knew Norman's schedule—he *set* Norman's schedule—and made sure the deed was done when your father wouldn't have an alibi."

"But couldn't you testify that Dad was home or wherever?"

She rubs the spot between her eyes. "You didn't notice because we were careful to keep it from you, but we weren't spending a lot of time together then. I think he suspected I knew of his cheating. We grew further and further apart, left each other alone to live our lives."

"So where were you?"

"Oh, lots of places. You remember. You were usually with me. New York or Boston at some fundraiser. Out on a girls' weekend. Trips like that."

"Trips Billy helped set up." The name tastes like bile on my tongue. He is the reason my life is so messed up.

"It's hard to be alone, Robin."

"I don't need you to tell me that."

She sighs again. "Well, I want you to understand this. Billy took the place that your father had held in my heart. I was thinking of divorce once Norman was out of office—I didn't want to sabotage his career. Back then divorce was a big deal for a politician. When he was arrested, I thought it was just for embezzlement and corruption, not murder. It was only when I heard the charges read that I realized Billy must have eliminated the problem by eliminating people. But in the back of my mind I thought that if Norman went to prison I could divorce him quietly and no one would blame me, and then Billy and I could get on with life." She looks at her hands. "I wasn't expecting them to come for me."

"You were going to run off with a murderer. And where was I in this scenario?"

"With me, of course."

"Boy, I sure am sorry it didn't work out with you and Billy. He would have been a great dad."

"Save the sarcasm, Robin."

I rub my temples. "Didn't you ever think of me, even once? Didn't you ever think about what would happen to me?"

Her face softens, and I can tell she wants to grasp my hand. "Honey, I was thinking of you. Your grandmother did give you what she was hiding for you, right?"

Big money, big money, no whammies.

"I found it. After she died. And I wish I had never laid eyes on it. It wasn't until after I'd already used some of it that 9/11 happened. And then it was too late."

She shakes her head. "That's not what that money was. It didn't come from arms sales or terrorists."

I frown. "What do you mean?"

"That money came from Billy. I thought it was a gift to help us out. It turned out to be a bribe— to keep quiet about his involvement."

"Wait a minute. Let me get this straight before any other revelations." I place my palms on the table in front of me. "I've spent $500,000 meant to quash the very evidence that would exonerate my father and save his life?" I throw my hands up, drawing the attention of one of the guards. "Oh, that's much better, thank you."

My mother puts a hand up to the guard to signal that everything is okay. "Robin, I know this is a lot to take in, but you wanted the truth. And the truth is, nothing was going to save your father after 9/11. After the mistrial, I thought he'd just go free, and that thought made it possible to live with myself. I was the one who'd asked for Billy's help. I was the one who'd put it all in motion. But you know what it was like after the attack. Everyone was out for blood."

My mind is sifting through evidence, trying to figure out what to put in that folder marked "The Truth." Yes, my father was a bad man, but he was not a murderer. And my mother? She was worse than I'd thought. She wasn't just a weak wife loyal to her husband to a fault. She was as disloyal as he apparently was. And worse, she knew the truth and hadn't spoken up. She left the once love of her life to an unjust fate.

"Robin, I know you're angry."

"Oh, you know I'm angry? Angry? As if I don't have a right to be? You could have said something to save him. You could have turned Billy in. You still could! I didn't need money, I needed parents!"

"Hey! Settle down!" the guard barks.

"Don't think for a second I'm just sitting on this information, Robin," Mom says in an almost whisper. "Why do you think they granted the stay of execution? They're searching for evidence to support my claim about Billy."

This is almost too much for me to take. "Billy was there—in my store. I could have called the police if I'd known."

She sits back and lifts her hands. "How would you know? How would you ever know anything if you never open one of my letters?"

I swallow hard. She's right. And I have no excuse beyond holding on to my bitterness longer than any grown woman should.

The guard gives us the five-minute warning. Tears are beginning to swell in my mother's eyes. As if that could help. As if that could change anything.

"I know my sins all too well," she says. "The chaplain here made sure of that. But she also told me they could be forgiven."

"No."

"Every one of them. And I know it will be hard for you to forgive me, but that's what you need to move forward. The truth isn't enough. Truth never made anyone feel better. That's why people lie—to protect people from the truth. What you need is to forgive."

I bury my face in my hands. "How can you expect me to do that?"

"I know it won't be easy. But easy things aren't worth your time. It's the hard things we really love in the end. The hard things we managed to do despite everything."

I wait for Mom to continue her speech, but she is looking at me with pity in her eyes. There's nothing worse than getting pitied by a complete train wreck of a person.

"Does Dad know about you and Billy? Does he know the truth?"

"He knows."

"Do you think he's forgiven you?"

Her moist eyes search mine. "I hope so."

I stand up. "Yeah, well, I wouldn't count on it."

Our time at an end, she shuffles out to her cell. I wait impatiently for the guard to unlock the door. In the parking lot I dig my phone from my purse, open my browser, and search for a number I never thought I'd call.

"United States Penitentiary, Terre Haute, how may I direct your call?"

"I need to talk to someone about visiting an inmate."

28

then

I sat in the idling car at the end of Peter's street. I hadn't planned on coming here when I turned the key in the ignition. But then a reporter had shown up—one who knew my name. My real name. I stared at the blank page I'd torn from the back of the library copy of the 1972 Kennedy High School yearbook. I hadn't known what to say to my mother in a letter. Now I didn't know what to say to Peter.

No, it wasn't that. I knew what I wanted to say. That he'd betrayed me. That exposing me to the press was unforgivable. That I had warned him if he told anyone it would be over between us. That he could take back his mom's stupid books and go on believing whatever he wanted about her. I didn't want them anyway.

That he had crushed me.

But when you wrote something, it was forever. Sharp words spoken in anger might dull over time as memory twisted and things of the past faded and blurred. A letter never softened, never changed. It was always there to remind you, to keep the wound ragged and raw. Which was what I wanted.

Right?

The garage door opened. I ducked low in my seat as Jack Flynt slowly backed out and turned down the street. His taillights disappeared around a corner. I sat up straight and scribbled out my note. I inched the car up to the house and found the button to pop the trunk. As quickly as possible, I piled the tattered boxes and pillowcases and the Rubbermaid container on the porch. On top I placed the yearbooks we had taken from the school library, along with the note, tucked partway into the one from 1972.

My hand hovered at the doorbell, finger extended. Then it dropped. Better not to chance him actually opening the door before I could get away. I got back into the car and drove off in fits and starts.

I didn't know where to go except away from town. I filled the tank at a gas station, then loaded the counter with snack foods and drinks. When I handed the clerk a hundred-dollar bill he pointed wordlessly at a sign that said "No 50's or 100's."

"But I already pumped the gas, and when you add all this stuff up, you're not going to have to give me much change."

"Where you going, miss?"

I tried to look taller. "Excuse me?"

"Where are you running off to?"

"Nowhere. I'm stocking up for my grand-mother. She loves Hostess Cupcakes."

"Where'd you get that money?"

"Not that it's any of your business, but I got it from her. Now are you going to sell me this stuff or not?"

The man sighed but took the money. I left the store with two plastic grocery bags full of junk food for me, crackers and nuts for The Professor, and a full tank of gas. I wanted to start off right then, but I hadn't slept all night. I drove toward the Saginaw Bay, to an empty roadside park, and covered The Professor's travel cage with my coat. Then I slipped into unconsciousness.

When I woke, the sun was hanging in the western sky. Beside me on the passenger seat, the doll's face glowed red in the evening light. Her dusty little patent leather shoes rested on *The Complete Poems of Emily Dickinson*. The one book I had wanted to keep. The one book to which I had no rightful claim. I had never paid for it.

I should have left that one on Peter's porch too. I couldn't start fresh with that book hanging around my neck like an albatross. Even if I didn't know what my ultimate destination was, I knew I had to do one more thing before I left Sussex for good.

But I'd have to wait for the cover of darkness.

• • •

The police cruiser didn't have its flashers on, but I could tell someone was in the trailer when I was still far down the road because all the lights were on inside. I fumbled for the switch to turn off the headlights and slowed to a crawl as I pulled into the cemetery lot. Peter's reporter was nowhere to be seen.

I slipped out of the car and wove through the gravestones by memory until I came to Emily Flynt's, then knelt in the dead grass that had been so recently blanketed in snow. I placed *The Complete Poems of Emily Dickinson* in front of the headstone where I had found it seven months before and stood up feeling a little lighter.

The trailer door opened, and I ducked back down behind the stone. The house was now dark and the cops were shutting their car doors. I prayed that the sound would not set off a round of squawking that might alert them to the car that was shrouded in darkness in the gravel lot. But The Professor stayed silent as they drove off into the night.

The missing bird didn't necessarily mean anything. A parrot left to his own devices could escape, after all. But the missing car must have been noticed, must have attested to the fact that the girl who had been living there had run off. Probably the reporter had tipped them off.

Maybe they wouldn't be back. Or maybe they

315

would track me, trace every step I had made. Maybe they'd question the cheerless gas station attendant. Maybe there would be cops on every highway leading out of town.

I needed to get out while the getting was good.

I drove in no particular direction but *away.* Away from the dead house, away from the graves, away from Peter. If the police had issued an alert for a runaway or a missing person or a car thief, I couldn't stop anywhere near here to figure out which way I was going. And it didn't matter anyway. I had no plan.

Stopping at intersections, turning, correcting the car's natural drift toward the ditches that lurked invisible along the side of the dark road— all terrifying at first—got easier as I went along. I was afraid to go any faster than about thirty miles per hour, which felt like hurtling down the steep first hill of a roller coaster.

When the sky began to purple in the east so that I could tell what direction I was going, I stopped and pulled a map from Grandma's glove box. I traced thick yellow lines of highway to where they ended near the enormous blue blobs of the Great Lakes I had just seen. I was surrounded by water. South seemed the only way out.

But for some reason, my eyes kept drifting north, to that big lake—deep, cold, ruthless. I thought of the cliffs and the dunes and the trails. And I thought of the little visitor station we had passed.

Perfect.

29

now

I roll back into River City as the sun is setting. The streetlights are blinking on, and kids riding bikes push the limits of what it means to be in by dark. With my windows down I hear voices on porches, dogs barking, a lawn mower choking into silence. I cruise down Midway with my foot off the pedal. I brake lightly as I near the store, then change my mind and keep driving to the riverwalk. At the sprawling playground at Columbus Park, one last dad drags reluctant children from the swings and piles them into a Subaru. A couple teenagers rollerblade past my parked car. Then I'm alone.

The long drive back to Michigan has given me plenty of time to think, and my mother has given me plenty to think about. By the time I crossed the Pennsylvania-Ohio border, I had managed to forgive my mom for being taken in by Billy Ackerman's lies. It was so easy to allow another person to derail you. So easy to go on blaming the winds of chance for one's misfortunes. Hadn't I done that for most of my life?

What I couldn't forgive her for was not standing by my dad. The irony is not lost on me. I've spent half my life believing her loyalty to him had meant disloyalty to me. Now I know the truth to be the exact opposite. She had stood by me to the extreme. So why am I not happy? Why am I never really happy?

I get out of the car and place my hands on the rail at the water's edge. The river slips silently by at August's unhurried pace. On the other side, the last gasp of the setting sun reflects off the windows of the new loft housing where the gravel quarry used to be. Funny. Last time I looked at that building, there had been no glass.

In a town where nothing much had changed for decades, a sudden spate of new construction and renovation seems to promise better times ahead. Ugly facades that had been erected in the 1970s are being removed to uncover the beautiful stonework of River City's lumber boom years. Abandoned factories are being turned into luxury condos. Spruce up the old, and when it can't be saved, raze it to the ground and build something new. The question is, what is worth saving? And what must be destroyed to make room for something better?

I turn away from the river and lean back on the railing. On the darkening park lawn, a robin yanks a worm from the ground and flies away. He and his mate are likely on their second or

third brood of chicks. He'll work hard to provide for them until fall, when they'll all fly away
from here to someplace where the worms and
insects they feed on are plentiful. No one will
tell him when it's time to move on. He'll just
know.

The next morning, I open the store as usual,
pleased to read notes from Dawt Pi and Ryan
about how smoothly the weekend ran. A few
customers trickle in and out, including old Mr.
Sutton looking for more westerns. Everything is,
by all accounts, normal.

Yet something feels off, skewed somehow. It
must be the shelves behind the counter, empty
since I boxed up Peter's books. I hate empty
shelves. In fact, as I look around the store, many
of the shelves feel a bit on the scanty side, so
many books have been lugged down to the
marina. It looks like I'm already having a going-
out-of-business sale.

It's not until evening when I flip the Open sign
to Closed and start up to my apartment that I
notice that the boxes of books I stacked by the
stairs before leaving for Connecticut are missing.
I glance around the back room, but they're
nowhere to be seen. I don't find them back in the
store either.

I pull the notes from Dawt Pi and Ryan out of
the trash and reread them, searching for clues

about what they may have done with Peter's books. Dawt Pi's note is simple, short, and to the point: *Thank you for $. 12 custumers. Talk soon!* Ryan's is longer, explaining how far along they have gotten on the *Dreadnoughtus*. On the last line, my breath catches: *The legs are all covered and they look awesome!*

I rush down the sidewalk to the marina and through the unlocked door. The dinosaur skeleton is complete. The legs are indeed covered with books that look like colorful scales. In the southeast corner of the cavernous room are stacks and stacks of boxes, each one filled with books gleaned from all over River City and beyond.

"Didn't expect to see you here tonight," comes Ryan's voice. "How did it go with your mom?"

"Where are the books from the back room?"

"What?"

"I stacked six boxes of books in my back room and put a sign on them that said Not for Sale. Where are they?"

Ryan glances nervously at the *Dreadnoughtus*. "Um . . ."

"Please tell me you didn't—" I race to the trunk-like legs of the sculpture, my eyes darting like hummingbirds over the book covers.

"Let's not jump to conclusions," Ryan says as he follows right behind. "I did bring those boxes down Saturday. But that doesn't mean they've been opened."

"Why would you take those? Didn't you see the sign?"

"It said they weren't for sale. We've been bringing boxes of books from the store for weeks. I thought they were for the *Dreadnoughtus*."

I circle each leg. They are not here. I try to force my racing heart to slow. "Okay, where would you have put them?"

He indicates the mountain of boxes. "All the books are in there. But it shouldn't take long to find them."

Silently we open box after box. The first three boxes of Peter's books are fairly easy to find. The next two are more challenging. The last one seems to have disappeared altogether, but Ryan eventually locates it on the worktable by the *Dreadnoughtus*. Beside it is a nearly empty box. It's obvious that the books in this box were going to be used next. I nearly faint when I open it. *The Catcher in the Rye* sits right on top.

Silently we lug the boxes back up to the store, then up the stairs to my apartment.

"I can bring them in for you," he says on the landing.

"No thanks. I can manage."

He looks reluctant to leave. "Look, Robin, I'm so sorry about this. I didn't realize they were your personal books."

"It's fine. It was a misunderstanding. That's all. Nothing happened."

But we both know what could have happened.

When Ryan is gone, I drag the boxes into my apartment one by one and realize that, despite my best efforts, Peter has finally made it through the door.

30

then

Though it may have been quicker to follow one of those thick yellow lines of expressway north, I wove my way through forests and fields on the thin gray lines—county highways and country roads that seemed less attractive to law enforcement and generally less terrifying to a brand-new driver. I drove all night, pulling over every so often to recheck the map or pee at the side of the road. Things were going smoothly.

Until I reached the big bridge.

I filled up at a gas station just off the highway, then sat in the car, sipping on a coffee that was really half creamer with four sugars.

"You can do this. You can do this. You can do this."

"You can do this," said The Professor.

"No, I can't."

I waited for another avian affirmation, but none was forthcoming.

I pulled back out onto the nearly empty highway and started forward at five miles under the speed limit. On the bridge I moved to the left lane, away from the rails, and fixed my eyes on the space twenty feet in front of me. If I could just reach that spot and the next spot and the one after that, eventually I would get across.

The woman who took my toll money on the other side didn't even look at me.

After two more hours and fourteen deer sightings, the little visitor station I remembered from just a couple nights earlier came into view. The sun was rising, and I had no further elements to my plan. I'd had a lot of time to think on the drive. How to ditch the car. How to keep The Professor warm enough. How to stay under the radar for three years until I was a legal adult. But solutions to these problems were slow in presenting themselves.

I could lie about my name, lie about my age, lie about where I came from. I was already in good practice for all of that. I could cut and dye my hair, start wearing glasses, wear mom jeans and thrift store sweatshirts with patchwork pumpkins and embroidered butterflies on them. But where could I live? What would I do with my time? Could I get a job? Or would they need my social security number? Could I apply to get my driver's license in a year? Or would that give me away?

I couldn't just check into a motel and live there quietly, left alone as long as I paid the bill each week. I was too young to rent a room. The trip with Peter had taught me that.

What I needed was an older partner of some sort. Someone with a lot of empathy but not a lot of questions. Maybe someone who was a little slow, a little crazy. Someone with a protective streak who didn't trust the authorities. Someone who liked spastic, ornery parrots.

It was a lot to ask.

I parked in the back corner of the lot, license plate facing the forest rather than the road, and felt a jolt of fear in my chest when I saw that I wasn't alone. Behind the little brick building was a rusty old green pickup truck. Was this the truck of someone who helped people in need? Or the truck of someone who would say, "Sorry, sweetheart, but my hands are tied, and anyway, it's for your own good"?

Even with the sun coming up, it was too cold this far north to even think about sleeping in the car. Maybe if I had left The Professor behind. But I hadn't. I had to take a chance.

With the blanket-wrapped travel cage in my arms, I headed for the back door. I knocked lightly. Then harder. Then I pounded. I was looking for a rock I could bash against the metal lock when the door opened a crack and an ancient man about my height sporting a grizzled, scraggly beard peered out.

"Well, hello there." He glanced at the bundle in my arms. "Whatcha got there? Raccoon? Bad time of year for 'em. Just getting up and hungry and sluggish and not looking where they're going."

He opened the door wide and motioned me in but didn't stop talking. "Hit it with the car? I see a lot of 'em starting round about this time. I know you're probably upset about it, but most of the time they're not worth saving. Too many of 'em around anyway. Too much trouble to nurse 'em back when you know once they're healthy they're just going to turn around and make more work for you, digging through trash cans."

He set the cage on a messy desk in a cramped back office and pulled the blanket away, still talking. "Now if it were an eaglet fallen out of the nest, that would be worth saving. But let's take a look at him anyway and see what's what."

The bent old man opened the cage door and peered in. "Now what the heck is that? I'm gonna need my specs." He patted the pocket of his khaki shirt and pulled out a pair of glasses. "Well, missy, that ain't no raccoon and it sure ain't no eaglet. What is it?"

"What does our survey say?" said The Professor.

The old man cackled. "Well, I'll be. You got yourself a parrot here! You didn't find this thing out in the woods, did you? Poor thing's missing half his feathers! Well, come on out, little guy. I ain't gonna hurt you. What are you doing out here? You should be in a cage with a bunch of toys. You escape? I hate it when people don't take care of their pets. Don't you worry. Someone's not a good enough owner to keep you safe, I won't go looking for him and send you back there to him. You're safe here for the time being."

The man finally turned and looked directly at me for the first time. "What's the story, morning glory? Where'd you find this bird?"

My mind raced for a plausible answer. I couldn't say I'd found him, because then I'd have no more claim over him than this old man. What if he took The Professor away because he didn't think I could care for him? What if he changed his mind and put a notice in the paper about a missing African Grey parrot, and some police officer had just read a notice at the station about a girl who stole a car and a parrot and ran away?

Then it struck me. I didn't have to lie. I didn't have to say anything at all.

He had already decided that the parrot had escaped, that he'd had a bad owner. Before that he'd decided I must have hit a raccoon with my car without even looking in the cage, without even looking to me for confirmation of his assumption. If I just didn't answer his question, wouldn't he simply answer it himself?

I stood in the doorway of that little office and smiled at him. Just smiled.

"You speak English?" he finally said.

I continued to smile.

He frowned. "You okay?"

Just kept smiling.

The old man screwed up his wrinkled lips and took off his glasses. "You look like you could use some coffee. Follow me." He leaned back over the cage. "You too, Polly."

I followed him into a small break room with a refrigerator, sink, and coffeemaker. A table and three mismatched plastic chairs filled almost all the space in the room. A hand-scrawled sign admonished coffee drinkers, "Turn off the burner when the pot is empty—this means you, Dave." Posters on three walls identified freshwater mussels, poisonous plants, mushrooms you could eat, and mushrooms that would kill you given half a chance. The fourth wall was taken up by an enormous map with zillions of squiggly lines and numbers.

The man poured me a cup of coffee and then opened the fridge. "Where's that bird? Got some grapes in here. You good with that coffee? I'll just go see if I can get your bird to join us."

There. He was my bird. Safe with me.

The man grabbed a handful of grapes and left the room. I stared at the map with the squiggly lines. Little triangles marked camping sites along a footpath labeled NCT. A number of spots along the lakeshore were named: Sand Point, Miner's Castle, Mosquito Beach, Chapel Rock, Hurricane River, Au Sable Lighthouse.

Log Slide.

The only thing that stood between me and the place Peter had brought me for my first glimpse of Lake Superior was about five miles of sand dunes.

"Here we are!" The old man walked in with The Professor on his gnarled hand. "Took a minute to get this rascal to come out, even for the grapes, but we're good friends now. Looks to me like your bird is stressed, plucked out all the feathers he could reach. And I saw through the window you have a car out there that looks pretty packed. So I figure you musta drove a long way and maybe the two of you could use a place to lay your heads, am I right?"

I smiled again.

"I thought so. It just so happens I got a place just off 72 on state forest land. I was born in Grand Marais, and I been moving south ever since. So far I've gotten about five miles."

Instead of laughing like I wanted to, I just shook my head. The old guy liked that reaction.

"You get used to jokes like that, honey. There's a lot more where that came from. What's your name?"

I almost said it. But I stopped myself. If I could speak a name, any name, I could answer questions. If I could write a name, I could write answers to questions. And that would mean the lying would have to begin.

"Okay, I'll go first. My name's Dave. Dave Dewitt. What's yours?"

I couldn't speak. Couldn't speak. Couldn't speak. Dave Dewitt would not make me speak.

He turned to the parrot on his hand. "What's your name, little guy? Polly? Bozo? Who's a pretty bird? Who's the pretty bird?"

"Professor," said The Professor under his breath.

"Professor? I'll be! Professor who? Professor Parrot?"

"Professor," the bird said again.

"Okay, Professor. Now who's that?" He held The Professor up toward my face and pointed. "Who is that nice lady?"

"Who," The Professor repeated.

"Yes, who?"

"Who."

"What're you, an owl? Who is—"

"Alex," said The Professor.

I knew he was talking about the host of *Jeopardy* because of how many times Dave Dewitt had said "who." But it didn't matter. I was Alex now. The name of Peter's football-star brother.

"Alex? Is that what he said?"

I smiled.

"Alex. Okay. Well, Alex, I don't know what your story is, but I know a damsel in distress when I see one. I seen plenty over the years. You wouldn't think so living out in the middle of nowhere, but I guess that's where your kind tend to go when they got trouble. Most the time it's about a guy. Sometimes it's about parents. You don't want to tell me about your situation, that's your business. I won't pry. But don't think you not talking will keep *me* from talking."

He motioned for me to follow him, walked back to the little office, and put The Professor back in his cage. He wrapped the blanket around it and shrugged into his heavy winter coat. "You follow me down the road a ways and I'll show you where I live. It ain't much, but it's better than sleeping in your car."

Dave Dewitt did indeed live just five miles away. A green mailbox adorned with the silhouettes of a family of three black bears marked the dirt drive, which wound through a pine forest that still held pockets of snow in the low places. The dingy house at the end of it was not much bigger than my grandmother's trailer. There was no yard to speak of, just trees and dirt and a fake deer eating nonexistent grass.

I parked behind his truck and took a moment to reexamine the situation. I had followed a strange old man to his remote house in the woods with $499,900 in my trunk. Beyond one neurotic parrot, no one knew where I was. The only way this could have been dumber was if Dave Dewitt were an able-bodied lumberjack of a man instead of an arthritic old codger.

There was still time to drive away. There was still time to drive south to someplace warm, where I could live outside and The Professor wouldn't freeze to death.

Then Dave Dewitt was opening the passenger door and removing the travel cage.

Even then, there was still time. When he shut the door I could peel out, leave the bird behind. He'd be a good new owner for The Professor. They were both old and gray with gravelly voices and too much to say. They were made for each other.

But then, wasn't he taking a leap of faith here? He had led a strange mute girl to his remote house in the woods. For all he knew I would kill him in his sleep and make off with whatever valuables he might have stashed away under his mattress or hidden in his freezer.

I turned off the car and stepped out onto the dirt driveway. If this was going to work, I had to trust him as much as he trusted me.

"Right this way, Alex. It ain't a palace, but it's warm in winter and sweltering in summer. You're welcome to stay as long as you need to. 'Til you get on your feet or your boyfriend's put in jail or whatever it was that sent you looking for peace up in the Great White North."

We entered a small sitting room, and Dave Dewitt let The Professor out of the cage.

"Not that I blame you. When you're looking

for peace, this is the place to find it. I'll take you out on the trail with me tomorrow, if you like. I walk the park a lot in the spring. Time to get all the branches cleared out from the winter storms before the hikers come through in the summer. Maybe you can give me a hand with that."

He looked at me for confirmation, so I smiled. I think I'd smiled more in the past twenty minutes than I had in the past twenty days.

"Spring's one of the best times in the park. The waterfalls are all raging, and there's no bugs yet and not so many people. It's quiet. Gives a person time to think. If you need it. Just gotta watch out for hungry bears, especially mamas with cubs. But don't you worry. Me and the bears got an understanding. I've known some since they were born, and now they're ten and twenty years old."

I wasn't worried about bears. I was worried that this peace and quiet Dave Dewitt mentioned would be subsumed by his insatiable need to talk. He talked during the entire tour of his little house. He talked as he helped me bring my bags into his den. He talked as he made up the squeaky hide-a-bed. He talked as he filled a bowl with treats for The Professor, who was given free range in the house.

My host talked through breakfast, lunch, and dinner. He talked on the drive back to the visitor station, talked as he arranged souvenirs and pamphlets, talked as he cleaned up the little kitchenette. I followed him everywhere, doing the small tasks he set out for me—sweep the floor, fold the brochures, alphabetize the mailing list.

When we left for the night, I turned off the coffeemaker.

By the end of that first day I knew his life story, his daily routine, his favorite and least favorite foods. I knew the names of the rangers and when they started working for the park. I knew the names of all the people who *used* to work there, when and why they left, and whether or not they were an asset to the park service.

When I crawled, exhausted, under the covers of the hide-a-bed, I could still hear his voice reverberating in the silence, like the echoes of a rock slide bouncing wildly up the sides of a deep ravine. The next day would be quieter. It had to be.

I'd already heard everything one person could possibly have to say.

31

now

There are days that end before you notice they've begun, and there are days that linger long after the sun is down. The days after I left Sussex at age fifteen were of the lingering variety. Days of hiking through forests and gathering wild blueberries and bathing in frigid waterfalls. Days of scrubbing sinks and toilets in the visitor center bathrooms. Days of chopping carrots and onions and rutabaga for Dave Dewitt's signature backwoods pasties. Days filled with occasional second-guessing but no second chances. The type of days you wished would get themselves over with because you were bone tired. But now as summer marches inexorably on, I'd give almost anything to have one of those unending days back.

Bit by bit, book by book, the *Dreadnoughtus* takes shape. Each day there are a few teenagers working alongside Ryan. Each evening after closing time, I continue the work late into the night, striping books with adhesive from one of the many caulk guns left on the worktable and pressing them into place. Sometimes I'm alone. Sometimes Ryan works beside me. Sometimes we talk about inconsequential things. More often we work in silence. If Sarah were there with us, we might get past the near-miss with Peter's books more easily. She would know what to say, how to cut through the unspoken tension. She never was one to be at a loss for words. But she never comes by anymore. She's too busy with her own ArtPrize entry as the deadline draws ever closer.

The frenetic monotony is broken when I open my postal box one morning to find an envelope with a return address in Terre Haute, Indiana. I rush back to the store and up to my apartment to fill out the requested information and scan copies of the necessary documents. I stuff an envelope and run it back to the post office within an hour. I don't chance putting just one stamp on the thing in case it should be a tenth of a percent of an ounce too heavy. I cannot miss my window due to insufficient postage. I affix three stamps and slip it into the big blue box that indicates a pickup time of 5:30 p.m. At 5:20, I close the store again in order to go watch a man transfer the contents of the box to his little mail truck.

Two weeks later, I find another envelope from the prison in my box. I have been approved. I won't ask Dawt Pi to give up another Saturday, and Ryan can't spare the time now that we're so close to finishing the *Dreadnoughtus*. Brick & Mortar Books will simply be closed.

Early Saturday morning before it is light, I feed and water The Professor and change the newspaper at the bottom of his cage. I have no old used mass market romance or mystery to give him; they've all been taken down to the marina. Even the castle in the window is gone. I look around the room for something for him to destroy and come up empty.

"Sorry, buddy. I'll stop and get you a new toy on the way home."

He gurgles and grumbles under his breath. I head for the back room.

"Robin."

I stop. He's never said my name before. Ever.

"What did you say?"

The bird regards me silently.

"Robin?" I prompt.

Nothing.

"Fine."

I turn away.

"Robin."

I hold the back of one finger up to the outside of the cage. He tests it with his beak, but does not bite.

"I'll be back tonight, buddy. I promise."

As I walk away, I wish he'd say it again, even though I don't have time to stay and chat. He doesn't, though.

When I stop to gas up the car it's 5:00 a.m. With a couple stops for food, I should reach Terre Haute by noon.

1:17 p.m., Saturday, September 7th. He is the fifth and last prisoner to enter the room, and at first I think there must be some mistake. The gray, shrunken figure in wrist and ankle shackles that are linked together with a noisy chain is not my father. Yet this is the person who sits down across from me and looks at the table in front of him. As my hair has grown unchecked, his has receded until there is nothing more than a shadow of stubble ringing a waxy bald crown. It's clear his nose has been broken and healed badly. Across his face run lines of dejection, anger, and resignation.

He is not a monster. He is barely a man.

1:18 p.m. I have already wasted a minute. Twenty-nine left. I cannot waste any more. What must be said? What should I have said to him in the letters I never sent, the calls I never made, the visits I never scheduled? What do you say to someone you've blamed for everything? What do you say when you've been so very wrong?

"I'm sorry." It comes out of my throat in nothing more than a croak.

He looks up at me, and memory squeezes my heart—of the last time he looked at me, across the table, over our empty plates, his lips smiling,

339

his eyes sad, excusing himself to answer the phone ringing in his office.

Then it's gone.

He looks down at his hands. "It's good to see you," he says.

I wait for more, for some indication that he's heard my apology.

"I'm sorry I didn't keep in touch," I say. "I thought . . . But I know now that you didn't do it, and I'm sorry I thought you were capable of such things."

He scratches the back of one hand. "Oh, everyone's capable."

"Okay, but still. You didn't . . . and I assumed that if you were arrested you must have. You shouldn't be where they put people like Ted Kaczynski and Timothy McVeigh."

He nods. "I appreciate that."

1:20 p.m.

"I've talked to Mom. She told me everything. About Billy, about the bribe. If I had known what that money was, I would never have used it."

"It wouldn't have mattered."

"It would. I found it in March. That was months before the new trial. I could have brought it to the police. If you'd been exonerated before 9/11, they couldn't have tried you again."

He is shaking his head. "Sure they could have. In the first trial I was charged with the murders and embezzlement, not with treason. Different crime, so additional charges cover facts that weren't known before. The outcome may have been the same either way. There's no way to know."

"I think it would have been different."

We are quiet a moment. 1:21 p.m.

"What happens now?" I ask.

"Who can say? Some people get a stay and hours later everything goes ahead as scheduled. Some people get a stay and their lawyers battle things out a little longer, and a few months later they're dead anyway."

"What are your lawyers doing?"

"Buying time. Looking for evidence to support your mother's latest statement."

"What evidence is out there?"

"Mainly a letter from Billy to your mother. She spoke to my lawyer about it back in February. She sent it to your grandmother along with a number of other letters from him just before she was arrested. In it he may allude to two of the murders."

"This February? Why wouldn't she have told someone about a letter like that when she first got it?"

"Why would she?"

"Why? Because if Billy confessed to the killings—"

"I didn't say that. It's not so cut-and-dried. It takes interpretation to see it, and at that point she didn't have the right context to understand it. Billy was good at fooling people into trusting him. It probably won't be enough to exonerate me, but it might be enough to get my sentence commuted."

I frown. "Still, why wait so long? She'd have to have wanted you to . . ."

He puts a hand up to stop me from saying it. "I don't think that's it. Prison gives you time to think. Too much time. You go over things enough in your mind, and you make a lot of trips between anger and despair and blaming and denial. You cover a lot of ground. But sometimes you don't look in the one dark little corner that's always been there because you just don't want to consider it."

He picks at his thumbnail.

"It took me a long time to come to grips with the fact that I really was a bad guy, that I'd used a lot of people for my own gain and hadn't cared who I hurt on the way. I spent the first five years here feeling like I'd been sorely mistreated. There were all sorts of people out there doing the kind of stuff I'd done and they weren't in prison, so why was I? Seemed pretty unfair and unjust. And the other people in here? They were all actual bad people. I wasn't like them. I wasn't psycho or bloodthirsty or ruthless. I was clever. I was someone who gamed the system and got ahead, and all the money and the women seemed like things I had a right to because I was a big shot."

He sends an apologetic look my way. I nod for him to continue.

"But you're inside long enough and one day you're going to stumble into that dark corner you've been avoiding because it's the only place left to go. And that's when you realize what you really are. A monster. After that you can deny it or embrace it. Or you can do what I've done, what your mother did—accept it and repent of it."

He laces his fingers together on the table. Each knuckle fits snugly in the cradle of two others. Neat, symmetrical, natural, like the teeth of a zipper. Here on death row my father has found a kind of settled peace that still escapes me.

"Grandma's been dead for a long time," I say. "That letter could be anywhere—or nowhere."

"My lawyers are trying to track it down, talking with the company that handled her estate, talking to friends who might still be alive. That's why the judge ordered the stay. She was quite generous, and my legal team is top-notch—Joel is the only reason I've lasted as long as I have—but we're running out of time."

"Why wouldn't they contact me?"

"They have a list. I'm sure you're on it. But it's been my understanding that you disappeared for quite some time—I have to say I'm glad to finally know you're okay—and I guess they just started with adults who might have had something to do with closing up her house. You didn't go through her things after she died?"

"No."

But someone had gone through her things right before she died.

"Oh my gosh," I breathe. "It was Billy."

Something in a crisis acts as a firebrand, imprinting details on your brain you can't account for, and I have never been able to forget the precise arrangement of my grandmother's belongings strewn throughout the trailer after the break-in. I rush from room to room in my mind. Where had Grandma put the stack of letters from my mother after I told her to get them out of the kitchen? There were no letters of any kind in the mess on the floor.

"He knew I had been sent to live with her," I say. "He said it, but I wasn't listening. I can't believe it was right in front of my face all this time."

I feel suddenly sick to my stomach. He hadn't just killed three unfortunate strangers. He had killed my grandmother. And I'd been alone with him in my store. I glance at the clock. 1:27 p.m. Talking faster than I ever have before, I tell my father the story of the break-in, of my unconventional trip across the river on Independence Day, and of the man in the boat who mistook me for my mother. With each additional revelation of how his chief of staff had betrayed and undermined him, his expression darkens a little more.

"The Professor knew," I say. "He flipped out when he saw Billy. And the only other time he'd been that agitated was right after the break-in when he pulled out all his feathers. He knew!"

I feel like throwing up.

"I thought whoever broke into the house must be looking for the money—and maybe he was, maybe he was just going to take it back all along—but what if in searching for the money he found the letter?"

My father leans forward, all business, the way I remember him being when I'd pass by his office door at home in Amherst as he was working late into the night to make deals and secure votes. "So you don't have any of your grandmother's papers?"

I sit slack-jawed, empty. "No."

"Is the trailer still around?"

"I don't know. I haven't been there in forever. But I'll check. When I get back into town, I'll go out there and look. But . . . chances are slim I'll find anything. There would probably be someone else living there."

My father's lips press into a line, and he looks down at his shackled hands.

"Oh, Daddy, I'm so sorry."

He shakes his head. "So where is Billy now?"

"Gone. He told me he was heading north to the Soo Locks and Lake Superior, but that was two months ago. He could be sailing around the Caribbean right now, free as a bird."

We're both quiet for a moment. I look at the clock, and my father follows my gaze. 1:44 p.m. Three minutes left.

He gives me a weak smile. "It might just not be meant to be, Robin. Someday he'll get what he deserves."

"No, *you* are getting what he deserves."

"Someday. It'll come. And I'm not getting what he deserves. I'm getting what I deserve."

Two minutes.

"Who do I contact if I find something?"

He rattles off a name and phone number, but they didn't allow me to bring anything into the visiting room, so I have nothing to write on.

"I'll mail it to you," he says.

I don't want to ask the next question.

"What should I do if I can't find anything?"

"Nothing. Live your life. That's all you can do." He places his hands flat on the table. "And forgive your mother."

I stare at the keyholes in the manacles around my father's wrists. "How?"

"If I can do it, you can."

"You never told her."

"Told her what?"

"That you forgave her. She doesn't know."

He shifts in his seat, rattling his chains.

"You should tell her," I say.

"Yeah," he says.

The guard gives us the one-minute warning. The backs of my eyes begin to burn. My father's eyes too are filling with tears.

"I love you, Robin. And I'm so sorry. You can't imagine how sorry I am."

My facial muscles rebel. My eyes overflow. My nose drips. I wipe the moisture away with my sleeve and take a deep breath to regain control.

"I love you, Daddy. And I forgive you."

He smiles through his tears. "Good. Now forgive her."

32

then

My first day out on the trail started at sunrise. With a walking stick in one hand and an honest-to-goodness machete in the other, old Dave Dewitt led the way through what he called "his leg" of the North Country Trail, a crooked line of earth that stretched 4,600 miles from New York to North Dakota. Dave's portion consisted of the forty-two miles displayed on the large map in the visitor station break room. It rambled past dunes, through forests, and along the quivering lips of cliffs, crossing rivers and marshes, skirting waterfalls and towers of ancient stone.

For one week each spring, he walked every inch of the challenging terrain, marking large trees for removal and cutting through the smaller obstructions himself using the chain saw that hung from the back of his pack. Normally he slept outdoors in his hammock and lived off unfiltered water and something he called GORP—"good old raisins and peanuts"—to which he'd started adding M&Ms twelve years ago.

"But we can't leave your parrot at the house

alone for a week," he'd said that morning over oatmeal, "so I guess this year we'll have to drive in to a few sites and do day hikes until we've covered what we need to cover."

We packed up his truck with supplies and I went to put The Professor back into the travel cage, but Dave stopped me.

"He don't want to be in there all day. Better to let him have his run of the place. Anyway, I ain't got nothing he's going to ruin any more than it already is."

I wasn't in complete agreement, but it was his house and I couldn't argue without talking. Leaving The Professor to his own devious devices, I hopped up into the passenger seat and settled in for a long day of listening to Dave Dewitt's unceasing monologue.

He did talk constantly on the drive to the trail-head in Munising, yet once we were prowling through the trees he was strangely taciturn. It was as though the great, brooding silence of the landscape had packed all of his many words back down his throat and into his belly. And because I wasn't hearing him, I could hear other things.

All the other things, in fact. The swish of denim and vinyl. The jingle of zipper pulls. My increasingly labored breaths alongside his steady ones. The sound of every footfall, which was one sound on dirt and another on pine needles and another on damp leaves and another on rock. The hiss of spray paint—blue to mark the trail, orange to mark the dangerous lurching trees that would be removed later by a team of young volunteers.

When we were in deep forest, I heard the rush of snow-bloated rivers and the whisper of Lake Superior somewhere beyond, somewhere I could not see. But when we came up to a bluff and there was nothing but gray-blue water stretching to the clouded horizon, I realized that the lake had not been whispering at all. The matrix of tree trunks and air pockets in the forest had deadened the roar, but it had always been a roar.

There was peace here. But not quiet. A pleasant reversal of the cemetery back in Sussex, where it was always quiet but never quite peaceful. Creeping like mist through the maze of bare brown tree trunks was so much like weaving through the dark gray headstones. Except here I did not wonder at what was missing in death, despite the fact that there were few signs of life around—no grass, no flowers, no leaves.

This forest was not dead. It was merely sleeping. More than that, it was about to wake up. That thing that was missing from the bodies in the cemetery? Nearly all of these trees had it, even some that Dave Dewitt had marked for destruction. It was stirring in their roots, coursing upward through channels deep within their stiff trunks, squeezing out into every branch and twig and waiting bud.

And I felt it stirring in me.

Two days ago, I had thought my life was over. Just as I had thought it was when my father was arrested, and again when my mother was arrested, and again when I had to move to Michigan. My grandmother was dead, my home had been ransacked, and my best friend had betrayed me. Every one of those moments felt like the last autumn leaf had plummeted to the earth, like all my life from that point forward was destined to be an eternal winter.

Yet here I was. Alive. In springtime. Blood running through my veins, oxygen filling my straining lungs, sweat seeping from my skin, though it was cold to the touch.

Maybe my life was really just starting.

Dave Dewitt and I worked all week in the woods and along the shoreline of the best of the Great Lakes. He showed me how to build a fire, how to identify animals by their scat, what to do if I saw a bear. Though I would not have thought it possible from such a chatty person, he taught me how to disappear—to walk unheard, to stay upwind, to blend with the background. Useful skills for someone on the run.

As the weather warmed and the calendar pages turned and the trail filled up with hikers, I moved as Dave's shadow, a silent partner in everything he did. He quashed the questions of other park employees and acted like it was perfectly natural for an old man to spend his every waking moment with a strange mute girl who had appeared out of nowhere.

Soon no one noticed me at all. The summer flowed over us like Bridal Veil Falls flowed over stone into the sink of Lake Superior—fresh and reckless and beautiful.

And then four hijacked planes changed everything.

Summer was over. No one was hiking. To a person, the nation was glued to its TVs, yearning for answers, looking for someone to blame.

In October, I helped Dave close up the facilities for winter and saw the first newspaper headline linking Norman Windsor with al-Qaeda. Then one about a new trial. Then one about a verdict. In my room late at night I choked on gallons of swallowed tears as I thought of my father, of all those people in the towers, of people in mountain villages on the other side of the earth being blown up, people who'd had nothing to do with the attacks. I gripped my sorrow tighter and tighter until I had controlled it, like a rat snake squeezing the life out of its prey.

I was glad Dave had insisted that The Professor get the run of the house. It had meant a lot of unpleasant discoveries followed by Windex and paper towels, but at least I would not have to see terrible news stories staring out from the bottom of a cage every day. Instead, I watched the news of my family's shame burn up every night when Dave started the fire.

The other blessing of that time was that Dave didn't own a TV. While everyone else was watching the invasion of Afghanistan and coverage of the second Norman Windsor trial, we spent the long cold nights in front of those crackling fires, Dave reading westerns, me slowly working my way through his library of wilderness guides and botany texts and geological surveys.

I tried to put terrorists out of my mind. I tried to put my parents out of my mind. I tried to put Peter and Emily Flynt and the stacks of beautiful books I had left behind in Sussex out of my mind. I memorized facts and figures, the unchanging properties of nature, the things that could not be affected by ideologies and arms deals and resentment.

Alone in my room at night I considered writing my mother to tell her where I was, to tell her I was safe and I was making a new life for myself. I wanted to tell someone about Dave Dewitt, about all the things I was learning, about how I'd kayaked beneath stone arches and into watery caves, about how I'd seen the northern lights dance over Lake Superior.

But what if the people who ran the prison read the mail? What if they alerted the authorities? Or what if my mother did? I loved it here, and I would not risk being found again. Anyway, who would care to read my thoughts about a grizzled old chatterbox or the exact hue of the water at the moment the sun is submerged in it? In the face of national tragedy, what else mattered?

Eventually the world moved on. The Professor's feathers grew back. The months became years. Grandma's car was slowly swallowed up by the forest. I never did cut and dye my hair, never wore glasses or sweatshirts with patchwork pumpkins on them. I helped pay for groceries and gas, and Dave never asked me where my money came from. He had offered me a paid position at the park, which I didn't take. He may have guessed why, or he may not have. But he was a gracious enough person not to ask.

On my eighteenth birthday I considered speaking, telling the truth. I was the daughter of Norman Windsor, who was now on death row for aiding and abetting enemies of the state. But by that time, I hadn't talked to another human being in three years. I'd had a number of whispered and rather one-sided conversations with The Professor on the rare occasions I was alone in the house, but talking to a bird didn't count. Birds, even parrots, didn't ask uncomfortable questions, and they didn't feel the temptation to share juicy gossip with their friends.

Anyway, something in me said the truth was worse than the lie, that there wasn't really a lie at all until I told the truth. I had never told this kind old man I couldn't talk. I had never told him my name was Alex. I had never told him anything at all. But if I told him who I really was, how would he feel about having taken me in? Dave Dewitt was not a fool. And I didn't want to be the person to make him one.

So I left things as they were. Because things were good.

Nine years into my stay with my surrogate grandfather, he suffered a stroke that robbed him of the use of his right arm. The park staff, smaller in recent years because of the recession, gave him a lovely retirement party. But Dave was not the type of man who retired. Though I worked hard to make him comfortable, I could not make him happy. He deteriorated at a steady rate over the next two years until I could not care for him any longer.

Before I could quite decide what to do for him, whether to get him into an assisted-living facility or hire a live-in nurse, Dave died uncharacteristically quietly in his sleep. When I found him the next morning, emptied of that mysterious essence that had made him alive, that had made him who he was, I finally let out all of the tears I had swallowed for nearly a decade.

A legendary figure in the UP, Dave would have been pleased to see how well attended his funeral was. As he had no family, I paid for everything— the plot, the casket, the headstone—with money

I now believed to be tainted with the blood of thousands of innocent people. I watched them lower the box into the hole, the last autumn leaf falling to the ground.

What now? Did I stay where I was? Did I remain Alex, the eccentric, mute, amateur naturalist? Did I reclaim the identity of Robin Windsor, daughter of the most hated man in America?

Or was there a door number three?

33

now

I've been in churches only sporadically since my childhood. Even then we were never regulars. We were Episcopalians because that's what Massachusetts politicians were if they weren't Catholic, and we managed to get to church for the big days—Christmas, Easter, and the month or so leading up to election day. But after a sleepless night during which I teased out all possible results of my errand to the old trailer in Sussex—none of them ending in success—I know I cannot begin this task without help.

Though there are plenty of lovely old churches with fancy altars and beautiful windows to choose from in River City, I opt for one that doesn't look like a church at all. Presentation isn't what I'm looking for. I'm looking for Dawt Pi. Because of all the people I know, she's the only one who has ever made me wonder if perhaps God must be real despite everything.

I see the back of her head from outside the large picture window of the storefront church in a run-down and unfashionable part of town. She is one of a couple dozen people seated in folding chairs set in two small blocks—four rows of five chairs on either side of an aisle of scuffed linoleum. I tap as quietly as I can on the glass, but she doesn't hear. I tap a little harder, and the entire back two rows turn around. The man at the podium at the front of the room waves, then beckons me in. That old familiar feeling—*bolt*—comes over me, but Dawt Pi is already on her feet and heading for the door.

"Robin! How good to see you! Come in!"

"I didn't mean to disturb the service."

"No, no! Come in, come in!" She is tugging at my arm, pulling me through the door, guiding me to the chair next to hers, which some helpful person has just vacated for me.

I lean over to whisper to her, "Will you come with me somewhere after church?"

She is staring straight ahead as though she didn't hear me. I tap her leg. Her head pivots slightly, but her eyes do not leave the pastor, who is saying something about a storm or a boat or something.

"Will you please come with me somewhere after—"

"Yes."

I know when I'm being shushed. I sit back in the uncomfortable chair and focus my attention on the man in the front.

"And Peter said to him, 'Lord, if it is you,

command me to come to you on the water.' And Jesus answered, saying, 'Come.' So Peter got out of the boat and walked on the water. But when he saw the wind, he was afraid, and started to sink."

The pastor pauses and looks around the room into the faces of his little flock. And then he looks at me, the black sheep in the back who is just thinking, *Why does it have to be about Peter?*

"Isn't that how it so often is?" the pastor says. "We ask God for something, he grants our request, and almost immediately we begin to fear. We fear the dangers around us, we fear the unknown, we fear he'll let us drown. We don't trust him to keep us safe. We don't trust him to follow through. And as we sink into the raging water, there are two things we can do." He pauses and holds up one finger. "We can forget about God—ignore the fact that he's standing right there, within reach—and instead flounder around on our own, trying to keep our heads above water as we slowly sink. Or"—he holds up a second finger—"we can call out to him. And that's what Peter does. He cries out, 'Lord, save me,' and immediately Jesus reaches out to him. Immediately. He takes hold of him and says, 'You of little faith, why did you doubt?' And they get into the boat . . . and the wind stills."

The wind stills.

That's how it feels. I had trouble articulating it to Sarah back when we were all stuck in my apartment the day my father was supposed to be executed, but that is what Brick & Mortar Books has been to me. A still point in a storm. Dave Dewitt had been one. And for a little while, that was what Peter was. That was how it felt to be with him—in his car, in the motel, at the precipice of Niagara Falls, at the edge of the abyss of Lake Superior. Each time a new book appeared in my locker. Each time a padded manila envelope appeared on the counter. A moment of peace, a moment without doubt, a moment I felt that, were I called to, I could walk on water, I could hold back the wind.

After the sermon comes to a close and everyone else sings a song, I force myself to be polite and shake some hands—every hand, in fact. I am enthusiastically invited back by everyone there. Each of them smiles. Not one of them stares or whispers off in a corner. When Dawt Pi and I can finally extricate ourselves from the proceedings, she follows me to the car.

"We have to stop at the store first and get The Professor," I say.

"Where are we going?" she says.

"Sussex. Where I used to live."

"You lived here?" Dawt Pi says as we pull up to the trailer.

It is rustier even than when I last saw it, and if Mary and the gnomes are still there, they are obscured behind a thick curtain of summer weeds stretching nearly up to the windows. The cemetery has been kept mowed, though the grass is brown and a few of the trees have been cut down. And beyond it, the dead house still slumps, its wood siding practically bare, its roof caved in in places.

"Yes. I lived here." It takes a moment for my hand to obey my brain's command to open the car door. "Let me just look. I'll be right back."

As I step up onto the porch I see a note on the door, faded from years of unfettered sunshine.

Property of St. James Catholic Church
NO TRESPASSING

The door is locked. I step down to where Mary used to stand, push through the weeds, and cup my hands around my face at the window. The blinds are closed, but one slat is gone, no doubt the work of an unsupervised parrot sometime in the distant past. Through the dirt and the narrow opening I can see that the place is empty.

The puzzle pieces come together in my mind. Grandma had likely left her worldly goods to the church, and they had probably brought everything to their thrift store where Grandma had volunteered each week, using the proceeds to pay for her burial after she had been so cruelly left behind by her ungrateful "cousin." There's nothing to find here.

I turn to go back to the car, but my foot catches on something and I pitch forward. A gnome—just one—lying on his back, forgotten. The red paint of his hat has faded to pink, and the blue of his coat has been chipped away by time and weather. But his smile is still there, as are those vacant eyes.

I step around the trailer and consider the dead house.

Dawt Pi is standing at the open passenger door. "Is it locked?"

"Yeah. But nothing's in there anyway." I open the back door of the car and pull out the travel cage we picked up on the way out here.

"What are you looking for?"

"A letter."

"Why did you bring The Professor?"

"You'll see."

I lead the way through the cemetery, only glancing at Emily Flynt's grave out of the corner of my eye. When had Peter last knelt there?

Through the metal grate at the front of the travel cage, The Professor has a clear view of our destination as we clear the gravestones and start across the expanse of weeds to his childhood home. I can feel him flapping and hopping around in there. I lead the way around to the back, then open the cage.

Dawt Pi pulls him out. "What are we doing with him?"

"He's going to help." I pull a folded envelope from my back pocket and hold it up to him, just as I had the key to the lockbox all those years ago. "Find the letter, Professor. Find the letter."

But he's not interested. The envelope drops to the ground. I pick it up. "Let's bring him inside."

"We are going in there?"

"Yes. Well, you don't have to if you don't want to, but The Professor and I are."

She looks up at the house doubtfully, then sets her mouth in a line. At my questioning eyebrows she gives a little nod, and we step out of the sun and into the musty dark.

It's all as it was, only worse for the intervening years, a tomb filled with the dusty artifacts of a mundane life. Every few steps I hold the envelope in front of The Professor and repeat my request. "Letter. Find the letter." But he gives no indication he's heard. There are no mysterious incantations from some long-forgotten game show. Nothing but the sound of the house crying out weakly under our feet.

In the kitchen, we open every drawer. Nothing. We search rotten couch cushions and dusty tables. Nothing.

"Let's go upstairs," I say.

We enter the sanctuary of my mother's childhood. Light streams through the window where the doll once sat. The bedspread is faded on the corner from the decades of constant sunlight. I kneel at the bed, offer a hasty prayer to Dawt Pi's God, and bow down to the floor. I run my hand along the floor in a pattern, back and forth, farther and farther into the space, then turn it up to the underside of the box spring and do the same.

"Big money, big money," says The Professor. "No whammies."

"Yes!" I say, straightening and pulling the envelope back out of my pocket. "Put him on the floor, Dawt Pi. Letter, Professor. Find the letter."

The bird scrapes around on the floor for a moment, but he doesn't seem to be looking for anything. He nibbles at the corner of the bedspread. I hesitate. Visions of my grandmother's bed askew and slashed, of her broken body stuffed into the small space between it and the wall, of the trails of blood running down her face.

I scoop The Professor up and put him on top of the vanity, then begin systematically dis-assembling the bed, layer by layer. Dawt Pi helps me fold what's left of the moth-eaten bedspread, then the blanket and the sheets. We move the mattress and check for holes along each seam, looking for a hiding place. Nothing. Coughing in the thick air, we put it all back together and start on the dresser. Drawer by drawer we paw through whatever Lindy left behind when she made her escape from Sussex. Nothing.

I sit back on the floor in defeat.

"The Professor is gone," Dawt Pi says.

She starts for the door and I follow. We look through the two other bedrooms, she for the bird and I for the key to my father's freedom, but the objects of our respective searches elude us.

I'm closing the last drawer in my uncle's room when I hear Dawt Pi call up the stairs that she's found The Professor. I have found nothing. Perhaps there is nothing to find. How can I tell my father that I've failed?

I pick my way down the treacherous steps. Dawt Pi is standing at the fireplace, The Professor on her shoulder, gazing at the yellowed family portrait over the mantel.

"This is your family?"

"That is my grandmother, a grandfather I never knew, an uncle I never knew, and my mother."

"You look like her."

"Yeah, I do."

"She is in prison too?"

"Yes, but not for much longer."

"Will she come back here once she's out?"

"I—I don't know."

I have never considered what my mother might do once she's released. Where does one go after more than two decades in prison? Would she try to reclaim her life in Amherst? How could she? No one is waiting for her there—no job at the university, no grand home on an oak-lined street, no swanky rooms filled to bursting with money and influence. No daughter. She wouldn't be welcome back in Amherst. Would she be welcome here? Would she return to River City as I had?

"Let's go," I say. "The letter's not here." I start for the hole in the back where the door had once stood.

"Wait, Robin. You should have this." She takes the photo off the wall and holds it out to me. "This is your family."

I tuck the photo under my arm, and we head for the car.

"Want me to take you home?" I ask.

Dawt Pi looks at the time. "Take me to Bob Evans."

"Bob Evans?"

"It's where we eat lunch after church. They will still be there."

"Bob Evans it is."

I head for Magellan Bridge and feel a sudden affinity toward the Spanish explorers after whom River City's bridges were inexplicably named. They never quite knew where they were going, and when they got there they sure made a mess of things. But at least they answered the call of the horizon. At least they took a chance. They set their course for the unknown, weathered hardship

and rough seas, and made an indelible, if sometimes ignominious, mark on human history.
They surrendered to the will of the wind and the
strength of the sails, looking to the heavens for
guidance through the dark nights. And there was
something to admire in that.

I pull up to the door of Bob Evans to let Dawt
Pi out.

"Park the car," she says. "In the shade. There."

I park as requested but do not turn off the car.

"Let's go," she says.

"Me? No thanks. I can't leave The Professor in
the car."

"Yes you can. It's not hot and you are in the
shade. Open the windows. Let's go."

I suppose after dragging her around that death
trap of a house on a fool's errand, it's the least
I can do. And if a bunch of men can get on a
boat while the crowd is warning them about how
they'll fall off the edge of the world, surely I can
eat at Bob Evans with a few friendly strangers.

34

then

A lot can change in more than a decade, so I was surprised and a bit disappointed when I returned to Sussex's main drag on a gray and windy November day in 2012 to see that it was all basically the same—the same houses, the same fences, the same businesses—only dingier. I guess there were a few differences. The video store was gone. A Chinese restaurant had become a Mexican restaurant. The giant willow tree at the corner of Spruce and Centerline Road had been felled. But the meat market was there, and the bakery, and the chain fast-food restaurants. I did not drive by the school or the cemetery or the dead house. I wasn't ready for that, and I wasn't sure I ever would be.

Nearby River City, however, had changed. Some storefronts were now boarded up, but I couldn't remember what had been there in the first place anyway. A long-defunct factory was being turned into something other than an empty shell. Most of downtown had gotten a new coat of paint. The number of pharmacies seemed to have doubled.

Across Cortez Bridge I turned down Riverside Drive and passed by the old playground, which now sported a prominent warning sign about arsenic in the wooden play structures. Beyond the marina I turned left onto Midway Street. The bars were all still there, as was Mystic Rhythms Aromatherapy Shop. I parked in an angled spot right by the entrance, slipped The Professor a few peanuts to keep him occupied, and pushed through the heavy shop door. It smelled exactly the same— like sandalwood and what I now recognized as marijuana. The lady with the long gray hair and the scarves drifted in from the back. She looked like Sussex did: basically the same, but dingier.

"How can I help you?" Her voice still sounded like feathers.

"I'm just browsing."

The sound of my own voice at a conversational volume startled me. I moseyed around for a few minutes, aware that she watched me from behind the register.

"You know what," I said, stronger now, "maybe you could help me. I'm just back in town after a long time away, and I'm looking for a place to rent."

"Oh? What brings you back?"

"I'm not exactly sure. I kind of had a feeling about it, is all."

"Oh, I understand that. I have psychic leanings myself."

"That's not exactly what I meant." I hesitated and tried to line up my jumbled thoughts into something that made sense. "I mean, I realized that I'm an adult and it's probably time to stop running."

She tilted her head but said nothing.

"So do you know of anything? I'd prefer not to be in a big apartment building, but I'm not really looking for a house either."

"Just up the road there's an apartment above the old art studio. That whole building's for sale, actually."

"I don't remember an art studio on this street."

"It was only there for about three years. It's been empty now for quite some time. It's too bad it failed. Mark was a fine artist and a regular customer of mine. But it's one of those cursed places, you know?"

"What do you mean?"

"Nothing works there. I've been in this location since the 1970s, and I've seen ten or twelve businesses in that storefront. They all fail. Some don't even last a year, but usually they go under around year seven or eight."

"That's a bummer. It's up the street?"

"Yes. Nearly the top of the hill. Same side."

"I'll check it out." I picked up a lilac-scented

candle and took a deep breath of its intoxicating bouquet. "Oh, I've got to have this."

"Good choice."

She rang me up, wrapped the candle in paper, and popped it into a little bag along with a book of matches. I left my car at the aromatherapy shop and walked up the hill to Chestnut Street. It was easy to tell which building had been the art studio. The brick on the side of the corner storefront sported an enormous mural of a billowing American flag that took up almost the entire wall. There was no sky behind it or landscape under it, and the edges of the flag were somewhere out of frame.

I came around to the front and was somehow not surprised to find that it was the very same building that was for sale when Peter and I had gone Christmas shopping in 2000, the first and only other time I'd been in the Mystic Rhythms Aromatherapy Shop. The striped awnings were gone, but the beautiful leaded glass door was still there. I peered through the glass between cupped hands. Except for some empty shelves that lined the walls, the place was devoid of furniture.

"What would you put there?" Peter had asked me.

A bookstore.

And why not? I didn't have a job or the prospect of one. I had lived so frugally with Dave Dewitt,

I still had plenty of money. The recession had hit hard in Michigan, and the real estate market in most towns still hadn't recovered. Maybe this was why I was here. Maybe this place had been calling me to come back and breathe new life into it. The woman with the voice of feathers said nothing worked here. But all that really meant was that nothing had worked here *yet*.

Within the week, the place was mine. The realtor was dubious when I warned him that I wouldn't have a credit history because I'd never gotten a loan or used a credit card or even had a bank account. But when I told him I could give him the asking price in cash, he didn't question my finances further. After all, he'd been trying to unload the place for years.

The day I moved my few belongings into the apartment, River City had its first dusting of snow. I gave The Professor free rein of the place, just as he'd had up in Dave Dewitt's house, until I could buy a nice big cage, cleaning up his messes whenever I came upon them. I emptied my suitcases, hung my wrinkled clothes in a closet, and lined up a few pairs of shoes. I laid an old quilt on the floor where I would sleep until I got a bed and set my mother's old doll against the wall. On my belly on the quilt, I looked into her sunbleached face.

"What do you think?"

She didn't answer, as I hadn't for so many years.

The doll and The Professor were my only company now. I felt a little silly addressing them like humans, but after I'd listened to Dave talk practically nonstop for over a decade, the silence in the apartment was deafening. Now that I was talking again, I couldn't stop myself. From the doll I got silence. From The Professor I got occasional mimicry and frequent bites. We'd been through a lot together, but that didn't exactly make us friends. It simply meant that all of his bad memories were associated with me.

I busied myself that first week with cleaning. I stood inside the big picture window downstairs with a bottle of glass cleaner and a roll of paper towels, watching fat snowflakes drift down from the clouds. I swept the floors. I dusted and oiled the shelves. I got down on my hands and knees with a bucket of soapy water and scrubbed. The dirt came off, but the splatters of paint—evidence of an earlier chapter in the building's story—were there to stay.

I spent the next several weeks scouring thrift stores and the nooks and crannies of the big antique mall across the river, looking for second-hand shelves and tables for the store and furniture for the apartment. I read books and articles about all the boring legal stuff associated with running a business. I filed permits and stood by as inspectors poked around and gave me advice about old plumbing and the ticking-time-bomb electrical system.

The first books arrived in January, and I spent much of the month lovingly arranging them and making handmade signs to help customers find what they were looking for. In February, I took out ads in the newspaper and on WRST declaring the grand opening of Brick & Mortar Books on March 1st.

The night before opening day I could hardly sleep. Against my solitary nature, I had contests and giveaways and activities planned—it was what the internet at the library told me to do— but would anyone actually come? Or would people be indifferent? It was still hard for me to think of most of the world as anything but hostile.

Thankfully, my fears were unfounded. Though there was a slow moment or two, all in all it was a great turnout on opening day, and every-one who walked in walked out with at least one book. The customers were friendly and happy to see a new business had moved into the long-empty storefront. Many of them shared stories of the businesses that had been in this location before.

What I hadn't expected was all the questions they had for me. What was my connection to River City? Had I grown up here? Why had I left? Why had I decided to return? And the most frequent refrain: What was my name?

The first time the question was asked, I held out my hand and said without thinking, "I'm Robin Dickinson."

Somewhere deep inside, I wasn't done running.

That was the first time I'd ever had a headache. It may have been nothing more than a coincidence—it had been a long and taxing day, after all. But when I waved goodbye to the last customer and flipped the Open sign, I realized that my head was throbbing. I sat down on the wooden stool behind the register, rested my elbows on the counter, and put my head in my hands. Could I leave the task of counting up the day's profits for the morning?

The bell tinkled, and I looked up to see a tall, slender blonde walk through the door.

"I'm sorry, miss, I forgot to lock the door, but we're closed now. We'll open again tomorrow morning at nine o'clock."

"So it is you," the woman said. "I didn't believe it."

"Excuse me?"

"Robin Dickinson."

"I'm sorry, do I know you?"

"You did." She rested her arms on the counter and looked me hard in the face. "Come on. You know me."

I was sure I didn't. Then I saw a shimmery

white scar on her forearm. Snippets of the past emerged from wherever they had been hiding in my brain and linked up, and instantly I knew.

"Sarah Kukla?"

"Bingo."

35

now

O n a painfully beautiful September morning, the big semitruck pulls up in front of the marina. The entire Science Olympiad team is there. After taking pictures of everyone with the dinosaur, tricky in the half-light of the cavernous boathouse, the team carefully dismantles it and loads it into the truck as I look on nervously. It feels reckless to immediately take apart something that took so much time and effort to build, even though I know it will all be put back together again soon.

Ryan and a parent volunteer follow the semi down the highway in a van full of giddy teenagers. I follow them alone in my car. Three and a half hours later we pull up to a museum on the west bank of the Grand River. The *Dreadnoughtus* is to be installed in the huge atrium beneath the skeleton of an enormous whale. It's a lovely venue and one of few indoor spots around the city that could accommodate a sculpture of this size. But when we begin unloading, it strikes me that putting the *Dreadnoughtus* in a museum is completely counter to the message I want it to send to people. A week ago I might have seen that as a sign that Brick & Mortar was doomed like every other business that had been housed at 1433 Midway. But perhaps not now.

When I slid into a chair next to Dawt Pi at Bob Evans that Sunday, I intended to have one cup of coffee, then skedaddle back to my apartment the first chance I got. Instead, I found myself fielding a barrage of questions about the store and the *Dreadnoughtus*. Everyone at the table seemed sure that it would win. Then the pastor's wife spoke up.

"But if it doesn't win, that doesn't mean it's God's will that your store should close. It just means that the prize money is not the way you'll keep it open. Sometimes we're handed adversity for our own good, so we'll grow. Just because something's hard doesn't mean it's not worth fighting for."

Whatever happened as the result of this contest, it didn't have to determine my fate.

Even with the help of the museum staff, reconstruction is not without its hiccups. But by dinnertime, the dinosaur is back in one piece and the robotics are functioning. I watch the head tilt and turn, watch the tail move slowly back and forth. With a little imagination I could make myself think it looked alive. But I know better. There's no life here. If it's not just breath and it's not just electronic pulses in the brain, it's certainly not wires and industrial batteries.

The job done, the teenagers scatter throughout the museum, some to the exhibits, others to ride the enormous carousel overlooking the river. I circle the colossal sculpture, this incredible creation that a few months ago had been nothing but an idea. Not even my idea. Sarah's idea. And Caleb's. And Ryan's.

"It looks amazing," Ryan says as he comes up beside me.

"It really does."

"Is it how you envisioned it?"

"Oh, I never really did envision it. You did."

"Nah. You caught the vision."

Had I? I'm not sure. I'd believed it could happen. I'd worked to make it happen. But that isn't the same as catching a vision.

"The kids all want to go out for pizza before getting back on the road," Ryan says. "You in?"

The last thing I want to do right now is go out to eat with a bunch of rowdy teenagers, but I can't refuse. These kids had made it all happen. There was no way it could have been done without their help.

At the restaurant I listen to talk of classes and teachers, clubs and teams. I think of my interrupted childhood when, for a while, I walked the very same halls these kids walk. One of them might have my old locker, never knowing what a sacred space it had been for a short time. How many kids over the intervening years must have dumped backpacks and textbooks in the very spot that Peter had once placed the hearts of Virginia Woolf and John Steinbeck and Harper Lee?

And there, squished between Caleb and a lithe, tattooed girl with blue hair, I suddenly know. I know why some books live on forever while others struggle for breath, forgotten on shelves and in basements. The authors of those books that now serve as raw material for a ridiculous animatronic dinosaur a few blocks away— they might have told rollicking good tales and sketched out characters who were fun to follow for four hundred pages, but they hadn't bled. They hadn't cut themselves open and given up a part of themselves that they would dearly miss. They hadn't lost anything in the writing.

That's the difference between the books that I could never aptly explain to Dawt Pi and the ones I let The Professor shred. That's the difference between the dead and the living. I hadn't put anything but a little elbow grease into the *Dreadnoughtus*. I hadn't given it my heart. The only things I had ever created that had cost me some essential part of myself were the poems I'd written for Peter to pay for the books that are still stacked in boxes just inside my apartment door. Those verses were as true and as honest as I could make them.

And there was fear in the writing. Fear that they would be misinterpreted, yes, but greater than that was the fear that they'd never be interpreted at all. That no one would read them and find me there.

Was that also what made a person or a bird or a frog alive? Was there a part of God's heart that animated each otherwise insignificant part of the world? Had he given something up in creating me? In creating my father? Would that part return to him when death finally claimed Norman Windsor? Or was it lost forever?

The talk around the table eventually turns to the upcoming homecoming dance at Kennedy, who is going with whom, and who is likely to be named king and queen. I can't help but think of that long-ago homecoming night.

Somewhere in another part of this city, Sarah installed her entry yesterday. A few weeks ago, I'd driven across the river to her house to see it. It was exactly as she had described it in the spring—a wall of car parts and broken glass with black and red paint spattered everywhere. It was built up on four large wooden structures that could be pulled apart for transport and then locked in place again.

"What do you think?" she had asked.

"It's . . . frightening," I finally said. "It's eye-catching, but also frightening."

"Yeah. It is."

I looked at the woman who had been my friend for seven years and realized with some shame that I had no idea what made her tick. "Are you happy with it?"

"Almost. I have one more element to add before it's done."

"What's that?"

"You'll see."

As Ryan generously pays the bill, I wonder what that last element is.

"You're going back in the van with them tonight?" I ask.

"That's the plan."

"Are they leaving right away?"

"Yeah. It's a long drive."

"Bummer. I was going to ask if you wanted to see if we could find Sarah's piece."

"I'd love to. But I don't think I can ask them to wait. It's been a long day."

"You could always ride back with me."

His eyebrows shoot up. "I certainly wouldn't mind a quieter return trip. I'd have to see if Carolyn was up to being the only adult in the van."

Ryan works out the details with Carolyn in the parking ramp as I consult the map that came in the ArtPrize welcome pack. Sarah's piece should be on the east side of the river, affixed to the outside wall of a building.

"Should we take your car?" Ryan asks when the van has driven away.

"Let's walk."

We exchange the fluorescent lights of the parking ramp for the friendlier glow of street-lamps and make our way across a footbridge over the river. Like River City, Grand Rapids is bisected by water. But this part of the Grand River is narrower and shallower than the Saginaw. No sailboats or freighters drift by. The bridges that traverse it are not drawbridges. They have no proper names apart from the name of the street they transmit from one side to the other. In a dry year, a man in waders can fish the middle of the stream and not worry about getting his elbows wet, let alone losing an entire pickup truck. It's a nice enough feature, but somehow it feels tacked on. Like the city planners were examining their maps, dissatisfied, until one innovative fellow added a streak of blue right down the middle and said, "What if there was a river?"

We wind through the streets along with the Saturday night crowd, which is far more fashion-able and seems less inebriated than River City's, until we come to a small parking lot beside a strip of one-story shops.

"There it is."

About twelve feet high and perhaps twenty feet wide, the three-dimensional mural is lit from below by floodlights directed up and in.

"Oh, wow," Ryan says.

I follow his gaze to the lower right corner, where

one might expect to find the artist's signature. There, crumpled, torn, and bloodstained, is the pale pink dress Sarah had worn to homecoming nearly twenty years ago. It has been crudely stitched back together with wire where it must have been cut from her body at the hospital. She has kept it all these years.

I replay that horrific night in my mind. The almost kiss, the screeching tires, the crunching metal, the smell of rubber and coolant and gasoline. The blood, the tears, the sirens, the lights. Sarah told me not long ago that Brad Ellis had not caused that crash. It hits me now, looking at this wall of destruction, that if he hadn't, Sarah must have—maybe not the way the rumors had it happening, but somehow. The knowledge that she'd had a hand in the death of a friend must have haunted her. And I never took the time to understand. I never even asked her about it after she revealed her secret to me in the bar. I was too concerned with Peter and his books, believing that my problems were bigger.

I know that I will not win this contest. And I suspect Sarah won't either. But I don't think it will matter to her. She may have created this piece of art for the contest, but really it was for her. A part of her is stuck in some moment in the past, a moment when everything changed and childhood was gone and an uncertain future unfurled in front of her. And part of her heart is here, in this disturbing work of art. Sarah's creation is alive in a way the *Dreadnoughtus* could never be, and when the *Dreadnoughtus* is dismantled and recycled, Sarah's piece will live on.

After a few silent minutes of appreciation for her realized vision, Ryan and I turn away and begin the trek back to the car. Halfway across the footbridge he takes my hand and urges me to stop walking.

"What?"

"Look." He points to the museum where the *Dreadnoughtus* can be seen through the wall of windows. "Nice work, Robin."

"That's your work."

Ryan turns to me and smiles. In his glasses, I see the lights of the Grand Rapids skyline.

"I'm glad I got to know you this summer," he says. "Since school started up again, I feel like we haven't had as much time together. But I want you to know that when this is all over, whether you win this thing or not, whether you can save the store or not, I want to keep seeing you. I really enjoy spending time with you."

He really is a nice guy.

"I've enjoyed spending time with you too."

He closes the small distance between us and folds me in an embrace. I put my head on his shoulder and look out over the river to the museum, still awash with light. To the left of the atrium where the *Dreadnoughtus* stands I can see the carousel coming to a stop. Horses of white and pink and pale blue. And one red horse with a golden bridle. Enveloped in Ryan's warm arms, I watch a man lift a little girl off the red horse and lead her out of the bright room. I pull away from the hug that has gone on too long and walk on, Ryan by my side.

Holden Caulfield couldn't protect his sister. My lies about my past couldn't protect me. Life finds us, no matter how we try to push it away. It found me. It found Sarah. Innocence ends for all of us, in different ways and at different times. But it must end. And no one is really to blame. Because if it were not that person, that event, it would be another. If my father had not been taken away in handcuffs, something else would have stolen away my unquestioning devotion to him. If Peter had not given away my true identity, something else would have.

My life isn't someone else's fault. It's just life.

I need to forgive my mother. I need to find that letter. And I need to talk to Peter.

On the long drive home, we sail by farmland illuminated by the harvest moon and talk about everything besides the embrace on the bridge. When we get onto I-75 going north, I tighten my grip on the wheel and take a deep breath.

"Ryan, I haven't been completely honest with you about those books."

36

then

The moment after I recognized Sarah Kukla, I remembered that the last time I actually saw her she was unconscious and covered with blood.

"Where the world have you been?" she asked with a bewildered smile. "I wasn't going to come down here today—this place has a little . . . baggage for me. But when Jennifer Wyrembelski told me she'd seen the incredible disappearing Robin Dickinson at my old art studio, I had to come see for myself."

"This was your art studio?"

Sarah looked off to the left. "Well, no. I didn't own it. I took classes here."

"Oh."

She fixed her gaze back on me. "Do you really think if you ignore my question you won't have to answer it?"

"What?"

"Where have you been?"

A nervous laugh escaped my lips without my permission. "Listen, Sarah, I'd love to catch up, but I've had a really long day and I've got a bad headache coming on. Would you mind if we continued this conversation another time?"

She narrowed her eyes. "Why don't I take you out for a drink?"

"Thanks, but I'll have to pass for now. Really, I need to get in bed with some herbal tea. I'm not used to being around so many people."

She stuck out her bottom lip in a pout. "Fine. How about tomorrow? What time do you close?"

"Eight o'clock."

"It's a date."

At 7:57 the next evening, after another busy day, Sarah Kukla walked through the door and flipped my Open sign to Closed. "Okay, Robin, time to go. It's ladies' night at Lucky's."

I locked the register and the front door and reluctantly led the way out the back, through the alley, and along Chestnut Street beneath the enormous American flag.

"I designed that mural, you know," Sarah informed me. Her tone was oddly argumentative, as though I had suggested that someone else had been responsible for the painting.

"Really? It's incredible."

"Mark painted it, but I designed it."

"Who's Mark?"

"He owned the studio."

"Oh, it's too bad he had to close it. Though I guess if he hadn't I wouldn't have been able to set up shop here. What happened, if you don't mind my asking?"

She turned a suspicious glare on me. "Why, what did you hear?"

I pulled back. "Nothing. That's why I'm asking."

Her brow unknit itself, and she offered a non-committal shrug. "Oh, you know. Sometimes people bite off more than they can chew. Mark made some . . . mistakes. And rather than stick around to fix them, he jumped ship and left other people to clean up the mess."

I couldn't tell if she wanted me to press for more information or mind my own business, so I fell back to my default: do unto others as you would have them do unto you. I didn't want anyone prying into my life, so I wouldn't pry into hers.

Sarah pushed through the door at Lucky's, releasing light and music and laughter into the night. I followed her to a vacant corner booth. She shrugged out of her coat and draped her thin arms across the tabletop. The patch of pale, shiny scar tissue shone where the bone had punctured her skin on homecoming night.

"What are you drinking?" she said over the din.

"Water with lemon."

"Don't you drink?"

"Not really, no."

Sarah rolled her eyes and waved a waitress over. "Two shots of tequila and a water with lemon." When the waitress left, she turned to me. "Spill."

Apparently Sarah didn't share my position on privacy. "There's not a lot to tell, actually."

She scoffed. "It was all over the news. They had people searching for you, cops were looking for the car, churches were holding vigils for you. Where the heck did you go?"

The waitress set a shot glass in front of each of us and put my water in the middle of the table. I pushed the shot over to Sarah and slid the water in front of me. I hadn't expected the third degree, and I wasn't sure where to start. I'd never really considered that people would be holding vigils on my behalf. How must it have felt when their prayers went unanswered?

"I was living with a friend." This was technically true. Sarah didn't have to know that he had started out as a complete stranger. "I haven't exactly been hiding." This was not true.

"But why did you leave?"

"Because I could. I didn't have any family. I didn't want some social worker to come tell me where I had to go and what I had to do. I didn't want to be a foster kid. I saw a short window of opportunity to take control of my own life and I took it. End of story."

Sarah put away one of the shots. "But why did you give all those books back to Peter? You left without even saying goodbye to him."

"That's not really . . . That's between me and Peter. It's no one else's concern."

"It was my concern, all right. It was my concern for three years when we were married."

For a moment we were the only two people in the bar.

Sarah pushed the second shot my way. I pushed it back. "You and Peter were married?"

On all of the nights I had lain on Dave Dewitt's squeaky hide-a-bed and wondered what Peter was doing, not once had I envisioned him with a girlfriend, let alone a wife—let alone Sarah Kukla. How could he marry her when he had told me straight-out that he didn't care about her?

"We got married in 2002. It was stupid. We were too young and not really in love, and we each thought the other one could fix our problems for us. We got divorced in 2005."

"I—I had no idea." I took a sip of water and tried to think of something intelligent to say. "Does he still live around here?"

"No." She downed the other shot and fixed me with a hard stare. "So that's it? Your cousin dies, so you steal her car and take off, but before you make your escape you take the time to bring all those books back to Peter's house and dump them on the porch."

I looked at my glass. "I was angry."

"About what?"

"I don't really want to talk about it."

"Fine. Keep your secrets." She flagged down the waitress and indicated another round.

The silence lengthened between us. I took another sip of water. "Well, it's been nice catching up, Sarah, but it's getting late and I still need to do some work tonight."

I made a move to slide out of the booth, but she put her hand on mine. "Your dad is that senator, isn't he?"

I frowned. Yet more evidence of Peter's betrayal of my confidence. How many nights had he and Sarah sat at the dinner table discussing my sad life?

"It was all over the news when you disappeared," she continued. "This connection to some corrupt Massachusetts senator who murdered anyone who had anything on him. Lots of people figured you got kidnapped or murdered by someone taking revenge for what he did."

I sighed. "Nothing so dramatic as all that."

"But you are his daughter?"

"Yes. So you can understand why I go by a different name. Just trying to make a new start. And please keep that to yourself." I checked the time. "I really have to go, Sarah. It was nice talking to you. Come by the store anytime."

This time she didn't try to stop me.

Back in the apartment I fed The Professor and lay down on my bed with a notebook and pen. I reread the little poem I'd written the day before when I was putting the first roll of receipt paper into the register.

> There is a day
> that calls us
> into life,
> one that slays us
> with its strife,
> one that saves us
> in spite
> of all the death
> we've wrought,
> and brings us,
> gasping,
> to the light,
> bids us live again
> despite the ache
> of all the days
> that came before—
>
> and today is that day.

I grabbed on to the promise of those few verses, popped some aspirin, and began to write.

37

now

I pull into Ryan's driveway a few minutes after midnight. For forty-five minutes I've been spilling my guts, and now I am completely empty. I had never before given voice to the depth of my feelings for Peter, the intensity of the anger I felt when I left him behind. The second-guessing and regret. The wishing things had been different. I might have told Sarah at some point had it not been for her own relationship to Peter. After her revelation about their failed marriage, I was careful not to bring him up, and she returned the favor. I might have told Dawt Pi if I felt that our limited shared vocabulary could hold such vast emotions. *Sad* and *mad* and *love* are such weak words, drawn long ago from Germanic languages spoken by people who may have been more stone than flesh. The soul needs words rooted in romance languages, words like *despondent* and *ravished* and *adore*.

Ryan has never spoken any romantic words to me. I have never felt nervous in his presence. I have never looked at him and seen beauty or danger or freedom. He is a nice guy. A solid guy. Someone you can depend on. Which is what I want in life. So why don't I want him?

"Maybe I've been too cautious these past few months," he says. "Sarah said I shouldn't move fast. But maybe I was playing it too safe. I really like you, Robin. A lot. And I know you have trouble trusting people. I thought if we were friends first it would be easier."

We stare out the windshield at Ryan's closed garage door. Were it not for Peter's books, would our hug on the bridge a few hours ago have been a kiss? Perhaps. But it wouldn't have felt the way it had when Peter kissed me on the trailer porch the night he rushed away from the paper he was supposed to write, the night he believed the truth about my past and didn't immediately run the other way.

"You did everything right," I say. "Honestly. It's just bad timing."

Ryan lets out a slow breath. "What if things can't be patched up with this guy? I mean, you knew him all of six months, and it's been what, eighteen years? Then he sends you all these books, every day, out of nowhere. It's like he's toying with you. What if there's nothing there?"

"I don't know."

"You think I could keep coming around the store even though there's no dinosaur sculpture to work on?"

I give him a smile to hang some hope on, but my words don't match it. "If the store is still there."

"You really have no other options if you don't win this prize?"

"I don't know. Maybe I could figure something out, but maybe it's time to move on."

A crease appears between his eyebrows. "All that work this summer and you've already given up?"

"Moving on isn't synonymous with giving up. Sometimes things have simply run their course."

I can tell he doesn't agree with me. He opens the passenger door. "Well, if you're still around after the enigmatic Peter shows up and you want to talk, give me a call."

He shuts the door and doesn't look back. I drive home slowly, along streets that are empty save for fallen leaves the wind has set to dancing.

The news coverage of the *Dreadnoughtus* brings in more customers for a couple weeks. But with so few books on the shelves for them to choose from, I don't make much of a profit. Perhaps enough to cover the cost of entering the contest. I tell people the stock will be replenished in November, but in my heart I know it's a lie.

In the evenings after the store is closed, I try to focus on writing Emily Dickinson's story, but in the back of my mind I am writing a letter to my father, trying to explain my failure, trying to tell him all the things I wish I could have done differently. As I lay in bed at night I walk through each room of the dead house, looking for the dark little corner I might have missed. But I cannot find it.

The ArtPrize winners are announced the second week of October. I'm not surprised that the *Dreadnoughtus* didn't place. In fact, when I scan the list I don't even look for my name. I look for Sarah's. And find it. Her piece, "Turning Point," didn't win the grand prize in either the people's choice or the juried categories, but it did win the juried prize in the 3-D category, netting her a tidy $12,000. I know she will be thrilled about the money. But more than that, I'm sure, she will feel deep down in her soul that her work has meaning, that it's alive.

The same day the winners list is published, I go to the post office to pick up what I know is the last padded manila envelope I will receive from Peter. I had stopped checking for packages after days with nothing following the delivery of *Moby-Dick*. I was tired of getting sympathetic looks from the round little postal worker with the big hair and the eighties glasses when she reported that no new packages had been delivered. Eventually I told her to give me a call if anything came in. The phone never rang, and I was so busy with the *Dreadnoughtus* I sometimes went days without thinking about it.

Then the phone did ring.

At the post office, Doris hands the padded envelope to me with two hands, like a nurse handing a newborn baby over to their mother for the first time. Its slim profile belies its weighty contents. I bring it back to the store and lock the door. I pull the red tab, and a tiny cloud of paper fibers shivers in the air.

It's as beautiful as ever with its gilded cover and marbled page edges. Like a fine casket. The tragedy of tragedies. *Romeo and Juliet*.

38

now

There's a finality in the closing click of my laptop I've never heard before. The story is finished, the last line written, a small piece of my heart sealed forever inside. The last scene had been the hardest to write. Emily Dickinson was dead. Susan and the rest of the family were in mourning. And Emily's younger sister Lavinia was kneeling at the fireplace, feeding page after page of Emily's correspondence into the flames, obliterating forever the other half of thousands of conversations. I don't know what I'll do with it. Probably nothing. But having finished it, I can now move on to something new.

There's no real reason for me to stay. Not for Peter. Ryan was right. I'd known Peter Flynt for less than a year. I'd shared books with him, but not my life. He'd married Sarah barely more than a year after I left Sussex. He could be married even now. There's no reason to think he wants me or to think I want him. I know absolutely nothing about him.

And not for Brick & Mortar Books. Sarah and

Ryan and even Dawt Pi's pastor's wife had all been encouraging me to push forward, to fight on to keep the store open. But as the shelves had slowly emptied out over the past few months, something strange happened: I got used to seeing them that way. Where empty shelves used to gnaw at me, I now found that with every book that left and was not replaced I felt just a little lighter. No longer did I fear not being able to stay here, cocooned in books. Instead I began to feel a yearning that must be akin to the force that prompted those explorers aboard their ships. A desire for something beyond the comforts of home. For something a little more frightening and a little more grand. They had set their sights on the western horizon, on the place beyond the edge of the map.

I set mine to the east. To Amherst.

I had thought that returning to River City seven years ago meant that I had stopped running from my past. Only River City wasn't really what I'd been running from. Sussex either. It was merely a detour, a place to stop and catch one's breath before the next leg of the journey. And I am ready for that next leg. I will not close my eyes and point to a spot on the map. There's no question now in my mind where I must go. If I am ever to make peace with the past—with my mother—I must live where it still lingers in shadows. I must face it each day.

It doesn't take long to pack; there's not much I need to bring with me. Some clothes, some bedding, an ornery old parrot. I dig through the front closet until I find my mother's doll where I stored her away not long after I realized I was never going to get Sarah Kukla out of my life. At least, I had reasoned at the time, I had another human being to talk to, even if we couldn't be more different, and even if many of our conversations are on the combative side. I tuck the doll into a paper grocery bag with a few odds and ends. I edge everything past the boxes of Peter's books that are still blocking the doorway and fill up the back seat of my car in the alley behind the store.

Then, for the second time in my life, I fill a trunk with Peter's books. They would make the trip with me this time, but I would not keep them forever. One by one I would reread them as a tribute to what might have been. When I closed the back cover, I would let them go. I'd leave them behind—on park benches, at bus stops, in mailboxes, near gravestones, on diner tables—a trail of bread crumbs to follow. Some other soul would pick them up, and the story would live inside of them as it had lived inside of me.

When the car is fully packed, the back end is riding low like a seagull in the river. At the very last, I strap The Professor's travel cage securely into the passenger seat. The twilight of impending dawn makes everything around me gray as I drive beneath Sarah's fading mural of the American flag and turn left onto Midway. It's still early and the street is empty. I put my foot on the brake, roll down my frosted window, and take a last look.

It's one of those cursed places . . .

I had once thought of my mother's childhood home as something that must have been beautiful before it was cursed, along with the little girl in the picture.

The picture. I forgot the picture.

I roll up the window, pull into a parking space on the south side of the street, and leave the car running. In the back room of the store, I find the family portrait where I had left it after coming home from my doomed errand with Dawt Pi. I tuck it under my arm and start for the door. Then I stop.

I never looked behind the photo.

Heart pounding, I rush to pry up the thick staples that hold the stiff cardboard backing, tearing a fingernail in the process. I wrench the back away, fully expecting to see a yellowed envelope taped to the inside. It's what would happen if my life were a movie.

But it's not, and there's nothing.

I will not cry.

I pull the photo from the frame and put my hand on the door to leave. Then the phone on the counter rings. I almost don't answer it. But then . . . "Brick & Mortar Books."

"Robin? It's Peter."

There are many types of quiet. The quiet when you first open a book and prepare yourself to enter a story. The quiet of the seed underground, waiting for spring. The quiet that follows the moment the past rips through time to invade the present.

"Peter?"

"Wow." A pause. "It's so good to hear your voice."

"Peter, I—I can't talk."

"It will only take a minute. I don't want to talk over the phone. Would you meet me somewhere?"

"You're here?"

"I'm in Sussex. Meet me at Kennedy? Under the bleachers?"

I cannot meet him. I cannot see him. I have already boarded the ship, put out from land. I am already on my way to the future.

"Robin?"

I open my mouth and the words spill out.

"I'll be there in fifteen minutes."

I pull into an empty parking spot not far from where I'd been interviewed about the book drive. I zip up my winter coat, leave the car running for The Professor, and crunch my way across the frozen lawn to the football field. The gate is padlocked shut, so I walk around to where the fence is shorter and climb over it. The chain link chinks against the posts, and beneath the bleachers the wind picks up an old popcorn bag and sends it skipping across the patchy grass. No one waits for me there.

Then, through the fog of my own breath, I see a figure approaching from the parking lot. He is bigger than I remember, his chest and arms filling out his coat in a way they hadn't when I knew him. His hair is cut short on the sides, a little longer on top, revealing only a hint of the wave it used to have. He easily swings his legs over the chain-link fence like a gymnast on a pommel horse. This close, the fine lines criss-crossing his face are plain, as is the shadow of stubble, sprinkled with gray.

I only ever knew Peter the boy. The man before me is a stranger. I shouldn't have come here.

"Wow," he says as he walks over to me. "You look exactly the same. Hair's longer."

There are so many words between us, so much that has been left unsaid, that it's hard to find the end of the string to start unraveling the silence.

Finally I say the first full sentence that forms in my mind. "Why did you send me those books?"

He smiles, but the smile does not quite reach his eyes. "What do you mean? They're your books. You paid for them. I figured you were

404

giving them to me for safekeeping while you were gone."

"No you didn't."

"No, I didn't." His eyes search mine for a moment, and his expression turns sad. "Why did you leave?"

"Are you kidding?"

"No."

"You didn't read my note."

"I read it. I read it a thousand times. But it never made any more sense than the first time I read it."

He looks so sincere that a little pit begins to form in my stomach. "The reporter? At my door? The very day after I freaked out on you and your dad about your mom?"

Two deep thought lines appear between his eyes. "I had nothing to do with any reporter. I'm not going to pretend I wasn't mad at you, but I never told anyone who you were."

The pit is getting deeper. "Then how would she know?"

"I don't know. When your grandma died, couldn't there have been some record of you as Robin Windsor? Maybe your grandma said something about it to a nurse."

I cross my arms, tucking my cold hands beneath them. My mind races for some other explanation.

"Anyway, you were wrong," he says. "About my mom."

I swallow hard. "I was?"

"Yeah. Dad and I were having an argument about . . . something, I don't know. We were always arguing then. You got in my head with that theory of yours. I went through all of the books you returned. The pattern was there, just like you said. I accused him of lying about it, and he stormed off and came back a minute later with the death certificate and the thesis she was working on for these graduate classes she'd been taking—some extension or correspondence program. Her thesis was on mad women characters in classic literature. That's why she had all those things underlined."

All the breath leaves my body. A master's thesis? Notes for a paper? It was as simple as that?

"That doesn't mean she wasn't having a tough time," he goes on. "I mean, there's probably a reason someone would gravitate toward that topic, and Dad told me she was under a lot of pressure and he wasn't always very understanding of it. He blamed himself for the aneurysm for a while. That was part of why he was trying to erase all trace of her—just trying to stop thinking about how he'd killed his wife. Then a doctor finally got it through his head that it had nothing to do with him. It runs in families, tends to happen to women more than men, she had high blood pressure, stuff like that."

The pit in my stomach is a chasm. I feel light-headed. "And I come along and twist the knife a little more. I—I am so, *so* sorry. I've been wrong about a lot of things."

Peter shrugs. "It can't be changed now."

"Does he still live around here? Your dad?"

"He moved to Arizona not long after I graduated college."

I look at my feet. "It was really none of my business."

Peter puts his hands in his pockets. "You were fourteen. Well, fifteen, I guess."

"Old enough to know everything and nothing." I pause, wondering if I should tell him about my parents, about the letter I failed to find. "How did you know where I was?"

"I've known for years. Sarah told me she ran into you when you first moved back."

I let out a long breath. "You married her."

He rubs the back of his neck. "Yeah, I did. That was a mistake."

"Why?"

"What do you mean, 'why'?"

"Was she pregnant or something? You didn't love her."

"No. The girl I loved skipped town and left everything I'd ever touched on my doorstep. Sarah was there for me. For a while anyway."

I swallow down all of the questions I want to ask him, all of the things I could never bring myself to ask Sarah because it would have meant talking about Peter when all I'd wanted to do for so long was forget him. Instead, I focus on the present.

"If you've known where I was all this time, why wait so long? Why send the books now?"

"I'd been watching the news. I knew the execution was coming. I thought maybe you'd need a nice distraction from it."

"Oh. And now? Why are you here now?"

He closes some of the distance between us. "Robin, I think about you all the time. I thought I could forget you if I got married. When that didn't work, I thought maybe I could forget you by going to war. But you were still there in my mind every day. And when I came home to divorce papers sitting on the counter, all I could think about was finding you."

My heart rate quickens. When I had been hiding in the north woods, Peter had been searching for me? The girl who'd taken every one of his manifold kindnesses and shoved them back in his face?

"I didn't know where to start," he continues. "I got a job where I could travel. I think somewhere in the back of my mind I thought maybe I'd run into you somewhere or at least come across some sort of sign you'd been somewhere—something so that I could at least be sure you existed, that you weren't some figment of my imagination.

But everywhere I went, I could tell right away you weren't there."

He takes another step toward me and reaches out to grasp my arms.

"The night Sarah saw you in the bookstore she called me in Wyoming. I was halfway to Michigan the next day when I thought maybe you wouldn't want to see me, so I turned back."

"I wish you'd come."

"Really?"

"I don't know. Maybe. Maybe not."

He furrows his brow, but his eyes never break contact with mine. "Is that how you feel now?"

I shake my head, afraid to speak for the knot forming in my throat. He pulls me into his broad chest and wraps his arms around me. In that embrace, the years of pain and anger melt into tears.

"Oh, Peter, I'm sorry. I was so hurt. I assumed it was you."

He cups my face in his hands. "It doesn't matter."

"But all this time wasted—I feel so stupid. It just seemed like there was no one else who ever knew about me or my grandma or . . . Oh."

"What?"

"It was Billy."

39

now

I fill Peter in on all my discoveries—the money in the Doll House, the truth about how my parents were and weren't actually involved in the crimes that took them from me, Billy's strange visit in July, the letter that had probably been thrown into a garbage bag as the old church ladies cleaned out my grandmother's trailer. When I say it all out loud, my life sounds far more exciting than it actually is. Never once does Peter look like he doesn't believe me.

Finally I run out of news about all the things I cannot change and focus on the one thing I can.

"Why not send the books all at once?"

"I thought about it. Briefly. I know how over-whelming that can be."

He smiles when he says it, but I can tell my rash and childish actions still sting.

"I thought maybe it would be easier if you had some time to get used to the idea of me again," he says. "Anyway, it took a lot of time to copy all the poems into them."

"What about all the different postmarks? How can you travel that much?"

"I work for the Department of the Interior. I've been doing an intensive tour of the National Park System this year to assess staff needs and management of the resources. Before I left DC, I filled up the back of my Explorer with everything and started working my way through. It's been a fun little puzzle to match the poems up to the books and copy them in. Took a little guesswork at times. Your handwriting was terrible."

"It still is."

The side of his mouth quirks. "Good."

"Why the big gap between *Moby-Dick* and *Romeo and Juliet*? I was waiting. I was hoping when they all came, you'd follow." Yes, I can admit it now.

"That was always the plan. But Sarah told me about the art contest thing and how busy you were. And she told me about that Ryan guy. I thought you had enough going on. I didn't want to be one more thing when I showed up. I wanted to be the only thing."

I look directly into his sky-blue eyes. "You are."

Peter places a hand on the back of my neck and pulls me into a kiss worthy of Shakespeare, worthy of poetry. Everything fades. Billy, the lost letter, Sarah, my failure. For just a moment, none of it matters. I feel nothing but his arms, his lips, this singular perfection.

"I can't believe you kept all of those poems," I say when it ends.

"I did more than that," he says. "I probably should have asked, but I figured you'd say no. So I went ahead and submitted the entire collection to a contest."

I take a step back. "You what?"

"Don't be mad. I wanted to do something nice for you that I figured you probably wouldn't do yourself. I wanted you to be able to see your name—your real name—associated with something positive."

The old familiar feeling of being deceived and exposed creeps across my skin.

"Peter, you had no right to do that."

"No? Those poems were mine, right? I gave you the books and you gave me the poems."

"You know that's not how writing works. Those were my intellectual property."

He takes my hand in his. "It's done. And what's more, you won."

"What?"

"Ten thousand dollars. And all the poems are being collected into a book that's going to be published next year. It's another reason I had to get ahold of you now. You'll have to start working with the publishing company and signing contracts and stuff."

I pull my hand away. "Wait, is that why you came back? Because I had to sign contracts?"

"No, it's not. It's not why I came back, it's why I came back *now*. Don't twist this into something it's not. I thought you'd be happy."

How could I know what I felt anymore? Everything's so tangled up, so complicated. Why did I pick up that phone? I could be halfway to Ohio right now.

"So, your store has been struggling," he goes on, "but now you've got some more money to keep it afloat."

The store. It really could all work out, just as everyone kept insisting it would.

I shut my eyes. "No. There's no store. Not anymore. It's done."

"But I thought—"

"I'm leaving, Peter. I'm leaving town. When you called, I was on my way out the door for good."

"You sold the store?"

"Not yet."

"Then there's still time."

"No, there really isn't. It's over. That chapter . . . it's done. I'm moving back to Amherst."

His eyes search mine for the barest moment. "Come with me instead."

My breath hitches. "What?"

"I'm heading north to visit Pictured Rocks and then flying to Isle Royale. I'm spending the winter there to help with a study of how the latest wolves relocated to the island are doing. Come with me. I'm sure they'd have room for you up there. It would just be a few months. Just to see if there's something here worth saving."

North is not my direction this time. East is. East to see my mother again. East to Amherst to prove to myself that my house is still alive. East to the Atlantic.

Peter is still looking at me, eyes pleading, waiting for an answer. "It's just a season, Robin. Amherst will be there in the spring. But this chance won't be. And if things work out . . . well, it's only an hour flight from DC to Massachusetts."

"Peter, I—"

My cell phone rings in my pocket. I check the number. Sarah. I press ignore. But her name on the display has knocked loose an idea.

40

now

W e have to make two stops before we leave,"
I say as we transfer the contents of my
still-running car to Peter's Explorer, starting with
the books.

"It's a good thing I pack light," he says. "You're
really going to leave the car here?"

"I'm bringing it to Dawt Pi—the car and The
Professor. He always liked her better anyway."

Maybe she could teach him some Chin words
before her family came. They would come. I
would make sure of it. Half of the money Peter
had told me I'd won for my poems would go
to her. Five hundred would go to Ryan for the
Science Olympiad team. The rest I'd save for
myself, a little nest egg for the future.

"I never thought I'd see this creepy thing
again." Peter is holding my mother's old doll
by the neck. He tucks it back in the bag and
shuts the liftgate of the Explorer, accidentally
severing the head from its body. It bounces twice
and rolls to a stop near my feet.

I let out an involuntary gasp.

"Shoot, Robin, I'm sorry," Peter says, opening the liftgate again.

I pick up the head and examine the stubby neck for damage. Except for a chip and a bit of extra dirt it seems to have survived.

"I'm sure it can be reattached," I say.

"What's this?" Peter pulls a short stack of folded paper from the body's stuffing and hands it to me.

I open one up. It's a letter. The salutation, *Lindy, Darling;* the closing, *Yours Always, Billy.* I frantically open and scan the rest of them. They are all from Billy. And surely one of them is the letter that will save my father's life. All this time it had been hiding behind those unseeing eyes. Every time I had spoken to my mother's doll, she'd actually had something she wanted to say back.

I rush back to my car, dig through my purse. The lawyer's card had arrived just a few days after I visited my father in Terre Haute. I fumble with my phone, drop the card. Peter picks it up.

"A lawyer? What's going on? What are those?"

I snatch the card from Peter's hand and punch in Joel Staub's number. It rings once, twice.

"Mr. Staub? This is Robin Windsor. I think I may have the letter you're looking for."

I tear down Centerpointe Road, past the stately homes of nineteenth-century lumber barons. I had once thought of Sussex and River City as nothing towns full of boring houses and farm fields. I'd been wrong. I just hadn't ventured far enough from home to know what I'd been missing. But I don't see the houses now as I speed through yellow lights.

Incredibly, Peter manages to keep up. He pulls into a parking spot right next to me outside Dawt Pi's salon downtown and rolls down his window. "Should I wait here?"

I give him a nod. The bell dings as I rush in.

"Robin!" Dawt Pi comes around the desk. "I'm so happy to see you. Do you need a haircut?"

Actually, I do. The reason I've let my hair grow so long is the same reason I have never purchased lattes or cappuccinos at a coffee shop—because I dread being stuck in a chair or at a counter while a stranger asks me personal questions.

"Probably, but that's not why I'm here. I want to give you something. A few things, actually. But first, do you have a scanner here?"

She leads me through an invisible but pungent cloud of hair product chemicals to an office in the back of the salon. I scan the letters one by one, then email the lot of them to the address on Joel Staub's card. When it's all done, Dawt Pi grips my hand and I realize with a pang how much I will miss her quiet support, her fierce determination, her faith.

"Now, about the other things. I'm leaving

417

town for a while, and I want you to watch The Professor for me."

She furrows her brow. "How long will you be gone?"

"I'm going up north for the winter. I won't need the car there. I may be back for it in the spring. We'll see. But for now, you can use it."

I hold out the car key and give it a little shake. Dawt Pi makes no move to take it, so I grab her hand and press it into her palm.

"What about the store?"

"I'll see to that. Don't worry. I have to run now. Peter's waiting for me."

"Peter? Book Peter?"

I smile. "Yeah."

She rushes to the front window. I feel my phone buzz. The text is from Joel Staub.

Scans received. Will keep you updated.

"Can you bring The Professor inside here?" I say. "He's in the car and it's too cold to leave him there. You can get all of his things from the store later. Sarah can help you move the big cage out." I hand her another ring of keys. "Give the store keys and the key to my apartment to her."

Dawt Pi slips into her coat and follows me onto the sidewalk. She crushes me in a hug. "I don't want you to go."

"I'll be in touch," I say, tears welling up in my eyes. "You have my number. I doubt there's reliable cell service where I'm going now. But I promise I will get ahold of you somehow and let you know how I'm doing."

"Okay."

She retrieves her avian charge from the car as I get into the passenger seat of Peter's Explorer and roll down the window. Dawt Pi hoists the cage up to my level.

"Goodbye, you cantankerous old curmudgeon," I whisper. "I'll miss you."

The Professor lets out a little gurgling noise. I wave to Dawt Pi as she takes him into the salon and roll up my window.

"One more stop."

"*This* is your store?"

"Funny, huh? It was for sale again when I moved back to town."

Then I remember that Peter has a different coincidence on his mind. This is where Sarah met Mark—and conceived Caleb. For a moment my grand scheme doesn't seem so grand anymore. Sarah must have bad memories of this spot as well. But she'd never really avoided the place, and she seemed to be upset that I was even thinking of leaving it. The plan could still work. I retrieve the deed to the building from the lock-box and lead Peter around to the back alley. I pull the spare key from its hiding spot in the crumbly mortar between two bricks.

"I see your grandmother taught you well," Peter says.

I give him a knowing smile.

Inside I pull out a clean sheet of paper. I'll figure out the particulars of switching ownership at some point, but for now I just need to write a letter.

Dear Sarah,

Thank you for your friendship these past seven years. A friendship I'm sure I didn't deserve. You forced your way into my life—and I'm glad you did. You've given me more joy than I think you realize, certainly more than I ever allowed to show. Now I want to give something to you. I know you were thinking of using your ArtPrize money as a down payment on a studio space. But I think you should save it for something else. Maybe supplies. Because you already have a studio space.

Peter and I are going to Isle Royale for the winter. And after that . . . ? So I'm deeding the building that currently houses Brick & Mortar Books over to you. You once studied art here as a student. Now you will be the teacher. Dawt Pi should have given you the keys. There's a spare in this envelope. We'll work out all the technical details later. For now, sell everything you don't want—books, shelves, my furniture—and use that money to set up shop.

Give Ryan my best when you see him next. And apologize to him for me. He's a nice guy. But he's not Peter.

I'll be in touch,
Robin

I slip the letter and the key into an envelope, seal it, and write Sarah's name across it. I place it on the old wooden counter and then follow Peter out the door and into the next chapter of my life.

41

now

No one notices the last robin of fall. Because of course, you can never be sure which one will be your last. But I am fairly certain that the one I see hopping from branch to branch in the white pine tree at the foot of the trail will be the last one of the year for me. He should have left already. I watch closely, trying to burn him into my memory. But Peter's gone on ahead and I must catch up.

"There you are." He puts an arm around my shoulders. "I thought I'd lost you."

"I could never get lost here. I know these trails better than anyone alive today."

During the long drive, I had filled in the blanks of my life, telling him all about my silent years with Dave Dewitt, working for Pictured Rocks. It's remarkable to think that, had I just stayed there, Peter would still have found me eventually, just as he'd hoped.

Now we walk side by side down the wide path to where it disappears in the snow-covered sand. Beyond the sheltering trees, the wind stings my face as a snowstorm sweeps down from Canada and over the big lake. My lake. Along my own personal leg of the North Country Trail.

Just as the first time I saw these waters, I hear the waves crashing against the shore before I can see them. We crest the top of the hill and brace ourselves against the wind. To the right rise the Grand Sable Dunes. To the left, the cliffs stand firm against the relentless lashing of the icy waves.

"You know I've been down there?" I say, pointing to the strip of shore three hundred feet below. "When I lived with Dave all those years I used to come up here now and then to watch the sunset, and I did go down the Log Slide once. They're not kidding with those warning signs. It took a couple minutes to get to the bottom and a couple hours to get back up to the top. It was pitch-black and freezing by the time I got back up. Dave never came looking for me, and I couldn't call for help because, of course, he didn't think I could talk."

"I cannot believe you didn't talk for eleven years," Peter says. "That is by far the most unbelievable thing you have ever told me."

"Well, I talked to The Professor. And if you knew Dave, you'd realize how very easy it was to do."

Peter gazes out across the dunes. "It's incredible to think that in a few hundred years or so this shoreline will look completely different."

"What?"

"These dunes will have moved inland or be gone entirely. The cliffs will have a different shape altogether. Arches will collapse and become pillars, and then they'll wear away to nothing but sand. The wind and the water are always changing the landscape in a place like this."

"I'd never thought of that."

"No? Your Dave Dewitt never talked about that?"

"He probably did, but when someone talks constantly, you kind of tune them out sometimes. And he was much more interested in the flora and fauna anyway." I survey the shoreline to the west. "I'd always thought of this shore as something I wanted to be like."

"How so?"

"You know, stable. Unmoved. The water churns and crashes, but the rocks stand firm."

"These cliffs are anything but stable. A few years back they lost a whole section of the North Country Trail near Grand Portal Point. Just collapsed—boom!—disappeared into the lake."

"I wish Dave had been around to see that."

Peter smiles. "You can't fight the elements. Wind and water always win. Even against stone. It's why we have the Grand Canyon and the Arches in Utah and Niagara Falls. You can't tame the waves and you can't hold back the wind. You've got to move with it. But that's not to say you have to let it take you wherever it will. Think of a sailboat. The wind moves it, but it's not what steers it. The captain of the ship decides where it will go. You're the captain of your ship."

"That's awfully philosophical for a Saturday morning."

Peter laughs, and the wind sweeps the sound away to some other place. "I'm freezing, and we've got a long way to drive yet before the really bad weather hits."

We start back toward the parking lot.

"You're sure I'll be able to get calls up there, right? I have to be reachable in case my dad's lawyer calls."

"Don't worry. There are reliable landlines. You can call him the minute we get there and give him the number."

"And if they need me to testify about—"

"Yes, I told you. You can get off the island in winter. It's just a little pricey." He stops walking. "You're not backing out on me, are you?"

"Not at all. Winter was one of the best parts of living up here. I loved being snug in a cabin under twenty feet of snow for five months. It's a good thing we have all of your books."

"Your books."

"Our books."

He smiles and the lines around his eyes deepen.

"I almost forgot to tell you. I do have one more."

Back in the Explorer, Peter cranks up the heat. He reaches back around his seat and pulls a messenger bag onto his lap. "Close your eyes."

I do. A moment later, something heavy is on my lap.

"Okay, open them."

The Complete Poems of Emily Dickinson. I flip through the pages. The marks and underlines, the dog-ears—they're all there. It's the same copy I stole from—and then returned to—Emily Flynt's grave.

"I'll *loan* that to you," Peter says. "That is, unless you have the means to pay for it."

He puts the Explorer in gear and heads out of the parking lot. It feels like the whirling snow outside the car is whizzing around in my stomach.

"I haven't written a poem in a really long time."

Peter reaches into the pocket behind my seat and produces a spiral notebook. Then he pulls a pen from the console. "Now's the perfect time to start."

He turns his attention to the road, leaving me in contemplative quiet. Not a word is spoken as we cut through the snow to Copper Harbor where we will board a small plane to Isle Royale. There, two tiny cabins await us, along with a second chance at what might have been. As the forgiving snow covers the evidence of life in this forbidding landscape, I let go of the encumbering past and feel, for perhaps the first time, that I am truly home.

Then I put pen to paper and invite poetry back into my life.

acknowledgments

To all of the authors, dead and alive, who have been part of my literary upbringing, I offer my gratitude. Whether your books made me smile or cry, whether they woke me up or put me to sleep, whether they promoted lively discussion or caused fractious arguments, they have worked their way into who I am as a person. They live on, even when their creators do not. And I am so grateful to be part of the conversation.

To my high school English teachers, especially John VanLooy, Ilse Irving, and Kevin Discher, and my college English professors, especially David Alvarez, Rob Franciosi, and David Ihrman—thank you, from the bottom of my heart, for sharing your passion for literature with me. Your words helped determine the course of my life.

To my mother, who took me to the library any time I asked, and the librarians who helped me find stories to fall in love with—thank you for feeding my insatiable desire for books.

To those who read early drafts of this story and offered their critique—Valerie Marvin, Andrew Spector, Heather Brewer, Twila Bennett, and

Orly Konig—I extend my heartfelt thanks for your encouragement and your input.

To Alma Staub and Joel Spector, thank you for sharing your legal expertise so that I could make the experiences of Norman and Lindy Windsor true to life (and for lending your names to the lawyer in the story . . . By the way, is it okay if I name the lawyer after the two of you?).

To my agent, Nephele Tempest, for pushing me to make this manuscript better. To my editor, Kelsey Bowen, for her unbridled enthusiasm for this story. To eagle-eyed Jessica English, who is the most aptly named copyeditor in the business. To Michele Misiak and Karen Steele for their ongoing work to introduce readers to my writing. To everyone else at Revell Books for the integral parts they have played in getting *The Words between Us* into the hands of readers.

And to Zachary, who has shared my story since I was fifteen. May each new chapter bring us something else to celebrate.

about the author

Erin Bartels is the author of *We Hope for Better Things*. She grew up in the Bay City, Michigan, area, upon which River City is based, and has spent much of her life waiting on drawbridges. She lives in Lansing, Michigan, with her husband, Zachary, and their son.

Find her online at www.erinbartels.com.

Center Point Large Print
600 Brooks Road / PO Box 1
Thorndike, ME 04986-0001 USA

(207) 568-3717

US & Canada:
1 800 929-9108
www.centerpointlargeprint.com